To L

The Grommets:
Big Island Justice

2013

Mahalo
for Da Kine
Food

The following story is fiction. The characters are fictional and any resemblance to any event or person alive or deceased is purely coincidental.

MARK-ROBERT BLUEMEL

THE GROMMETS:

BIG ISLAND JUSTICE

2013

The Grommets:
Big Island Justice

2013

This book is dedicated to Gerry Spence, 'America's Winningest Lawyer.' In the courtroom, as in life, we stand on the shoulders of giants.

INTRODUCTION

This is the second installment of the surfing mystery series. This one takes us to Hawaii, "The Big Island". As with the last book I would like to thank my friends and family for al their support and encouragement, as well as all the readers who gave me positive feedback and the inspiration to write this book.

The Hawaiian people have managed to survive on a tiny island chain in harmony with nature for many years. Hopefully, they will continue to preserve the natural beauty of their island home.

Keep reading! Book three in this series, "The Grommets: Toxic Tides", is in the works. Thanks to all of you readers for your continued inspiration and support.

Special thanks to Kris Kezar for his amazing original artwork for the cover and interior sketches!

CHAPTER ONE
The Big Surprise

'WWHHIIIRRRRRR' the high-pitched sound of the extension of wing flaps fills the passenger jet's cabin. The loudspeakers crackle: "Attention passengers, this is your Captain speaking. We are beginning our descent into Hilo International Airport. Please secure the overhead compartments, fasten your seatbelts and return the tray tables to their upright position... Flight crew, please prepare for landing, Aloha, and welcome to Hawaii." A loud click concludes the message from the cockpit.

In the seats to my left are my wife and son, Buzzy. Across the aisle in the middle row to my right, Oz and his family are locked in excited conversation. Jimbo and his gang are seated a few rows in front of them. This isn't the first trip we've taken to Hawaii together. We usually try to rent a big condo every few years and have all of our families come together. The very first time Oz, Jimbo, and I went to The Big Island, we were still "Grommets."

The adventure began near the end of the school year. My dad came home with an excited look on his face. At the dinner table he announced: "I have good news for all of you. The research grant was approved and we will be spending six weeks on The Big Island of Hawaii." Dad was, and still is, a marine biologist specializing in the study of the squid. He is absolutely crazy about them! Recently after recovering from a long illness, he returned to his office at the State University's Marine Sciences

Lab. He is still very popular with his students. My father is a really cool guy!

"Can I surf there?" was my immediate response to this fantastic news.

"Sure son; after all, surfing was invented in Hawaii." Dad replied before putting a forkful of salad in his mouth.

My little brother Eric sat in this high chair picking the lettuce with his fingers. He looked like a miniature version of our dad.

"Okay, everybody eat now, before your food gets cold. We'll talk about our trip later." Mom commanded.

After that, everything seems like a blur. "I'm going to surf in Hawaii;" I thought, visualizing myself shooting through turquoise blue cylinders of water, just like the photographs in the surfing magazines.

The next day in school, I met my surfing buddies and best friends, Jimbo and Oz, during lunch. They had already claimed our favorite table in the lunch yard.

"Howzit, Buzz?" Oz greeted me.

"Um-Hmmm," Jimbo nodded with a mouthful of his bologna sandwich.

Opening my lunch bag I couldn't contain myself. "My dad got a grant and we're going to Hawaii for six weeks this summer!"

Jimbo's mouth opened to reveal its chewed contents. Oz looked equally surprised and was the first to respond: "That's so cool!"

"Yeah, I'm gonna be able to surf in Hawaii!" I beamed, but looking at my friends my heart quickly sank. It hadn't occurred to me that I would not be there surfing with Oz and Jimbo. Alone without my buddies, the prospect of six weeks in Hawaii was suddenly not appealing. "I wish you guys could come along."

Jimbo gulped his food down and said: "Why not? We won't take up much space. Maybe instead of going to my grandparents' farm this summer, I can go with you. What about you, Oz?" Jimbo said appointing himself travel director.

"Ah, I don't know. Six weeks is a long time and Mom is pretty strict about me being at home with the family." Oz shrugged his shoulders.

"Tell your parents it will be an educational experience. Besides, we have that reward money we got last summer of which we haven't used any. We can tell our parents, we'll pay our own way!" Jimbo declared.

"That would be awesome!" I encouraged my friends. "My parents would probably be happy to have you guys come along."

"I don't know." Oz repeated: "My mom is pretty strict." Then he smiled. "It's worth a try, it can't hurt to ask; but I'd better come up with a good reason to give my parents to let me leave home for six weeks. Remember, even though we got the reward money for solving that mystery and finding that corpse, I got in huge trouble and my parents don't trust me as much anymore." He lost his confidence again.

"Aw, come on Oz, where are your cojones?" Jimbo exclaimed drawing from his arsenal of unsavory Spanish vocabulary. "Buzz's parents are strict too. You can tell your folks they are stricter than them and that you will be supervised the whole time. Just look at how Buzz turned out. And don't forget to tell them that this is a unique once in a lifetime opportunity!"

We didn't leave the bench for the rest of the lunch period, discussing every strategy in the hopes that my friends' parents would allow all three of us to go to Hawaii together. It was exciting. The school bell interrupted our discussion too soon. We arranged to meet at The Shack and go surfing after school, before running off to class.

Later that afternoon, I pulled my bike into Nana's yard and leaned it against the back wall of The Shack. They were already waiting for me with their wetsuits on. Jimbo was still lecturing Oz on the strategies of approaching his parents with the big question. He turned to me and said: "Hurry up!" Grabbing my wetsuit off the hanger I quickly changed inside, rolled up my clothes, and put them on top of my tennis shoes against the wall. I grabbed my board and joined my friends outside in the alley. "We won't ever need wetsuits in Hawaii. It's so tropical and warm there. Trust me, you would be foolish to waste space in your suitcase." Jimbo remarked as he pulled the back gate shut behind us. Then we walked down to the beach barefoot, wearing our wetsuits with surfboards under our arms.

"Puny" would be the best description of the waves we saw when we reached the top of the stairs at Main Beach. Walking down the steps, we looked anxiously at the shore hoping to see a fun wave making its way through the mush. Not one did. It was practically flat. Silently, we waded out at our usual spot in a V-formation. Oz went ahead with Jimbo. I was a few feet behind them in the center. Oz jumped on his surfboard and began paddling out. We followed almost simultaneously. Only three other surfers were in the water with us, trying to catch almost non-existent waves. Jimbo was the first to try to catch one, but it didn't have the force to propel him forward. After slapping his arms into the water trying to keep up, it crumbled into white foam meandering towards the shore. I didn't have any better luck on the next wave. Paddling feverishly, I felt the wave pull my board a little, then weakly pass around me as it too broke into white foam. Oz caught the next wave, but just stood on his board as it pulled him a few feet then left him standing high and dry before falling off.

"That was the wave of the day!" Jimbo shouted sarcastically.

We attempted to catch waves for the next hour, but the surf was simply too weak. Still, it felt good to be in the water, paddling around.

"You see, this is the reason we have to get our parents to let us go to Hawaii with Buzz. Wouldn't you rather be surfing crystal blue Hawaiian barrels than riding these miserable ankle-slappers all summer?" Jimbo was committed to his goal. "The Grommets will surf in Hawaii together!" He declared.

That night at dinner, I gently eased my parents into the idea of having Oz and Jimbo travel with us. It didn't take much convincing, they liked the idea. It was as if they had been thinking of it all along. So, now everything rested with Jimbo and Oz getting permission. I called them both that night, excited to let them know my parents agreed. Jimbo was confident. Oz sounded unsure on the phone. We arranged to talk more about our plans at lunch the following day.

The next mid daybreak, I was the first at the lunch table. My Spanish teacher had let us out of class a few minutes early. Jimbo was the next to approach trotting with his brown paper lunch bag swinging back and forth under his arm. He threw it onto the bench and raised his arms as if he had just won a title fight.

"Yup, I'm going to Hawaii! I'm going to Hawaii! I'm going to Hawaii!" He chanted, nodding his head up and down while still jumping with his arms stretched out over his head.

Oz walked up calmly and sat down next to me during Jimbo's goofy victory dance. He quietly pulled the Thermos out of his lunch box, unscrewed the cup and poured himself a drink. Then he pulled out his sandwich, unwrapped it, and started eating.

"Well?" Jimbo was the first to break the silence after calming down.

"Well, what?" Oz replied, acting nonchalantly.

"You know! Are you coming to Hawaii with us or not?" Jimbo snorted impatiently.

"I didn't ask yet." Oz mumbled, looking down at his lunch.

"Awwww come on, don't make me feel like a freak going alone with Buzz and his family." Sensing that he had snubbed me Jimbo added: "No offense Buzz, but you know, it will be more fun with Oz there, too."

I nodded.

Jimbo continued: "If you need help, we'll help you come up with a plan for asking them."

"I thought that's what you have been doing since yesterday." Oz replied. "The thing is that if I ask my parents and they say 'NO' it's final. Then, there is no turning back! Until then, there's still a chance."

"My parents need to know by the end of next week, because of airline reservations. You can't wait too long to ask them." I prodded Oz.

Jimbo was far more frank: "That's the stupidest thing I ever heard. Just figure out a plan, the best way to ask them and then GO FOR IT! I told my Mom how it stinks not having a Dad and how Buzz's Dad is cool and I'd know what it is like, for once. After a couple hours of nagging, the answer was – YES!"

"Yeah, Jimbo that works for you, but it's not like that for me. I can't just talk my way out of things like you can. Besides, my parents are really strict." Oz sounded calm, intently staring at his Thermos.

"You still have a few days to figure out a plan," Jimbo urged before the topic of our discussion changed to the afternoon surf session and the hope that the waves had improved from the day before.

We met at The Shack at the agreed time. After changing into our wetsuits and grabbing our boards we headed out. Reaching the top of the steps, the sight of three-foot peaky mushy waves greeted us at Main Beach.

"That's more like it." I cheered.

Oz was already halfway down the stairs and Jimbo not far behind him. I hurried in order to catch up and jumped from the fourth step with my surfboard under my right arm, onto the soft warm sand. The afternoon sun, which had heated the sand, was getting lower, and we didn't have much time before dinner. Enough to catch a few fun waves, though! By the time my toes touched the tepid water, my friends had already made the fifteen-yard paddle. I saw a wave come through about thirty yards down shore and decided to walk a little further in that direction before wading into the water and jumping on my surfboard, because I thought it might be a better spot. The waves that day were generated by the wind. Most surfers would call it a "wind swell." Generally they are mushy and have short faces, but still can be a great deal of fun. The present day new generation of surfers has taken these waves to a new level popping out of the wave and doing complex aerial maneuvers we only dreamed of as Grommets.

At first, I paddled and paddled against the incoming small walls of white water. After what seemed like a long time I looked back. To my complete dismay, I was still close to shore. Feeling foolish, I stood up only to find that the water was only knee deep. Sheepishly, I looked around. Nobody was looking at me, so I grabbed the nose of my board and quickly shuffled into deeper water before jumping back on. Luckily, there was a lull in the waves so the trip back out was quick. Jimbo and Oz didn't seem to react to my choice of take off spots, they appeared locked in conversation. I sat alone enjoying the peacefulness of the warm sun and the afternoon onshore wind against my face. There was a long wait between sets, so I just sat there. Glancing over at Oz and Jimbo, I noticed they were looking at me. Jimbo shrugged. I signaled 'okay' to them and looked out to the horizon just in time to see the first signs of the approaching waves.

My hunch paid off. The reward was a three-foot peak that rose before me. I spun my surfboard around and with four arm strokes felt it pulling my board into it. At that instant I sprung up, dropped down the small face of the wave and was propelled forward. As it slowed, I cut back turning back to the breaking part. Once I reached the sweet spot, I turned my board back in the direction of the breaking wave with renewed speed. As I raced further it rose up in front of me. At that point, I felt the joy of riding this powerful little wave. After kicking out of that one and a short paddle up the beach, I caught another almost identical wave. It only took two more like that, for Jimbo and Oz to paddle over to the spot where I was surfing. We spent the next half hour riding these juicy little waves before the wind completely blew out the fun, ending our session by turning the ocean shore into white water mush. Tired and happy, we returned to The Shack, rinsed our wetsuits, and went home.

CHAPTER TWO
Travel Plans

The next morning, I was surprised to see Oz waiting for me outside my first period class. He was beaming from ear to ear. There were only a few minutes left until the first morning bell, so I peeked into the classroom, Mr. Peaves the algebra teacher was already writing endlessly long equations onto the black board.

"Did you ask your parents?" I asked, with the hopes he would be joining us on our trip to Hawaii.

"Nope," Oz replied coyly. Before I could express my disappointment he slapped me on the shoulder and said: "Nope, but your mom did. She rocks! I'm going to Hawaii with your family. I am stoked! We're gonna surf!" Oz was interrupted by the bell. "Duty calls, I must run," he flashed me a thumbs up as he jogged away to his first class.

The rest of the morning dragged as I couldn't wait to see my friends at the lunch break. Finally, the noon bell signaled my release. I grabbed my backpack and raced to our bench. Oz and Jimbo were already sitting next to each other with the contents of their lunch bags scattered out in front of them.

"I'm stoked! You really are coming on the trip with us?" I said as I plopped myself down on the bench across from them.

"Yes!" Oz was grinning from ear to ear. "Your mom called my mom, last night. She called Jimbo's mom the night before last." He turned to our friend, who had just taken a big bite into his sandwich and was trying to look innocent. "Yeah, our great salesman over here had some help, I think." He nudged Jimbo, who ignored being confronted with his bragging the previous day. Turning to me he said: "Your mom called mine the night after she asked Jimbo's mom." We both giggled at our friend. He just kept on chewing swallowed and then said: "My mom said if I don't get at least a "B" grade in History you'll be going without me. And don't think you'll have much fun then." He chewed solemnly.

Jimbo was not a bad student, but he really just had a mental block with History for some unexplained reason.

"You better study, Jimbo." I looked at him with dismay. "Don't be a knucklehead! Mr. Jones will flunk you, especially after that stunt in the library last semester," referring to a previous time where Jimbo, in a moment of boredom, took one of the white rats from the biology class and let it loose during a lecture on library research for History papers. Mr. Jones just stood there in shock; while Ms. Wizzel the librarian stood on the table screaming, until Jimbo grabbed the rat and put it on his shoulder. Jimbo received detention for a week. I thought for sure, he would get expelled. "Besides, you know the famous saying: 'Those who don't know history are bound to repeat old mistakes!'" I rather enjoyed telling Jimbo off, for a change.

"Yeah, yeah, I'll study. You can quiz me before the final exams." Jimbo responded flippantly. He got up and threw his trash away. "I'm going to see Mr. Jones now to ask for extra credit. Maybe I should pick up the rat from the Biology classroom and bring it for a visit. The rat misses him." He saluted as he turned to walk back to the building. We followed.

When I got home after school, that afternoon, my mom was in the front yard working on her rose bushes. Snipping a wilted branch with her clippers, she asked me: "How was school?"

"Great, mom! Thanks for asking Oz and Jimbo's parents. I am so stoked that they are both coming to Hawaii with us." I stated beamingly.

"You don't seriously think that I would leave such an important decision to you three boys, do you?" She laughed. "At first, Oz's mom was concerned that six weeks is a long time, but then she considered all of the positive aspects. Just so you know, we will need to do a lot of preparation for this trip. A foreign professor and his family will be staying here in our house for a month while we are in Hawaii. We have to get this place in tip-top shape. So don't make plans with your friends for this weekend. We have a lot to do."

"Okay, I'm going surfing, now." I ran into the house to drop my books in my room, then leaped down the stairs to the kitchen grabbed a banana off the counter, and jumped out of the door and onto my bike. "We're going surfing at Main Beach. I'll be back before dark." Pedaling as fast as I could down the driveway, I passed mom, who was still pruning her rose bushes. I caught her frown, but made it down the street before she could think of something to sabotage or delay my surf session. Unfortunately, we were disappointed at the beach. The surf was flat.

"We should have checked it first, before putting our wetsuits on." I remarked, feeling a little silly standing in my wetsuit with my surfboard under my arm. The ocean looked more like a lake.

"Awww, heck!" Jimbo sighed.

"Well I guess we can get some of the yard work done at Nana's. She lets us use The Shack, so we need to keep up our end of the bargain and keep her yard looking nice." Oz was right.

"Yeah, the grass is getting a little tall and the hedges need trimming." I added.

Jimbo sighed gloomily. We gave the beach a parting look and headed back to The Shack. There we changed out of our wetsuits into our street clothes and stored our gear. Then Jimbo grabbed the lawnmower and started cutting the grass in front of Nana's house. Oz handed me clippers and grabbed a pair for himself. We began trimming the top of the hedges that were already sending new shoots up above the windowsills.

Oz, Jimbo, and I met Nana when we were surfing one morning while she was doing one of her ocean swims. She got a cramp in her legs and held on to my surfboard while we waited for the lifeguards to rescue her. As an expression of her gratitude, she gave us each cool watches and offered the use of The Shack in exchange for our taking care of her yard work. A great deal, since her house was only a block from Main Beach. We were glad to be able to hang out and store our surfboards and equipment there.

"Oh that is wonderful, boys." Nana's voice yodeled as she walked around the side of the house with a pitcher of lemonade and three mugs, admiring our efforts. "I brought you some refreshment."

"Thanks Nana." All three of us replied in unison. We each dropped our gardening tools and grabbed a mug from Nana.

"Thank you boys, the front was looking like it needed a little hair cut. I picked some lemons this morning." She said pouring lemonade into Jimbo's mug. After each of us had some, she smiled and walked back to the side of her house. "I'll be in the kitchen if you need me."

"What are we going to do about Nana's lawn when we are in Hawaii? It's going to need to be cut at least three times in the six weeks, we are gone." Oz contemplated, before taking a swig of Nana's sweet and tart lemonade. He gave Jimbo a glance and then looked at me.

"I never thought about that." I confessed. "Any ideas, at least we have two weeks before school ends, we'll be leaving right after that. My Dad is already flying out next week. He's going to find a place for us to stay before he starts working on his research."

"Tell him to get a place on the beach!' Jimbo exclaimed.

We agreed that would be awesome and worked for another hour until we finished all of our jobs. I went back and pulled two rakes and the broom out of The Shack. We quickly removed the clippings and swept the walkway clean, while chattering about our upcoming adventure in Hawaii. Now, there were only two hurdles to overcome before we would all have the surfing adventure of our lives. The first, getting someone to take care of Nana's lawn, which shouldn't be too difficult. The second, though, could be a problem: Helping Jimbo get a "B" grade in History.

The solution to Nana's yard came surprisingly easy the next week in my English class. Our assignment was to prepare a resume for a summer job. The teacher posted the best ones on the bulletin board. Stephanie Long was in the same grade and almost all of my classes. Under "work experience," for the class assignment she listed landscaping, gardening and yard work. Stephanie's grandmother and Nana were friends.

After English class I caught up with Stephanie, who was already opening her locker. She was wearing a purple sweatshirt with a matching headband in her dark brown hair.

"Hey, Stephanie."

"Hi Buzz." She smiled back at me.

"I saw your resume on the bulletin board in class."

"Oh?" Stephanie looked at me a little surprised.

"Yeah, well you know Jimbo, Oz and I help your grandmother's friend Nana with her yard work. Well, we are all going to Hawaii this summer and I was wondering if you could do some of the light yard work while we are gone. All you'd really have to do is water and cut the grass a couple of times and maybe sweep." I stammered, suddenly feeling a little flushed.

"Sure," she smiled again. "I didn't think I'd get a job from that resume without even applying for one." Stephanie giggled pulling out a pen. "Here's my number." Then, she grabbed my left hand and wrote her phone number on my palm with her purple ink pen. I froze. My heart skipped a beat. Stephanie flicked her hair back with one hand, with the other she grabbed her backpack, closed her locker and said: "You have to bring me something back from Hawaii as payment, though and…" she paused, "I want you to give me surfing lessons, too."

"Okay, sure." I agreed, still feeling awkward.

Stephanie waved goodbye as she walked off down the hallway to her locker.

Jimbo noticed Stephanie's phone number on my hand before I even sat down at our usual lunch spot.

"What's this?" He grabbed my hand to look at Stephanie's phone number. "Ooooooohhhhhhhh Buzz, did a girl write her number on your hand?"

"Jerk," was all I could say feeling embarrassed. "Stephanie is going to take care of Nana's yard while we're gone. And all I have to do is bring back something nice for her from Hawaii." I retorted, and then immediately regretted giving him that last piece of information.

"Will you bring back a ring for her? When's the wedding?" Jimbo teased. "Are you going to move in with her grandmother?"

I turned and feigned interest in watching the highly contested kickball game that was taking place on the adjacent field. Ignoring Jimbo's teasing, I concentrated on trying to not feel so self-conscious.

"Nice job!" Oz broke in saving me from turning even redder. "Nana has known Stephanie since she was a baby. She even babysat her parents. That was a brilliant idea, Buzz! But, does Stephanie know how to do yard work?"

"Yup, as a matter of fact, she does the yard work at her grandmother's place." I regained my composure. A loud cheer erupted from the game at the other end of the schoolyard.

"I was just joking bro." Jimbo recanted. "Stephanie is cool. She will be great."

"By the way how's your History class going?" Oz looked at Jimbo.

"Oh shoot, I'm late. I'd better run. Mr. Jones is tutoring me during lunch. I forgot!" He stuffed the sandwich in his mouth threw the rest of his lunch back into the bag and a muffled: "See ya," as he quickly trotted away.

Oz and I sat quietly eating our lunches for a little while. Oz was the first to break the silence after finishing his sandwich. "That hit the spot. So Buzz, I'm glad that you solved the problem of finding someone to help Nana while we are gone. Jimbo is really trying hard, but maybe we should help him to make sure he gets that "B," in History."

"What do you think we need to do?"

"Tutor him." Oz answered frankly.

"What?"

"You know, we should give him tutoring, like private lessons. We can help him. But you need to be cool about it." Oz gave me a stern look.

"What do you mean? Don't you think I'm cool?"

"That's not it, Buzz. Reading and that stuff is easy for you, but for Jimbo it's really tough and you always act arrogant towards him about school. He is scared he is going to flunk History and go to his grandparents' farm over the summer, when we are in Hawaii." Oz confronted me.

We didn't speak to each other much after that. The rest of my day went by in a mixed fog. The feeling of Stephanie writing her phone number on my hand, along with the guilt of Oz telling me that I was being too hard on Jimbo, filled my head. That night I couldn't sleep and decided to take action to help my friend. The next day, I left for school early to enact the plan that I had put together during the night. Mr. Jones was nice and let me borrow a History book, class outline and notes on what Jimbo needed to learn. At lunch I told Jimbo and Oz to meet me at The Shack an hour after school, but didn't tell them more. Then I went straight to The Shack. From the yard, I could see that Nana was in the kitchen.

She looked out, squinted, leaning on the windowsill and said: "Why you are here early. Is something wrong?"

"I have a favor to ask."

"What is it, Buzz?"

"My Dad is taking us to Hawaii for six weeks this summer. Oz is coming, but Jimbo has to get at least a "B" in History class, or his mother won't let him go on the trip to Hawaii with us. Mr. Jones his history teacher told me this morning that Jimbo needs help to make it. If he works hard he can do well on the final. I got the book and notes from Mr. Jones on what he has to know. You told us once that you and your husband studied History. I told Jimbo and Oz to meet me here in half an hour. They don't know about my plan, to help Jimbo."

Looking into her blue gray eyes, they had a twinkle. Nana chuckled: "My late husband was an archeologist. So, I guess you are right he studied ancient cultures. Our son Joey was always horrible at History. We really struggled with him. Archibald and Clara were straight "A" students. They loved History, and school in general. Joey didn't." She reminisced. "Well come on in, I have some milk and cookies if you can stomach it. I'll take a look at the book and the teacher's notes, and we'll see what we can do." Nana gave me a big hug.

Poncho, Nana's big old Rottweiler, who looked more like a bear, greeted me at the door with a slow wag of his stumpy tail. I patted his massive beefy head before putting the big History book on Nana's kitchen table and sitting down. She pulled a jug of milk from her refrigerator and poured a glass before placing it in front of me. Then Nana grabbed the cookie jar off the counter lifted the lid and placed two big chunky chocolate chip cookies down on a paper napkin.

"So, let's take a look at the book." She reached in the pocket of her apron and pulled out a pair of nickel rimmed glasses, glanced at the notes Mr. Jones had written for me and opened the History text. The cookies were delicious. Poncho sat under me resting his head on my foot. We chatted about History and Hawaii; we discussed that Stephanie Long would be looking after her yard while we were gone; Nana was very pleased. Finally, Oz and Jimbo arrived at The Shack. Poncho let out a little bark. When Nana heard them, she took her glasses off, placed them on the table and stood up to open the kitchen door. Poncho lifted his head and began the slow process of getting up to take the few steps to greet my friends at the door.

"Hello boys! Buzz and I were just enjoying some cookies and milk. Would you like some?" Nana hugged Jimbo and Oz on their way in. "Sit down. I'll pour you some."

"We checked out the surf. It is still flat as a pancake." Oz reported.

Jimbo took one look at the book on the table and recoiled in horror. He didn't speak, and shot me an angry look.

Nana broke the momentary awkward silence. "I am so happy to hear that you are all going to Hawaii together this summer. My late husband and I went on our honeymoon there. It was beautiful. You will really enjoy the surfing. The water is so warm and crystal clear." She had a dreamy look on her face for a moment then turned to Jimbo and smiled. "I hear we have a little task ahead of us though, I believe, a tangle with History."

Jimbo shot me another nasty glance.

Nana continued: "My son Joey had problems learning History and had a hard time with English, too. We even thought he was colorblind in kindergarten. It turned out the little devil was just stubborn and didn't want to learn. He wanted to play so he just made up colors whenever he was tested, just to get it over with. My husband and I had to take him to an eye doctor to find this out. Johannes was so mad at first, but then we just laughed and laughed. So Jimbo, if you have to do well in History to go to Hawaii, so be it. We will help you together." As usual, Nana relieved the pressure of the situation. Jimbo sat there crunching his cookie.

"Yeah Jimbo," Oz urged: "You can do this! We can help you."

Finally, I felt like I could break my silence. "Mr. Jones is pretty cool. I know you don't like him, but he wrote down stuff we can work on and lent me this book."

"That was very thoughtful of you Buzz." Jimbo exclaimed sarcastically.

"You are a good friend, Buzz." Nana sat down next to Jimbo at the table and put her arm around him. "We can start now. Oz and Buzz, why don't you boys leave us alone; I reviewed your teacher's notes and we can get through this material. We will make flash cards and you boys can help Jimbo memorize them when I am not working with him. So how about it, Jimbo, what do you say?"

To my relief, he smiled and said: "Sure Nana, on one condition. I want this to be our secret. Nobody else can know."

We all agreed and shook hands. Oz and I went home after one more check at the beach, which showed no signs of surf, while Jimbo stayed for his first History tutoring session. Hopefully, soon the three of us would be surfing great waves in Hawaii.

CHAPTER THREE
The Big Trip

Dad left for Hawaii about a week after Nana started tutoring Jimbo. It wasn't a teary-eyed farewell because one week later we were going to meet him on The Big Island. The day for final exams finally came; I took my tests without any problems. After studying really hard, they were a breeze. Then, I began to worry about Jimbo's History exam. To make matters worse, it was the last test administered by the school before summer break. Jimbo had a deal with Mr. Jones, who agreed to grade his exam immediately so he would know if he got the "B" or was not going to Hawaii. We waited outside the History classroom for our friend to finish. The door opened and a few of his classmates walked out looking exasperated.

"That can't be good." I commented. When the next student walked out, I asked him: "How was the test?"

"Hard," he responded coldly.

Finally the door opened and Jimbo walked out smiling. "Whew, I'm the last one to finish." He whistled. "That was brutal! Jones is correcting my exam now."

We waited outside the classroom. The suspense was awful. I could see Oz was a little nervous, too. Jimbo on the other hand, seemed perfectly calm. The importance of his exam grade didn't seem to affect him. At last, Mr. Jones opened the door and waved for Jimbo to come in alone. After five minutes the door opened and Jimbo walked out looking down at the ground.

"Did you get a 'B'?" Oz couldn't stand the suspense either.

Jimbo paused: "Nope."

My heart sank.

Jimbo exhaled deeply. "I got an 'A' minus." He snorted. "You know, I really studied, too much. All I needed was a "B." All that work on those flash cards that I had to do with you guys was a waste of time."

"Oh Jimbo," Oz growled. Jimbo smiled and made moves jumping around like a boxer, pretending to punch Oz's chest.

"Hey, we have to figure out what to do with our surfboards. I almost forgot mom told me the airline charges 75 dollars each way. Or, we can rent or buy boards there, probably used ones."

"Yeah, our boards will be important. I want to bring mine. It would take time for us to get used to different sticks." Oz commented. "We will have to wrap them up really well so they don't get dinged on the airplane. I have some ideas on what we might want to do. Bring your sleeping bags to The Shack. Wow, we're leaving in three days!" Our last meeting at The Shack was devoted to packing our surfboards.

The final three days passed like lightening. Mom made me clean my room, clear out my closet and drawers, and put everything that I wasn't taking to Hawaii into boxes. Then she told me to carry them into the garage for storage. A scientist and his family, who were relocating to our city from France, stayed in our house for a month while they looked for a house to live in. We said 'goodbye' to Nana and I made the arrangements with Stephanie to take care of her yard. Before I knew it we were riding with Oz's family in their van, which was loaded to capacity. Jimbo and his mom arranged to meet us at the airport. When we arrived at the airport terminal, Oz's dad stopped the van at the curb and got out. A man in a porter's uniform pushing a luggage cart approached him. They shook hands and we piled out. My mom with little Eric on one hip, approached the porter, pulled out our airline tickets from her travel bag and handed them to him. He counted the bags and began loading them onto his cart. Meanwhile, Oz's mom helped us get our boards off the roof racks. They no longer looked like surfboards. We had removed the fins, wrapped them in our sleeping bags and stuffed them full of clothes to add padding. Then we used rope to wrap around the sleeping bags so they fit snug around our surfboards. The result was a lumpy bundle, which one snide passerby described as 'dead bodies' and another as 'mummies.' I didn't care, the excitement of the trip was so overwhelming, I just wanted to scream.

"Here are your boarding passes and luggage claim tickets. Those surfboards will be hand carried onto the plane. You will need these tickets to pick them up at baggage claim at your destination," the porter informed us he put them on top of the luggage stacked on his cart. He stapled the baggage claim checks to the ticket envelope and handed them to my mom. She handed him a ten-dollar bill. He tipped the brim of his hat said: "Thank you ma'am;" and pushed the loaded cart away. Oz's dad parked their van, while our group proceeded to the gate area with our carry-on luggage. We had arranged to meet Jimbo and his mother there. When we entered the airport terminal, I noticed that Oz's mom was crying. Back then, you didn't have to go through considerable security screenings and even non-passengers were allowed to accompany travelers to the gate.

Jimbo and his mom were not there yet when we got to Gate 22. The board displayed that our plane was scheduled to leave in forty-five minutes. Oz's mom had her arms around him. Her eyes still looked swollen, clearly indicating that she had been crying. A few minutes later, Oz's dad arrived after parking the van. He put his arm around her. It looked like he was giving last minute instructions to Oz. My mom was sitting with Eric on her lap. I sat down next to her. The public announcement loudspeaker crackled: "Attention ticketed passengers for our seven o'clock flight to Hilo International Airport on The Big Island of Hawaii. Please be prepared for boarding in ten minutes."

Looking over at Oz and his parents in the seats facing us was a gloomy sight. Even my friend, who was about to depart on the dream trip for any surfer, was looking miserable. His mom's tissue paper was rolled in a ball and every few minutes she would use it to blot her eyes. Jimbo, on the other hand was nowhere in sight. We had told him countless times to be there on time and I had overheard the phone call between my mom and his, telling her the flight information.

After what seemed like an eternity, boarding was announced. We got in line at the gate. Mom, carrying a sleeping Eric, and I were in front of Oz, whose parents stood next to him in the queue. At last, Jimbo and his mother ran up to us. She was looking extremely frazzled.

"Okay, let's go!" Jimbo was waving his ticket envelope in the air as she grabbed him and smacked a kiss on his cheek, leaving a faint red lipstick impression.

"Be good, James," she spoke with her voice quivering. "Oh Honey, please be good!"

"Sure Mommy, I'll do my best to be good." Jimbo sounded almost innocent as he gave her a big hug before joining us in line. He shot me a sly look.

All of the excitement of that day was overwhelming; I felt a little dizzy and was looking forward to sitting down and resting on the plane. We walked up to the flight attendant. She checked our boarding passes and ripped off a portion of our tickets before returning the stubs to mom. Last minute hugs and kisses were doled out to Oz and Jimbo by their moms before they followed us past the gate and onto the tarmac. My little brother, Eric looked red faced and groggy holding my mom's hand as we approached the open door of the huge passenger jet. A pretty stewardess saw our group coming and waved to a man in the cockpit. The tall captain stepped out and introduced himself. He gave each of us a tiny plastic mold of the airline's emblem with a deadly sharp safety pin glued on, which he called our "wings."

Strangely, despite all of the anxiety and excitement over getting to the airport, once we were finally inside the plane the sounds of fans and the enclosed space suddenly made me feel sleepy. We walked past the first class seats and reached our row. Mom went ahead of us carrying Eric. She stopped at the center of row 78 and pointed to our seats. We occupied the entire middle row. At last, I was able to plop down off my feet. Oz sat to my right and Jimbo was next to him on the other isle, proceeding to test all of the buttons available within his reach. Eric had the seat to my left next to mom at the isle. Passengers kept pouring into the plane, placing baggage in the overhead compartments and claiming their seats.

"Young man, you need to move your seat up." A squeaky female voice commanded from behind Jimbo. All I could see was a mound of orange hair. "Young man, you need to push the back rest of your seat up!" The voice squeaked more demandingly. My mom looked over and gave him 'the look.'

"Certainly, ma'am," Jimbo replied in his politest voice and pushed the button on his armrest. He made a funny face once mom wasn't looking.

A big man with suspenders and a white ten-gallon cowboy hat put his attaché case in the overhead compartment, placed his hat on top of it and sat down in the isle seat across from mom. He greeted the lady sitting at the window to his left side; there was a vacant seat between them. Then the man turned his friendly smile towards us and said, "Howdy," with a deep bellowing voice. I returned the greeting with a wave. The man commented how Eric was the same age as one of his grandsons. He and mom started talking. Jimbo and Oz chattered nervously looking at a surfing magazine. Not wanting to talk, I was glad everyone was occupied and pulled a book out of my backpack. Feeling a little warm, I unscrewed the air vent above, and enjoyed the cool breeze on my face. Soon no more new passengers walked down the isle and it appeared that most of the seats on the plane were now occupied.

Cabin lights flickered as the sound of the jet engines began to rumble. The loudspeakers announced: "This is your captain Doug Sparks on behalf of myself, co-pilot Al Wright, and our crew we bid you welcome to our non-stop service to The Big Island of Hawaii. Please fasten your seatbelts and return your seatbacks and tray-tables to their original position. We will be taking off shortly." The plane jerked back and pulled away from the terminal before taxiing down the runway. After about five minutes the captain announced: "Flight attendants please prepare for takeoff."

"Next stop we'll be walking on the ground in Hawaii, surfing Mecca of the world!" Oz exclaimed, 'High Five-ing' each of us and even reaching over to Mom who was looking concerned about my little brother Eric, but still managed a weak 'high five' hand pat. We settled into our seats. I felt a little tired and shut my eyes. Before I knew it, I dozed off to the hum of the jet engines.

The plane rattled hard and I woke up, forgetting where I was at first. There was a small pillow behind my head and a short blanket covering my chest, now.

"Hey sleepy, you're missing all the fun," Oz nudged me in the side lightly with his elbow. "We're in a storm; you've been sleeping through a great roller coaster ride."

Jimbo was grinning from ear to ear next to him. Mom was pale and she didn't look too happy, but still managed a weak smile. Eric was asleep on her lap. The undertone of the drone of the engines and ventilation fans filled the cabin.

"You slept through the lunch service, but I wrapped this sandwich for you, Honey." Mom whispered as she removed the cellophane wrapper from a ham and cheese sandwich. She handed it to me. It didn't look good and I didn't feel like eating.

"No thanks, mom. I'm not hungry right now. But, I could use some water." My mouth was so dry, it felt parched.

Mom continued to whisper, re-wrapping the sandwich. She placed it in the large handbag at the foot of Eric's seat, while he slept with his seatbelt buckled and his head on her lap. "You can go to the back of the plane and the stewardess will give you some water. Please go out on Jimbo's side, so you don't wake your brother. He is not feeling well and has been fussing the whole time."

"I'll go with you," Jimbo jumped into the isle and motioned me to follow him. I climbed over Oz, who had turned his attention back to the book he was reading. "I know my way around here."

The plane wobbled a little and I felt like I was walking on a ship following my friend down the aisle to the galley in the rear of the passenger compartment.

"Hello Jane, my friend here would like some cold water." Jimbo nonchalantly asked the stewardess, who had met us at the door pre-flight. She looked up from her paperback and smiled.

"Why of course, James." The pretty lady stood up, straightened her blue uniform and filled a cup of water. Handing it to me she said: "Here you go, young man."

"Thanks." The water felt cool in my mouth, which was so dry it absorbed the liquid, like a sponge. "Could I please have a refill?"

"Of course, you are such polite young gentlemen." She giggled. "Are you going to surf the big waves in Hawaii, too?"

"Yup," I answered between sips. She smiled.

After another cup of water, I joined Jimbo, who had his face pushed against a small oval window near the back of the plane. "Check this out, we're over a big tropical storm! You know what that means... big waves!" He turned to me and looked up as if staring at a gigantic approaching wave. Below us faint flashes of lightning illuminated the gray sky from underneath. Looking out of the porthole next to Jimbo, the earth was covered by a dark blanket of clouds. The passenger jet that had seemed so huge in the airport terminal now felt like a tiny speck in the universe. Just then, the plane wobbled up and down.

The captain announced: "Attention passengers, please take your seats and fasten your seatbelts. We seem to be hitting a little more turbulence. There appears to be a rough spot ahead. Thank you." The intercom clicked off.

We made our way back to our seats like sailors on a turbulent sea. Oz pulled his legs back to let me pass him. As I buckled my seatbelt the plane took a long dip. My stomach and lower parts seemed to feel the fall the most. Several passengers let out a loud: "OOOOHHHH" in unison. It sounded like a choir. Then there was silence for a few seconds followed by a resumption of nervous chatter. It was amazing that as high above the cloud layer as we were, the forces of the tropical storm below us still reached our plane. Looking over to my left, I thought my eyes were playing tricks on me. The lady sitting by the window next to the stout man had an orange cat on her lap. She stroked its fur nervously while whispering to it. The man seemed unbothered by the turbulence. He was reading a newspaper.

"Cheddar has to go into quarantine for three months, when we get to Hawaii. He is so nervous about it." The lady noticed I was looking at her across the isle. I nodded acknowledging her.

"Oh, that time will pass by so quickly." Mom spoke encouragingly. She looked frail stroking Eric's hair. He was sound asleep in her lap.

The lady smiled weakly, and said: "You are right. That will give me time to find the perfect place for us to live and get everything just right, before we move in." She spoke to Cheddar and put him back into the pet carrier on the empty seat next to her.

Jimbo got up and tried to walk back to the rear of the plane, but was quickly ushered back by the male steward. Sitting in his seat, Jimbo looked around annoyed apparently searching for something to do. He grabbed the headphones he had purchased, put them on his head and began playing with the controls in the armrest of his seat. Following Oz's example instead, I grabbed my book from my backpack under the seat in front of me and began reading. I only looked up occasionally when the plane wobbled or took a dip. This was immediately followed by another choir of "EWWHH's" and "OOHH's." Occasionally, an isolated scream could be heard during the more severe drops. Immediately after that, there was always a brief moment of silence. The turbulence didn't bother me, it was rather fun. Despite the rough ride, the stewardesses who served us drinks and peanuts were apparently unaffected. I ordered an orange juice and gave the peanuts to Jimbo. My throat felt scratchy. Oz got a cup of water. Only looking up occasionally to take a sip, he was glued to his book. Eric on the other hand had awoken from his long sleep and was acting real grumpy. Mom was doing everything in her power to keep him still, but he refused all the usual treats. He just whined and sucked his thumb wiggling around on the seat next to me. A few times I got annoyed when my reading was interrupted by a whack or a kick from my little brother's flailing arms and feet.

Finally after about an hour, the captain announced: "Ladies and gentlemen, we are about to begin our descent. Fortunately, the weather on the ground in Hawaii has cleared. Unfortunately, in order to land we are going to have to fly through the tail end of this tropical storm. Please remain in your seats with your seatbelts fastened." And so began a landing none of us would ever forget. Within a few minutes, dark gray clouds replaced the bright sunshine that was illuminating the cabin through the oval windows. My little brother reflected the mood of most of the adults on the plane. He began crying, very loudly. His wailing was interrupted by the sound of rattling and the plane jerking left and right, followed by a sudden drop. This time, there was a collective scream. Once the plane stopped shaking to and fro, Eric resumed his tantrum.

"Can't you keep that child quiet?" The lady with the ball of red hair behind Jimbo implored loudly before letting out a scream: "IIIIEEEEEE!" as the plane plunged straight downward.

The man next to my mom chuckled, turned to her and said: "Don't worry, the more he fusses the easier his eardrums will adjust to the pressure change."

Mom nodded and stroked Eric's forehead. He had found temporary solace in his pacifier. The plane began to wobble and shake again. This time there was no drop. Instead, the captain got back on the intercom: "Attention passengers. We have encountered a slight problem. The good news is that we have priority for landing and will not have to wait; however, our touch down will be unusual in that our landing gear is frozen, so we will be forced to land without it." A shudder and murmuring filled the passenger cabin. Jimbo wore a sadistic grin; he seemed to be enjoying the whole spectacle. The captain continued: "Please assume the crash position with your head between your knees and your hands on top of your head." We all obeyed. Mom sobbed a few times before regaining her composure as she adjusted Eric in his seat and put her arm over his little body.

Oz, who had been quiet for most of the trip turned to us with his hands on his head and declared: "That's called a 'belly flop' landing and is actually not that uncommon. I read about it in a book on aviation. You know I'm thinking of becoming a pilot some day."

"Yes, the young fella is right. When I was in the Navy Air Corps, we used to call them 'pancake landings.' Everything will be just fine." The big man raised his torso and spoke reassuringly to my mom and the lady at the window next to him. He got up and quickly opened the overhead compartment, grabbed his white ten-gallon hat and slammed it shut before the stewardess could tell him to sit. Meanwhile the lady pulled Cheddar back out of his carrier and held him against her chest with his head tucked under her chin. "I can remember quite a few times, having to prepare for a pancake landing. On the ground crew, we had a routine." The man reminisced, carefully putting his hat under the seat in front of him before resuming the crash landing position.

"How do you stop the plane, if you don't have wheels to brake?" I wondered.

"Well, the wing flaps act as an air break." The man reassured us. "It takes a little longer, but the plane will stop."

The aircraft shuttered again and swayed back and forth. Two rows in front of us, one of the doors of an overhead compartment popped open and a purse and other bags fell on the head of a man leaning forward in the seat below. He rubbed the top of his baldhead and looked up frightened and annoyed. A stewardess rushed over picked up the carry on, and closed the compartment. She leaned over to the man's ear apparently making sure he was okay, before walking hurriedly back to the rear of the plane. The lights in the cabin flickered and went dim.

"Flight attendants prepare for immediate emergency landing." was the captain's final announcement, which didn't add much to boost the mood in the passenger compartment. My mom looked really worried holding Eric's pacifier in his mouth. His face was flushed and his eyes looked watery and red. I felt a little hot myself. The jet engines began to rev loudly as we neared the runway. A big 'BANG' filled the cabin followed by a loud scratching and squeaking sound. The cabin was filled with the sound of the bottom of the plane grinding on the runway surface. Maybe Cheddar thought it was too quiet, because all of a sudden he let out a loud screaming: "MMMEEAAOOWWW!" His owner cried out for him. All I could see was an orange blur, and then I felt him pouncing on the backrest of my seat.

"AHHH, get this beast off of me!" Cheddar had found camouflage and comfort in the bright orange beau font hairdo of the lady sitting behind Jimbo. The volume of the bottom of the plane scraping against the runway lowered. Finally we came to a halt. Just as the movement stopped, the oxygen masks plopped down in front of us hanging by clear tubes.

Jimbo broke the silence: "Finally! We made it. I'm going to write to the president of this airline. This treatment is outrageous!" He unbuckled his seatbelt, stood up and gently grabbed Cheddar off of the irate woman's head. "This is a pretty kitty, not a beast. You really should get your animal nomenclature straight, lady."

At that point some of the passengers began to race to the now opened doors, the captain made his final announcement: "Attention, we have safely landed. Please remain calm and exit through the open door nearest to your seat. The emergency slides are all inflated. Wait for the person ahead of you to step off the slide before, leaving the airplane. There is no danger. We have successfully landed. All of your luggage will be delivered to you at the terminal. Please leave your carry on items on the plane and exit immediately." Just then, the plane creaked as it began to tilt to the right. There was another group moan. We all froze for a second before unfastening our seatbelts.

"Okay, let's go!" The man next to us sprang into action with surprising speed considering his large frame. "Ladies, I'm going to get up and cover your backs. Boys, follow the ladies immediately." He commanded putting his hat on.

The man stood up in the aisle and took one step back. The lady jumped up and reached over us to grab Cheddar from Jimbo. Mom picked up Eric and grabbed my hand. Jimbo and Oz followed.

"Okay, we're off!" The man followed us down the aisle.

When I got to the door, it was already dark outside. A multitude of fire engines and ambulances lined the runway around the plane. Their lights made the whole scene seem colorful and almost festive. The air was warm and humid. It was filled with the smell of the fire retardant foam that had been sprayed around the runaway along with jet fuel and a hint of flowers. Mom forced the three of us to slide down the inflatable slide. Oz went first. It wasn't as fun or fast as I had imagined it would be. Since the plane wasn't standing on its landing gear, it was lower to the ground and we had to walk off the slide on flat ground for a few yards. Once Jimbo had deplaned, Mom slid down with Eric on her lap. She looked like a ghost. Eric had a pacifier in his mouth, clinging to her.

"Look at little Eric. He is so lucky. He didn't even have to wait to grow tall enough to get on one of the fun rides at the amusement park. He already rode a roller coaster on this plane!" Jimbo broke up the silence and we all laughed. Even mom, who was still pale as a sheet, managed to smile. Emergency personnel in blue jumpsuits approached us to see if everyone was okay. No one needed help except for the lady with the prominent orange ball of hair, which now looked more like a big bird's nest. She was put on a stretcher and driven off in one of the ambulances.

The firemen were still spraying foam on the other side of the plane. We stood at the base of the slide with most of the other passengers and watched as the man, who helped us stood up at the door. He assisted and encouraged other passengers to go down the slide. Finally he put his white ten-gallon hat on, before casting his big body down the slide. Many clapped when he jumped to his feet at the bottom. I couldn't help but join in, clapping loudly. The man tipped his hat in acknowledgement. We all shook hands; some people hugged each other as we were escorted to waiting buses and driven to the terminal. The lady and her cat, Cheddar, were not seen again.

Dad was waiting for us at the terminal. Mom hugged dad for a long time before we could get near him. Wearily, we waited what seemed like an eternity to get our carry-on bags, luggage and finally our surfboards. Oz and Jimbo bickered over luggage placement but we managed to load up everything on three carts.

"Okay you two, here is some change. Go and call your parents and let them know that you arrived safely. Tell them

'Aloha,' from us. We'll wait for you right here." Dad reached into his pocket and handed each of them several quarters. He then grabbed the now sleeping Eric from mom carried him on one arm, and put the other around her. We waited for Jimbo and Oz to make their phone calls. Then, dad guided our weary bunch to the van he rented for our stay. The three of us each pushed a cart of luggage with our surfboard on top.

We relived the crazy flight telling dad about all the details on the way home. Everyone pitched in with the story, even little Eric, who was now looking red in his face talked and pointed. My left ear felt numb and I couldn't hear well out of it. After a half-hour drive in the dark, we finally arrived at what was to be our new home on The Big Island for the following six weeks!

CHAPTER FOUR
Aloha Hawai'i

Waking up the next morning, I didn't remember at first that we were no longer at home. My eyes focused on our new surroundings. The beds, which Oz and Jimbo had claimed, were empty. From outside the half open window, soft guitar music and a woman's voice singing in a melodic unfamiliar yet comforting language drifted in. Feeling a little fuzzy in my head, I closed my eyes and dozed off listening to the soothing tones.

After what seemed like a few minutes, I heard faint sounds and voices coming from downstairs. The bungalow that the University had provided for us, while my dad worked on his research in the lab, was three stories high and had a view to the ocean from the top floor balcony off my parents' bedroom. My brother had a crib in the tiny room next to ours on the second floor. Below that on the ground floor were the kitchen and living room.

My suitcase was still lying on the floor next to my bed. I grabbed my new baggies, a t-shirt and put them on before heading downstairs. The smell of breakfast greeted me. Mom was at the stove in the kitchen, everyone else was seated at the rectangular table eating.

"Good morning honey, would you like some pancakes?" My mom was happily flipping the flapjacks with a spatula.

"Sure, mom." my stomach felt empty.

"We wanted to drag you out of bed, a long time ago but your mom told us to let you sleep." Jimbo informed me before shoving a forkful of pancakes with syrup dripping into his mouth.

"How did you sleep?" My father smiled, as I sat down next to him. He was reading a folded newspaper on the table. "Are you ready to go surfing?" He patted me on the shoulder.

I nodded.

Oz who had finished his plate of food got up, brought it to the sink and rinsed it. He sat back down and said: "A little more enthusiasm. We're in the birthplace of surfing. Except that some people say surfing was invented in Peru..." He paused and couldn't help letting out a giggle. His parents had come from Peru when Oz was just a baby. "Your dad is going to drop us off at a surfing beach."

"We're taking Eric to the doctor, but first we'll drop you boys off at the beach. We'll pick you up after the appointment." Dad added. Apparently, I had slept through what had been a rough night for my little brother, who had been crying and fussing until my parents let him sleep with them. Mom put a plate with two pancakes, scrambled eggs and bacon down in front of me.

"Mom, I don't like bacon," I complained looking down at the food.

"I'll take them!" Jimbo sprung into action. I nodded. He grabbed them off my plate and ate the crispy strips one by one.

"The beach we are going to has black sand." Oz looked up from a travel guide which he had bought before we left home. "We have to unpack our surfboards and install the fins before we leave for the beach."

"Finish your food. Then hurry and get ready. Make sure you take your surfboards outside. I do not want to see them in the house. All I need is wax and sand all over. Black sand or otherwise, I want you guys to help keep this place clean." Mom commanded from the stove.

We finally finished breakfast and got our boards. They were still wrapped like mummies lying on the living room floor where we had dropped them the night before. We carried them out to the driveway. Oz pulled a small red folding knife from his pocket and cut the thin rope holding the sleeping bag tightly against his board. After finishing, he handed the blade to me. I cut the main knot on the rope and passed it to Jimbo. Holding one end of my board up above the black tar of the driveway, I slowly unwound the white rope. The sleeping bag regained its old form. Finally, I held my surfboard again. The fins and Allen wrench were still taped to the deck. I pulled the tape off and began reattaching the three fins, making sure to put each into the correct slot. My old friend shined in the morning sun. For the first time since we landed on the island, I felt the excitement of our upcoming surfing adventure. It was finally a reality. We loaded our boards in the back of the van and went into the house to pack for the beach.

It started to rain for a few minutes and then the sun burst out through the clouds again. Some people move to that part of The Big Island thinking of blue skies, until they realize they now live in a rainforest. Time seemed to drag, as we waited for my parents to get ready and load up Eric and other stuff into the van. Finally, we were buckled up and headed to the beach!

"One of the grad students working with me is a surfer. He told me a good beach to take you to. There are only a few sandy beaches in the area. Most of the others have dangerous lava or rock bottoms." Dad paused as he stopped the van at an intersection and waited for a car to pass before turning. "You guys should have plenty fun at the sandy beaches. I don't want to hear about any shenanigans. You are surfing in Hawaii now. The ocean here is far more powerful and dangerous than what you boys are used to at home. You will only surf at the beaches we allow. Do you understand?" Stopped at a light, he turned around and looked at each of us until we all responded in unison:

"Yes, sir."

Not knowing better, we rolled our eyes at each other in the back seats, as soon as dad's attention was focused back on the road. As if sensing our insolence, mom turned around and gave each of us a stern look. Only Jimbo giggled quietly after she turned her attention back to the front of the van. Dad sensed that we had not gotten the warning. "This is no joke. If I find out that any one of you act carelessly or don't obey the rules of safety, you will be shipped back home the next day. There will be no exceptions!"

A silence fell over us, which was only interrupted by the sound of the motor. Outside the landscape looked almost like home, except greener. Occasionally we would pass a tree or shrub that looked alien. The houses were farther apart than at home and one story high. Only a few two-story buildings broke up the pattern. We headed through town, which almost looked like it was out of a western movie, except that it was paved and cars were parked in front of the stores. Beyond the urbanized area the road was lined with lush green vegetation. It looked like we were headed inland away from the beach.

"Isn't the beach in the other direction?" I complained, as Jimbo and Oz nodded in support.

"We ran out of time and have to get Eric to his appointment at the hospital now. We'll take you to the beach after that." Dad ripped at my heart with that statement. 'Wait at the hospital?!'

I was furious. Oz and Jimbo looked out of the window on their side. I resigned to looking out of mine.

The hospital appeared like a neat stack of giant white boxes on the right side of the two-lane highway. Dad pulled into the driveway and let mom and Eric out at the front door.

"I'll park and meet you in the waiting room." Dad kissed mom on the cheek and waited for her to walk into the entrance before driving to the back of the lot. After parking and pulling the keys out of the ignition, he turned to us and said: "Okay boys, hang out here. This shouldn't take too long." He jumped out, shut the door and trotted over to the hospital entrance.

"Welcome to Hawaii, ladies and gentlemen. Here we are in the back of a parking lot." Jimbo broke the silence. "What do we do now?"

"That's easy." Oz grabbed his backpack from behind our seats, unzipped it and pulled a flying disk out. "Let's play!"

We jumped out of the van. Stretching my stiff legs felt good as I ran down the empty part of the parking lot to catch the disk before it hit the ground. Winding up, I managed a toss straight over Oz's head to Jimbo. The gloom lifted and we had fun in the soft Hawaiian breeze. Whenever a car drove by I expected to get a dirty look. Instead, ladies in bright floral dresses who got out of cars, waved and smiled. Men smiled at us and waved, even stopping their cars to wait for us to catch the disk.

When my parents and Eric finally returned, I was almost disappointed to stop our game and get into the van. We drove back down the country road into town and stopped at the drug store. Mom ran in with the prescription for Eric's ear infection. Then we were finally beach bound!

My heart began to beat faster at the first glimpse of the ocean. The sky was overcast and the water gray, but each time there was a wave or the sight of white water the excitement level in the van skyrocketed.

After about twenty minutes, Dad muttered looking down at a hand drawn map: "I think this is it." He turned the van down a dirt road. Dense shrubs and old gnarled trees lined the way. At the end, there it was the beach! At last, we had made it. A few cars were parked off the dirt and Dad found a spot under a tree that overlooked the ocean. As soon as the van stopped, we unbuckled our seatbelts and raced out the door to the black sand beach. It really was black!

"It looks kind of mushy." Oz was the first to comment as the three of us stood at the waters edge. The water looked dark gray, not at all like the turquoise blue cylinders pictured in the magazines. These waves looked more like the ones we surfed at home. We were silent.

"Let's charge it!" Oz broke our silence.

"Last one in the water is a turd!" Jimbo called out his challenge.

We looked at each other and ran back to the car. Luckily, my dad had already taken my surfboard out of the van and stood it up under the tree. He was just pulling Oz's board out. After throwing my t-shirt into the van, I grabbed my board and ran down the short stretch of warm black sand to the shoreline. Since I was already wearing my baggies, I reached the water first. Oz walked in the water seconds before Jimbo made his splash.

"What is the last one in the water?" Oz looked at Jimbo smiling.

"Okay, I'm it. Who's got the wax?" Jimbo ignored his defeat.

Standing in knee-deep water, Oz pulled a bar out of his baggies and rubbed wax on the deck of his surfboard. He then broke the remainder in half and threw a piece to each of us. The coconut scented surf wax was sticky and left white bumps on my surfboard. I rubbed it on the areas where I place my feet to prevent slipping off the deck.

"You guys rushed off, without saying anything." Dad interrupted. "You are surf crazy. Check in every half hour. Look at the shore. I'll wave my towel over my head when it's time to go. Be safe out there."

"Okay, dad."

"Yes Sir." Oz replied.

"Aye-aye, sir." Jimbo gave an over-exaggerated salute.

Dad shook his head as he watched us wade into waist deep water. We jumped onto our surfboards and began paddling towards an empty peak. I was glad that there weren't any other surfers there. A few were sitting at the other spots, where waves were breaking further out. When we reached the spot we sat up on our surfboards and huddled together. Looking back towards the shore the vegetation looked tropical with all of the palm trees. My parents had set up two large blankets. Eric was plopped in the middle of one and my parents were laying on the other.

The ocean looked flat for a few minutes until the next set arrived. The sight of surfers catching the outer peaks alerted us. The first wave that hit us did not form a steep enough face for anyone to catch. The next rose up two feet higher and presented a nice push. Jimbo and Oz paddled and jumped to their feet riding on their first Hawaiian breaker together. Thirteen seconds later, mine rose up behind me. A few arm strokes and I felt the pull of the wave; it felt quicker and stronger than what I was used to. In an instant, I was on my feet racing towards the shore. A quick turn to the right and my board was gliding along the face of my first Hawaiian wave. Even though the waves looked like the ones at home, this was different. The speed and power was more than I ever had experienced on a wave that size. No fancy turns were possible. All I could do was to curl my toes and hang on. The wave ended as fast as it had begun, only fifty feet away from the take off spot.

Oz and Jimbo were paddling back out next to each other by the time I got back onto my board. I was stoked by my first ride. Before I got back to the peak, another set came through. This time, Oz was the first to catch one. He dropped down the face and made two off the lip turns before passing from my sight. Jimbo caught the next and went straight, hanging in the sweet spot of the wave. I tried to paddle faster but did not make it in time for the last of that set. Feeling a little tired I welcomed the rest sitting in the deeper water beyond the foamy remnants of the last wave.

Oz was the first to paddle back. "Whew, that was fun!" He sat up on his surfboard next to me. "We saw your wave, it looked like a zipper."

"Yeah, that was fast. I couldn't believe how powerful it was. They look like the waves we surf at home, but a lot juicier." I said.

"All right, this is great!" Jimbo was slightly out of breath.

Just then, the first wave of the next set peaked in front of us. I turned my board, grabbed the nose with two hands and pushed it backwards. As it popped back out of the water, the force of the wave pulled me, and I leapt to my feet instantly dropping down the face. "OOOOOWWW," Oz hooted. Again, the wave was too fast to do any turns. As it tapered a little, I turned my surfboard up and over the top. Realizing my error, I jerked the board back and to my surprise, reentered the wave took the drop and rode for another twenty feet before it fizzled out.

My heart was pounding and body filled with joy from the experience. My friends each caught fun waves. Jimbo took off first, and then Oz. Waiting for them to be dropped near me at the deeper water, I sat on my surfboard.

"YEAH!" Jimbo shouted as he dropped chest first onto the deck of his board immediately paddling back out, he passed by me nodding his head in triumph.

Oz attempted a lay back turn at the end of his wave and sunk backwards into the water instead.

"Nice one," I complemented my friend as he approached me. "My last wave was weird. I cruised up and over the top of the face and then turned back and dropped into it again."

"Wow, you did a round house cut back!" He explained. "You need waves with power to do that. These waves have power!" Oz exclaimed before we paddled back out together.

Jimbo, who was outside went further out to meet an even bigger approaching set. We watched as he turned around, and began to paddle. As he rose to stand, the wave broke and knocked him forward off his surfboard, which shot up in the air behind the white water. His head popped up a few seconds later in time for the next set to pummel him. Three more waves repeated the pattern before the ocean surface became calm again and Jimbo was able to get back onto the deck of his surfboard.

Paddling, I felt a little chilly. "I'm going in after the next one, it's getting cold." I informed Oz.

My friend gave me a questioning look, but then nodded. Oz looked out at the horizon and exclaimed: "Here it comes!" He pointed at the approaching wave.

Jimbo was too far out to take off. I was in a better position, so I spun around and scratched the water until I felt the strong pull of the wave on my board. I jumped up, and was able to make a few turns on the face of the wave, before it crumbled in the deeper water. Back on the beach, I wrapped myself in a towel to warm up and ate half a peanut butter sandwich. Jimbo and Oz only caught a few more waves before they also paddled in.

That afternoon and evening we sat at the house and relaxed watching TV and exchanging stories about the fantastic waves we had ridden that day. It was a great ending to our first day on The Big Island.

CHAPTER FIVE
A New Friend

In the middle of the night I awoke in a sweat, with a sharp pain in my left ear. Touching the lobe, it hurt even more and felt like I had cornflakes in my ear canal. It was impossible to fall back asleep. After tossing and turning until the sun came up, I walked downstairs and sat down at the kitchen table. Mom soon followed.

"Your father is going into the lab today. You don't look well. Are you feeling okay?" She felt my forehead. "You have a temperature, young man."

"And a bad ear ache, too," I added wearily. "It feels like there is a big splinter sticking in my left ear."

"Just like Eric. We'll take you to the doctor. I'll see if Dr. Yamaguchi can squeeze us in. He's an old friend of your father's from college. He said he would be at the hospital today, too. I remember his office hours from when we brought Eric in, yesterday." Mom grabbed her purse pulled out a little bottle, opened it and shook two little pink pills into her hand. "Here, take these baby aspirins."

"Uh-oh!" Dad walked into the kitchen. "Is some one else sick here?" He looked at me concerned and felt my forehead. I nodded miserably. "I'll call Hank, he should be at the hospital already." He turned to Mom and said: "Do you think I should call the lab and tell them I won't be in?"

"No, honey, we'll drop you off before we take Buzz to get checked out." Then turning to me she directed: "Go and lie down on the couch. You can watch TV. I'll bring you a damp warm cloth for your ear."

Lying down in the den area, I didn't even feel like watching TV. My mom brought me a hot washcloth. She wringed out as much of the water out if it, as she could, before gently placing it on my ear. The slightly damp, warm washcloth helped reduce the pain. It felt soothing. I dozed off.

Jimbo woke me, shaking my shoulder. "Hey buddy, wakeey-wakeey, time for breakfast. We're having cornflakes."

Rubbing my eyes feeling nauseous at the suggestion, I told him: "No thanks," and curled into a ball. It was like the energy had been sapped out of me. My head felt dizzy, and I didn't want to do anything but get rid of the pain in my left ear.

The ride to the university was short. We drove from there back to the hospital. Oz had left the flying disk in the van, so my friends jumped out and began tossing it in the parking lot before mom had even unpacked Eric and his stroller.

The inside of the hospital looked like any other. Mom, Eric, and I stepped through the entrance doors. We walked down the hallway to the doctor's office. I sat down in the waiting room while Mom checked in with the receptionist and overheard the young lady say: "Dr. Yamaguchi will be with you shortly. He asked that you wait a few minutes, for him." Mom gave Eric a pacifier in his stroller, picked up a women's magazine from the rack and sat down next to me. The waiting room was empty and I was glad not to have anyone else looking at me during my misery.

Finally, after about twenty minutes, a tall stocky Asian man with glasses wearing a white lab coat entered the waiting room.

"Well, hello Gina and little Mister Eric; I guess this must be Buzz." He looked at me and reached out his hand. I shook it.

"Let's get you into the examination room and see what's going on."

We followed him down the bright hallway. A pair of nurses passed locked in conversation. When they passed Dr. Yamaguchi, they said: "Aloha," smiling heartily at us. In my brain fog, it struck me; we are really in Hawaii!

"In here please." Dr. Yamaguchi stopped at a door that had a sign, which read: 'EAR, NOSE & THROAT EXAMINATION ROOM.' "I have a hunch that we are going to need to look at you through the scope so I figured we'd go straight to this room." He opened the huge door, and turned on the light. "Okay, come on in. Gina, you and Eric can sit here." He pointed to a chair by the wall. "Okay, Buzz please, sit here." It looked to me like a dentist's chair. I sat down. He put on a brown leather headband with a large round mirror on it. The mirror had a hole in the middle. The doctor seated himself on a short stool. He rolled it over to me and flipped the mirror down over his right eye from his forehead. Dr. Yamaguchi stomped his foot down and the light dimmed in the room. It felt a little eerie.

"Okay Buzz, so tell me how do you feel?" He asked.

"My left ear hurts and I feel dizzy." I replied.

"Let's take a look." He said as he looked into my right ear. "That one looks okay. Let's see the other. Oh boy, yes you have a full-blown ear infection in your left ear. Let me clean it out a little, so I can get a better look." He grabbed a light blue kidney shaped bowl and held it under my aching ear. "Okay, this won't hurt, but it may be a little uncomfortable." That was an understatement. He grabbed a small water hose from the console with his other hand. The cool water made gurgling and slurping sounds in my ear and felt very uncomfortable. No, he was wrong, it hurt! With curled fists, I gritted my teeth until it was finally over. The doctor gave me a paper towel to hold against my ear.

"Alright Buzz, now let's take a closer look." He put the scope into my ear. I cringed as he put a thin instrument with cotton on the tip into my ear canal. Hearing a squeaky sound in my ear, it hurt real badly. "There, now I can get a good look. Looks like you have a full-blown ear infection. But, the lucky thing is your tympanic membrane is still intact. That means you don't have a hole in your eardrum. Your brother wasn't so lucky." He picked up a silver instrument that looked like a pair of pliers and put the tip into my nostril. I felt it stretch open as he examined me further, and then the other nostril. "Okay, you also have a mild case of sinusitis. Looks like you have a deviated septum just like your dad." He put the instrument down, pulled a hose out of the panel and clicked a nozzle onto it. Then he held it up to my left nostril. "Okay Buzz, I want you to say 'cuckoo'."

As I complied and said: "Coo-CKOOOO," he blasted air through my left nostril and I heard and felt a blast of air in my left ear. It must have cleared something because I could hear much better. He repeated the process in my right nostril and ear and then flipped up the round mirror back up simultaneously clicking the lights back on with his foot. Then, he puffed some kind of a powder into my left ear.

"You are done. I'll write you a prescription for antibiotics. I want to see you back in a week and a half." He turned to my mom and said: "I'll see them both for a follow up. Hanna and I would also like to invite you up to the house this weekend. She'll call you to confirm." Then, he turned to me and spoke words that struck like thunder: "Okay, no water in the ear. No water in the ear." It echoed. "I hear that you are an avid surfer." I nodded. "Well, don't go surfing until after you come for your check up in ten days. If everything looks good then, I'll clear you to go back in the water. Make sure that you put cotton in your left ear when you shower. You must keep it dry. I'll send you home with a prescription for drops, too."

We said goodbye and walked out of the hospital. Oz and Jimbo were sitting on the curb next to the van.

"Alright, ready to surf?" Jimbo jumped to his feet.

I shook my head.

"What?" Jimbo looked shocked.

"What's the matter?" Oz walked up.

"He's got an ear infection and can't get water in his ear. Buzz won't be surfing for at least ten days until the doctor clears him." Mom interjected.

"AWW, that stinks!" Jimbo exclaimed.

"Yeah, that's foul." Oz sympathized, too. "Can't we plug up your ears, so you don't get water in it?"

Before I could consider that interesting possibility, mom answered: "No, he can't get water in his ear and there is still a risk of it with ear plugs."

"Let's put a bubble around his head." Jimbo added: "You'll be 'Buzz, the bubble boy,' cool!"

It wasn't funny to me. Everyone laughed, except for me. Even little Eric repeated 'bubble boy' and giggled. I felt lousy.

On the way through town, mom ran into the drug store again and dropped off my prescription. Then, we headed to the beach. I felt miserable lying on the blanket, watching my friends surf. The waves were even better than the day before. Both Oz and Jimbo caught some really good rides. Before going back to the house we returned to the pharmacy to pick up my medicine. When we got home, I went upstairs. Mom started to make dinner.

That night I had crazy dreams. Nana was driving her huge black dusty jalopy across the ocean to Hawaii. Stephanie was sitting next to her. Poncho, Nana's Rottweiler was wearing sunglasses and a Hawaiian shirt, coasting behind them pulled by a rope on a pair of water skis. I awoke to an empty bedroom. My ear no longer ached, but I still felt very groggy. After plopping back down and snoozing for another ten minutes, I got dressed and went down stairs. Mom was reading a book on the couch in the den and Eric was watching a children's program on TV.

"How are you feeling Honey?" She looked up concerned.

"Oh a little better, my ear isn't aching anymore. Maybe I don't have to stay out of the water that long." I sat down next to her.

"Yeah right, nice try Buzz. You're not going in the water until Doctor Yamaguchi says so." She felt my forehead. "You don't seem to have a temperature – that's good. Your father dropped your friends off at the beach and went to the lab. The dishwasher is not working, so I called the property management company and they are sending a handyman to fix it. Make yourself some cereal." Mom returned her attention to her book with the man with the long blond hair and the big muscles on the cover.

The kitchen at the house was unfamiliar, so I had to look around for a bowl and spoon. The cereal boxes were still on the counter. Just as I got the milk out of the refrigerator, there was knocking at the door. Mom closed her book, jumped up and went to the door. I finished pouring the milk, put it away and sat down to eat at the table.

"Aloha," a short thin gray haired Asian man with thick spectacles wearing a blue cap and overalls followed Mom into the kitchen. "I am Hiro, and this is my son Keemo." A big tall dark skinned boy walked in carrying a metal toolbox. His face was expressionless. He didn't say a word or even nod. "So, the dishwasher is giving you trouble?" Keemo's father asked.

"Yes, it doesn't seem to work." Mom walked over to the kitchen table and sat down next to me.

"Well, let me take a look." The man motioned for Keemo to put down the toolbox. His face was emotionless as he stood there watching his father work. "Okay." Hiro grabbed his flashlight opened the dishwasher and began tinkering. I watched while eating my cereal. Keemo stood with his arms on the side of his body motionless, watching. Hiro pulled the bottom rack out of the dishwasher and placed it on the counter. "So what's your name?" He asked looking at me though his round spectacles.

"Buzz," I answered.

"What are your sports?" He asked as he kneeled down in front of the broken appliance. After telling about surfing and my ear problems to him, Hiro said: "Maybe you want to come over and borrow one of Keemo's skateboards. I'll bet you didn't pack one in your suit case for your visit." He chuckled. Keemo nodded without any expression or emotion.

"Yeah, that would be cool! Mom, can I borrow one of Keemo's skateboards?" I begged.

"Sure, honey," she replied walking into the kitchen. "So what's the verdict?" Mom asked.

"I think the motor is burnt out. I'll have to see if we have one in storage or from the parts store that will work. Otherwise we'll have to order one from the mainland. That may take a couple of weeks. But don't worry; we maintain a lot of properties for the university folks. We might just have the part or I'll probably find one somewhere on the Islands."

Mom smiled: "I guess with all the young men in the house, I'll have plenty of help washing the dishes by hand."

"Except for me, remember I'm not supposed to get water in my ear." I mused.

"I'll be back when I find a replacement for this motor. We live just a few houses down the street. Keemo and I walked here. In the meantime maybe Buzz would like to come back to our place and borrow a skateboard?" Hiro closed his toolbox and handed it to Keemo.

Mom nodded affirmatively when I asked if it was alright. She hugged me and said: "Behave yourself, Buzz. And remember Dr. Hank said you can't get any water in your ear." Following Hiro and Keemo out of the house, we walked on the street. There was no sidewalk. Keemo walked on the grass, and Hiro was to my right in the street. A beat up pickup truck driven by a gigantic man in a red and white floral shirt slowed down. The man honked and waved at us.

Hiro and Keemo said: "Aloha." The man drove by shaking his hand with his thumb and pinky finger sticking out. Keemo did the same back.

"'Aloha,' means hello and goodbye, in Hawaiian." Hiro explained. "In Hawaiian words have 'Mana' that means spiritual or divine power. 'Aloha,' and also 'Mahalo,' which is how you thank someone, are among the most sacred and powerful words." We walked further down the street. "You must only use them when you really mean it, don't make fun of them or use them for your own personal gain." We walked quietly passing another five houses until we came upon a property that was overgrown with vines. Walking past the palms and bushes into the front yard, there were appliance parts littered all over. Three rusty refrigerators with their doors removed, were lined up on the side of the house with white chipped paint.

"Keemo, show Buzz your skateboard collection." Hiro walked into the screened porch in front of their small house.

Keemo walked mutely to the back of the house. All sorts of machines and parts unfamiliar to me obscured part of the yard. In the back stood a rusty metal shed. Keemo opened the combination lock and swung the double doors open. Inside were racks full of skateboards and parts, neatly stacked. In the far corner a shocking pink surfboard and a longer fluorescent green one were leaned next to each other against the aluminum wall. The shed looked impeccably organized unlike the rest of the yard.

"Wow, are these all of your skateboards?" I was amazed by the number and variety of skateboards neatly arranged on the walls and ceiling of this shack.

"Yeah, I collect skateboards, trucks, wheels, and bearings. I keep them all organized and in order. Here, this one will be good for you. Let me check the trucks." Keemo pulled down a wooden skateboard with red wheels, grabbed a tool from the wall and adjusted the metal axles.

"Do you surf?" I asked him pointing to the two surfboards in the corner.

"Those are my cousin's. I ride a surf mat." Keemo replied. "You want to go skate?"

"Sure, I have to go by my house and check with my mom. Is that okay?"

"Okay." Keemo handed me a helmet from the wall and a set of knee, and elbow guards. He picked a set for himself, grabbed a skateboard off the wall rack, and locked the shed. I followed him out to the street. There, he jumped on his skateboard in one leap and did a turn in a big circle ending back in front of me.

"We'll do easy hills first." He said before he took a big push from his front leg and rode down the street towards our vacation house carving smooth S-turns. I was never a very good skateboarder, so I just put the board down and stepped on it. After a few pushes with my back foot, there was enough momentum to follow Keemo, awkwardly.

Heeding mom's warning to 'take it easy,' Keemo and I agreed to only skate on our street. After about an hour, I got tired. My ear had begun to ache a little, too. We skated back to the house. Keemo and I arranged to meet the next day after lunch to go skating.

CHAPTER SIX
Trouble In Paradise

The next day, Jimbo and Oz again left early with Dad, who dropped them off at the beach. The day before, they were so exhausted from surfing, that all my friends could do was gorge themselves with food and fall asleep.

Listlessly, I passed the morning by alone. Lunch was 'blah.' I was getting irritable with boredom and maybe just a little jealous about not being able to surf. Finally, there was a knock on the front screen door. I recognized my new friend's frame, which looked like a shadow behind the screen door.

"Mom, I'm going skating with Keemo!" I shouted.

"Okay, be careful, honey, and be back before dinner," Mom was upstairs.

"Aloha!" Keemo greeted me.

"Aloha, I'm stoked to go skating!" I replied as we walked down to the street.

Keemo jumped on his skateboard and I followed. This time we rolled down the hill in the direction away from his house.

"Where are we going?" I asked.

"To a primo place for skating!" he replied nonchalantly weaving turns back and forth in the street.

At first, I tried to follow his example, my turns were not as graceful and a couple of times I nearly fell. When we got near the end of our street I started to get warmed up and my turns flowed more smoothly. We stopped at the corner and waited for the cars to pass. When the coast was clear, we crossed the busy street. Walking next to Keemo, I felt small. The skate helmet was making my head feel warm in the tropical air, but I resisted the temptation to take it off.

Then, the long march uphill began. After ten minutes, I had to take the helmet off and strap it to my board. We walked and walked… silently. Keemo took the lead. We were heading in a direction away from town. After another fifteen minutes I had to take off the knee, elbow pads and wrist guards. They felt hot and soaked with sweat. Keemo waited patiently at each stop. He seemed indifferent to anything else, serene, and spoke very little. I trusted him. We walked and walked at a slight incline and at other times up steep hills. It seemed like forever following my big friend. I felt strained and tired, but pushed on. My legs and lungs burned and my head felt like it was going to explode at times. Alongside the road the houses were replaced by dense brush, which was later replaced by sheer jungle. We walked and walked further up the hill. Finally, we came to what seemed like a plateau. I regained my breath and actually managed to keep up with Keemo, walking next to him.

"So do you think this is going to take much longer? My mom was expecting me back for dinner and I have to take this medicine for my ear so that I can go surfing again." There was no response from my friend. I got a little nervous. We kept on walking.

After another period of silent walking that felt like hours, I tried again. "Hey Keemo, how much longer is this going to take. I'm worried my parents are going to give me grief over being away too long. If I miss dinner there's going to be trouble, he-he." I tried to laugh.

"We're almost there," was his stoic response. "And the way back home is a lot faster." He pointed downhill.

Looking back down at the long steep way we had already come was a little scary. We walked further before coming to another street, which was level and had wide sidewalks. Keemo dropped his skateboard, which landed perfectly on its wheels. I tried the same maneuver without success, my board bounced up and flipped onto its deck. As I was bending down to turn it up, I noticed something shiny in the leaf filled gutter.

"What's that?" I pointed.

Keemo bent down and picked up a big gold clip-on earring with what looked like diamonds.

"Wow, I wonder if it's real?" I exclaimed.

"We should return it to its owner. She is probably real sad. It is important to return things to people when they lose them. I once lost my wallet and someone returned it to me with the money in it. That made me happy, but before that, I was sad when I found out I lost my wallet. The lady that lost this earring probably wishes she had it for her empty ear." Keemo said studying the piece of jewelry, holding it close to his eyes. He handed it to me to look at. After I handed it back he put it in his pocket, looked at me and said: "My dad will know what to do."

With long strides, Keemo pushed his skateboard forward with his back foot, while I struggled to keep up. The pavement in this neighborhood was nice, smooth and flat. I wondered where there could possibly be a good place to skateboard here in a neighborhood in what seemed like a jungle. After a few turns down a couple of different streets, Keemo stopped in front of an old abandoned looking gray house that had a battered 'For Sale' sign with a huge dumpster in the front yard.

"Here we are." He said. 'This place is being fixed up. My Uncle Lolo is working on it, but they are waiting for the owner to come up with more money to fix it." Keemo walked along the side of the house to the back yard. The structure was enormous and right behind the house was a huge empty swimming pool! So that's what he was talking about.

The pool looked like it was surrounded by jungle. In the back of the property, a huge Banyan tree overshadowed the dense overgrowth. The house in the front of the property was not even visible from the shallow end. We walked on the cracked cement to the steps. Keemo dropped his skateboard down in the pool and jumped on the deck. He pushed with his front foot and launched through the shallows to the deep bowl at the other end. Turning left, he rose up the wall about three quarters from the rim and gracefully rode his skateboard around the bowl until dropping back down and rising into the shallow end. Stepping on the tail, he grabbed the front wheel and said: "Your turn."

Swallowing my fear, I pushed off with my back foot and moved through the shallows at a comfortable speed. Dropping into the bowl, I had to lean forward in order to keep from falling on my rear. The momentum propelled me up the face of the wall at the deep end. When my board slowed I tried to turn the nose around 180 degrees and ride back down the wall, but I wasn't fast enough. Instead, my front foot slipped off the deck and I ended up running down the wall into the bottom of the bowl, almost falling on my left side. My skateboard rattled past me and rolled up the other side of bowl and back down again. Picking it up, I ran back to Keemo who was waiting his turn in the shallows.

Before he could jump onto his skateboard a flash of pink appeared at the other end of the pool. A girl with long jet black hair under a bright pink helmet and long tanned legs walked up. She stood at the edge, one foot on the tail of her skateboard. With a graceful move she put her other foot on the front of her deck and dropped into the bowl. With hair flapping back like wings under her helmet, she cruised up, down and around the vertical wall. Finally, she lost momentum and joined us at the steps of the dry swimming pool.

"Aloha, Cuz." The girl was dressed in pink from her t-shirt down to her socks and tennis shoes. "Uncle Lolo just dropped me off."

"Aloha, Leilani." Keemo greeted her in his inexpressive manner.

"Who's the haole?" She looked at me from the corner of her eyes. I felt a little uncomfortable.

"My friend, Buzz." Keemo's answer made me feel less intimidated. "We came here to skate together. He is staying at the University house down the street."

"Aloha," I greeted her sheepishly.

Leilani nodded coolly and pushed her skateboard back into the bowl. We took turns riding in the deep end of the pool, but after about ten times I was exhausted and took off my helmet. The light wind cooled my sweaty forehead. For the first time since we landed, my nose was clear. I could breathe through it again and smell the scent of flowers in the breeze.

A pretty black crow was busily pulling dry grass from the tufts that were growing out of the cracks in the cement around the pool. It would get a beak full and then fly off for a few minutes only to return and repeat the process. Every once in a while the small avian would stop and look at me, as if to make sure I wasn't a threat, before continuing with its industrious pursuits. The black bird flew into the giant banyan tree in the very back of the yard, making funny cat-like sounds. A feeling of happiness overcame me, sitting in this strange yard with my new friends.

"Are you ready to go home?" Keemo asked, panting after his final ride.

"Yes, sure!" even though I felt very comfortable there and really didn't want to leave.

We followed Leilani, out of the overgrown back yard. I hadn't noticed, but the large wooden side gate was leaning against the gutted house. Back in the street, Keemo, reaching up as she held on to her cousin's right shoulder, towed Leilani on her skateboard. I walked on the left side of Keemo along the curb. Just as I was about to break the silence with a comment about the pool we had skated in we heard a loud: "BEEP, BEEP, BEEP-BEEP!" A woman wearing a red scarf on her head, driving a red convertible raced around the corner and almost hit us head on.

"Hey, you kids get out of the way! What, it's you again!" She shouted and honked her horn: "BEEP, BEEP, BEEEEEEEE EEEEEEEEEEEEEEEEEEEEEEEEEP!" The woman leaned on her horn. "See, I knew that that dumpster full of garbage would attract rats!" It was obvious that she meant us.

Like a deer in the headlights, I froze until Keemo pushed me over to the safety of the curb. Leilani rode her skateboard around on the driver's side narrowing her eyes, she paused for a moment giving the woman a venomous scornful look.

"Don't you look at me like that, missy!" The woman took off her glasses and glared back at Leilani.

We continued walking, as the car engine revved behind us. The tires screeched. We watched the red convertible speed away.

"She didn't like my stink eye. I'll give that to that goat again next time I see her. Who does she think she is calling us rats and almost running us over?" Leilani watched the car speed away with a look of distain. "She lives next to the house where we skate. My uncle got permission from the owners, so there's nothing that she can do. We can skate."

The way home was a lot faster. Leilani was in the lead snaking long turns to keep from going too fast. We followed her example as we rode our skateboards down hill the entire way. At certain points it was a little scary going fast down the mountain hill. It was a good thing there were only a few cars on the road. We reached the main street that leads into town, in no time. After another ten minutes out of our way, we arrived at Leilani's house. It had a big front porch and a mostly dirt packed front yard with some patches of grass.

"Aloha! See you later," Leilani kicked up her skateboard in the air, caught it and ran into the house.

Keemo and I turned around and walked back to the street. We didn't speak very much until I broke the silence: "What's a How-lee?"

"A haole is someone who isn't Hawaiian." Keemo responded in his usual matter of fact fashion. He elaborated: "It's not a nice word and I don't like it. My dad says it's mean and he doesn't like it either."

When we got to my place, Keemo and I arranged to go skateboarding after breakfast the next day unless he had to help his dad, in which case maybe in the afternoon. Inside, Oz and Eric were sitting in the living room watching TV.

"Hey, Buzz." My friend greeted me.

"Aloha, Oz. Where's everybody else?" I wondered.

"They're upstairs. Jimbo is kind of bummed out. He got into a fight with one of the local kids at the beach." Oz reported. "Jimbo was getting a little aggressive in the water and got tangled up with a boy. On the beach, they got into exchanging punches and Jimbo got a black eye before the grown-ups could pull them apart. Now, he wants to fly home. He's balling upstairs in the bedroom and your parents are talking to him."

Mom came downstairs into the kitchen. "Hi Buzz, I'm glad you're back. If you are hungry, grab a piece of fruit from the counter. We'll be eating in about an hour. Jimbo needs to use his main course first." She opened the refrigerator and pulled a steak out. After throwing the wrapper into the trash, she rinsed it under the faucet and patted it with a paper towel, just as Jimbo walked back down the stairs. His right eye was shut and swollen. Jimbo's left eye was blood shot and his cheeks were streaked with tears. "Here, hold this on your eye." Mom smiled sympathetically as she placed the sirloin beef filet over Jimbo's shuteye. I grabbed an apple and left the kitchen.

"How was the surf?" I asked Oz before biting into the apple, after joining him in the living room.

"Oh, it was the best we've seen. You've got to get out there, soon. There were a lot more guys out, but the waves were unbelievable." Oz became animated.

"Oh, that's great." I tried to sound happy for my friends, but wished I could go surfing again, now.

"What did you do?" Oz inquired.

I told him about the pool and Keemo, and his cousin. Finally, we could hear the sizzling sounds of Mom starting to make dinner. Jimbo came into the living room shortly thereafter. He was holding the piece of steak on his right eye. I almost laughed at the sight. Three minutes later, Dad came into the living room. "We need your steak back." My friend handed him the slab of raw meat and revealed his swollen eye. "Thank you James, now I'll fry this up and you can eat it, too." Dad tried to cheer him up. "Go ahead and wash your face, and I'll give you an ice pack for you to reduce the swelling."

Dinner was solemn. Jimbo's right eye was still shut and very red. The beginning of a black eye was forming a half moon shape underneath it. My little brother Eric broke the silence: "Jimbo has a boo-boo on his eye." He had a look of concern.

Even Jimbo couldn't help but chuckle, too. It broke the ice and he was able to tell us his version of the days' events: "The surf was awesome today, but I ran into a real jerk in the water. Every time, I had a wave he was there yelling 'how-lee' this, 'how-lee' that. Finally, I had enough and when we were on the beach he punched me."

"Haole is the Hawaiian term for people who are not from the islands." I informed my friend.

"Yeah, you were dropping in on that guy and everyone else, Jimbo." Oz added details. "Including me, I was getting annoyed too."

"No way! First one standing up on the wave gets it." Jimbo's voice became heated: "You are just on their side. They never called YOU, 'Haole,' anyways, just because your skin is darker than mine." He snapped. "It's only because you look like you are one of them!"

"Well, now you know what it's like for me back home when I'm the only dark skinned person in the room and people treat me differently or even just stare at me." Oz retorted.

"Okay, gentlemen, that's enough." Dad stopped them in their tracks.

The rest of the dinner was silent. My parents talked about boring adult stuff and after we ate, everyone went off to do their own thing before bedtime. I picked up the book I had been reading. Jimbo and Oz did not look at or speak a word to each other. They just stared at the TV.

The next day all seemed to be forgotten. They left with dad after breakfast, to get a ride to the beach. Keemo came by about a half hour after they left.

"Aloha, missus," he greeted Mom at the door. "My dad told me to tell you he'll have the part for your dishwasher in a few days. He located one on Oahu."

"Aloha, Keemo and Mahalo for giving me that information." Mom patted him on the shoulder. I saw my big friend crack the semblance of a smile for the first time. "Why don't you come back and join us for lunch, today." She invited him.

"If my Papa says it's okay, Mahalo." Keemo replied.

"We'll see you later Mom." I grabbed the skateboard, helmet and pads from the hallway as we walked to the door. We headed back to the pool.

This time, the hike up into the mountains wasn't as hard and my skating seemed to be improving. I was able to ride up and down the vertical walls. It was a lot more fun. During one of my rides Keemo vanished into the dense vegetation. He left his skateboard and helmet on the first step of the pool. I fell on my butt trying to ride around the wall, as the skateboard shot out from under me. The helmet Keemo lent me was a little big so it slid over my forehead and obstructed my view. I heard giggling from above, while resting on my aching behind on the center drain grate of the pool.

"Nice try! Now hurry up and move. Did you come here alone?" Leilani frowned down at me from the rim above dressed in pink and purple. She was poised with one foot on her skateboard to make the drop.

"No, Keemo is here." I answered. She let out a faint snicker as I scurried out of the bowl, after clumsily grabbing my skateboard and pulling my shorts back up.

'Where is Keemo?' I wondered walking up the steps and out of the pool. The ball bearings in Leilani's skateboard wheels rattled while the urethane made screeching sounds as she carved up and around the walls of the bowl. I walked into the jungle where Keemo had disappeared. The light was dim under the green canopy. My eyes took a moment to adjust. It felt cool and still there. Pushing through the greenery the light from the clearing of the neighboring property became visible. At the edge, I could see Keemo standing under an open window. Just as a lizard was climbing up the wall, he grabbed it gently and turned back towards the foliage. Apparently, he didn't see me so I just retraced my steps back to the pool.

"What did you catch?" I asked Keemo who had the animal cupped in his hands.

"Mo'o!" he replied looking at a gecko resting in his hand. Keemo was standing in a small patch of sunlight that made it through the canopy. It looked like the reptile could have escaped, but it just rested there peacefully.

"Cool!" I admired his catch.

"Do you guys want to skate or stand around?" Leilani rolled over to us. When she saw the gecko in Keemo's hands, her tone softened. "Oh, you found a mo'o, our family's aumakua. Your Mom is watching over you."

Keemo nodded and gently placed the animal back onto a big leaf. He put his helmet back on and took his turn skating.

"What're a 'mo'o' and an 'aumakua?'" I asked Leilani.

With her eyes on her cousin, she told me: "Mo'o is an ancient Hawaiian legend about a giant guardian reptile that can change into different shapes like a gecko, and the aumakua is a family guardian spirit. Our family's aumakua is mo'o, the gecko. Keemo's mom died when he was a baby. We Hawaiians believe that our deceased relatives watch over us as animals. For our family it's the gecko, others may consider sharks or other animals as their aumakua."

"Oh," was all I could say in response.

We took turns skating for another half hour and then walked out of the yard. Once we were in the street an unpleasant female voice shouted: "There he is officer. There's the thief!" I froze. The woman, who almost ran us over with her red car the day before, was standing between two uniformed police officers pointing her finger at us! "There they are officer. Arrest those little rats!" Two black and white police squad cars were parked at the curb with their multi-colored lights flashing.

After that everything felt like a bad dream. The police officers asked us to empty our pockets. We did as they told us and laid their contents on the hood of the squad car. Keemo was still wearing the same shorts he wore the day before, when we came to the pool. He pulled out a skate key from one pocket, a few coins and then… The earring we had found in the street the previous day, bounced on the shiny black hood. The senior officer picked it up and walked back over to the woman.

"That's my earring! I've been missing it for a couple of days." Her shrill voice shouted. "See, I told you that overgrown kid is a thief. That boy is the leader of that gang of rats. He was snooping around my house this morning. Yesterday that kid stole my earring, today my diamond ring is missing from my kitchen window sill!"

My jaw dropped. "We found that earring in the gutter, yesterday on our way here. Keemo was catching a lizard at her house; he didn't steal anything!" I defended my friend.

"Should we arrest the little one and the girl, too?" The younger officer pointed at Leilani and me asking his senior partner with the three gold stripes on his shoulder. He shook his head.

"Turn around and put your hand behind your back." The other officer broke his stern silence and walked up to Keemo, who looked dumbfounded. The policeman firmly spun Keemo around and grabbed his arms. With a rapid series of loud piercing clicks, the handcuffs bound Keemo's wrists behind his back. I felt like I was having a nightmare. Keemo began to cry out, when he couldn't shake the cuffs off. He began to shout and swing his head around wildly. At one point he head butted the younger officer, who sank to his knees for a moment. The older policeman with the stripes grabbed Keemo by the back of his shirt and shoved him onto the hood of the squad car.

"Hey, leave him alone. He didn't steal anything!" Leilani recovered her composure and sprung into action. "Keemo is innocent. He is not a thief. That woman is crazy!" Leilani banged on the grey haired officer's chest with her fists as the younger one led Keemo to his black and white car. He opened the rear door, placed his hand on the top of my friend's head and gently eased him into the back seat. Leilani let out a cry and got to the squad car just as the officer shut the driver's door. She pounded on the side rear window screaming. Keemo sat behind the tinted glass looking at her with a stunned expression, his mouth wide open. The officer started the engine of the squad car and drove off. Keemo gave me an emotionless look through the rear window. As they drove off, Leilani raced after them on her skateboard, screaming.

Suddenly, I was standing there alone and in shock, watching the police car drive away with Keemo's silhouette in the back seat. Leilani was chasing the vehicle at break neck speed on her skateboard down the street, screaming. The higher-ranking officer walked into the house with the accusing woman. He came out a few seconds later and approached me. After a brief questioning including: "Where do you live?" He motioned me into the back seat of his squad car.

Needless to say, riding back home in a police squad car did not go over well with mom. She was in the front driveway with Oz and Jimbo unloading groceries from the van when we pulled up. I could hear her loud groan from the street, after the officer opened the door while I slid out from the back seat. The mood was very bad.

"Nice going, Buzz." Jimbo was kind enough to attempt smoothing out my entrance. "You got to ride in a police car!" But then he had to add: "And we haven't even been here a full week, yet. Nice friends you have been making!"

Oz just looked at me with his mouth open. Officer Ho clicked his pen and addressed mom: "Are you the parent of this minor?"

"Uh, yeees, unless you tell me otherwise; I confess I was at the birth. Yes officer, at least I hope so," Mom tried clumsily to soften the moment with humor. I felt so horrible. Officer Ho was kind enough to let mom load Eric into the house and direct Oz and Jimbo to take care of the groceries. Meanwhile, he unloaded two skateboards helmets and pads from the trunk of the squad car. Then as if on cue the raindrops began. We stood in the rain while Officer Ho took down my information. Mom returned looking distressed. Her hair got sopping wet before we moved to the front porch.

After the officer left, we finally walked into the house. Mom gave me a curt: "Go to your room. I'm calling your father." Jimbo sporting his black eye, Oz and even little Eric looked at me with stunned expressions as I walked up the stairs to the bedroom. Plopping down on my bed I stared up at the ceiling and listened to the sound of the rain pelting the windowsill. My thoughts were racing. Keemo didn't steal any jewelry; he was just catching a gecko, the mo'o. Some aumakua, what kind of a guardian spirit lets you get in so much trouble without even doing anything worse than chasing a lizard to someone's house and catching it? He set it free after all. Then, what happened to

Leilani? The scene of her chasing after the police car replayed in my head over and over again. At times, I felt embarrassed for just standing there and not doing anything while the police took my innocent friend away.

Dinner was a grim affair. Dad opened the bedroom door and summoned me to come downstairs. The chatter at the kitchen table stopped when I came into the room.

"Sit down." Mom commanded.

Looking across the table at my friends, they were quiet.

"So," Dad broke the silence. "Well Buzz, what do you have to say for yourself? The police are calling it residential burglary! You have gotten yourself into quite a situation. Your friend arrested for stealing jewelry and you are a suspect or accomplice. The police want you available for questioning. Who knows you may be charged with a crime, too." He was furious. Everyone else at the table was quiet.

I cleared my throat. "Keemo didn't steal anything. He was over at that woman's house to catch a gecko. The earring that was in Keemo's pocket, we found in the gutter yesterday."

"Way to go Buzz, you seem to manage to find treasure that turns into trouble." Jimbo chuckled but turned dead silent when both my parents simultaneously shot him a cold glare.

Undeterred, I continued: "You have to believe me! We were skating in the pool next to that woman's house. Then Keemo saw a gecko, which is mo'o in Hawaiian and his aumakua. You've got to believe me, we didn't steal anything!"

"That's enough of this nonsense! I want you on house arrest for the time being. After dinner, you will go straight up to your bedroom and stay there. Tomorrow, I'll try to find a good lawyer. What a disaster." My father sighed.

Dinner was so awful, I felt like I wasn't a member of this family. Jimbo got up and began collecting dirty plates to wash the dishes. I took that opportunity to make my escape. When I got up to the bedroom, plopping down in bed, the emotions took over my body forcing me to sob into my pillow for a minute, before catching my composure. 'This is like a nightmare!' I thought. 'But, then what was Keemo going through? He was probably locked up in a cold dark cell.' My daydreaming was interrupted by the bedroom door squeaking open. Oz walked in.

"Hey," Oz sat on the edge of my bed. "I just want you to know that I believe you. Jimbo does too."

Just then Jimbo walked in and sat down next to Oz. He looked over to me and said: "Sorry for the wise cracks about finding treasure. I didn't mean to get you in worse trouble with your parents. 'Guess, I just have a problem shutting up. You've got to admit your track record isn't great in the treasure department." Jimbo reminded me of our last adventure, which began when I found a mysterious chest on the ocean floor while we were diving.

"But, we are 'The Grommets' and we stick together. So, whatever we can do to help we will." Oz was sincere.

"Yeah!" Jimbo chimed in.

"Well, I'm stuck in here right now. There's not a lot that we can do until I am off restriction." Just then a gust of wind pelted our window with raindrops. "It looks like we are all stuck in here for the time being." I sighed. "Keemo is innocent. I know it. He needs our help!"

The next morning, when I awoke the previous day's trouble temporarily slipped my mind for a pleasant moment. Then, like a wall of bricks falling on me, the bad memory returned. For the first time since we arrived, I got out of bed before Jimbo and Oz. The ice-cold stare my mom shot me made me shudder, when I walked into the kitchen.

"Make some cereal for yourself," was her curt greeting.

As I grabbed the box, Jimbo came walking into the kitchen.

"Save some of that for me! So what's on the agenda for today?" He turned his attention to Mom.

"Since we won't send you surfing in a rain storm, I thought we'd go do something indoors today. Today we are going to visit the Tsunami museum. Tomorrow afternoon we are invited to Hank and Hanna's for a barbeque"

"Cool," Oz joined us. "Tidal waves are called 'tsunami's' they are generated by earthquakes."

"Alright, I want to ride a tsunami!" Jimbo piped in only to be contradicted by Oz:

"You'd drown." He stretched his arms out and groaned slightly. "I'm kind of glad that we are taking a day off. My shoulders are sore from surfing the last four days straight!" Oz exclaimed as he sat down at the table between Jimbo and me. Dad walked into the kitchen carrying Eric. He set him down in the high chair at the end of the table, fastened the safety straps and looked at mom and said: "So are you ready?"

"Yes, honey," Mom answered and turned to us. "I'm going to drive dad to the lab. Watch Eric. Give him some dry cereal on his tray." She glared at me momentarily before grabbing her purse off the counter, opening it and pulling out her keys. My parents left.

"What do you mean, I'd drown?" Jimbo resumed their conversation looking at Oz who ignored him. Instead, he poured milk over his cereal and grabbed the newspaper from the middle of the table.

"I wonder how Keemo is doing?" I pondered.

"Probably sitting in jail, where jewel thieves belong." Jimbo sneered. He had obviously forgotten he swore to support me.

"He's innocent." I protested. "Keemo didn't steal anything. He was just catching a gecko that was climbing on the lady's wall.

"Well Keemo made the local paper." Oz pointed to an article. "And it looks like you got honorable mention!"

It was upsetting when Oz read the entire newspaper article out loud:

A juvenile was arrested for jewel theft, yesterday. At approximately 10:45 a.m. Mrs. Van Der Snoot reported that her five-carat diamond ring, which she had put on her windowsill was stolen while she washed her hands. Mrs. Van Der Snoot stated: "The phone rang. It was a hang up. When I went back to put my diamond ring back on it was gone." Mrs. Van Der Snoot also stated that she had seen a local boy walking under her kitchen window while another boy sat in the bushes as the "lookout." Only one of the minors was taken into custody and is now in juvenile hall." A police spokesperson said that charges are still pending and may be filed shortly against the second minor, who is from the mainland.

"Keemo didn't steal any diamond ring. We have to help him!" I pleaded with my friends.

"Funny, how you find things and people get in trouble. If you ever find a metal box again Buzz; I for one am going to run for the hills!" Jimbo retorted snidely.

"The police are investigating the case. We are not even from here. What can we do?" Oz questioned. "They will be able to do a better job than us." He added.

"But, they already think Keemo's guilty. You just read it in the paper." I urged.

"Too bad about your friend and your ear; we came here to surf Buzz, not to try to solve anymore mysteries, or get in trouble thanks to your need to play Sherlock Holmes." Jimbo turned the subject to surfing. Tired of his tales of wave riding grandeur over the previous days, I went upstairs to read my book.

The rain was still pounding on the outside of the house. The water running down the gutter sounded like a fountain trickling. It was almost impossible to get into my book as thoughts raced through my head. Furious with Jimbo, the idea of giving him another black eye crossed my mind. My thoughts turned back to the crisis. How was Keemo holding up in jail? What was Leilani doing? Maybe she could help, but now, I was frustrated being stuck and grounded with no way to contact her. It felt miserable.

CHAPTER SEVEN
Law And Society

The Tsunami Museum was informative. Many people died when a giant tidal wave hit The Big Island in 1946. Maybe it was because of the black and white photos, but the museum was really gray and depressing. Now, there are more precautions all over the islands to warn people of future threats, but a tsunami could hit at any time. My mood was sinking. I was starting to wonder why they even call this place 'Paradise.' Mom was treating me differently. It made me feel like I wasn't even part of the group.

When we got back to the house at lunchtime, there was a business card on the front screen door. Mom frowned and looked at me before unlocking the entrance and letting us all in. I took the hint and made myself scarce by running up to the bedroom. My book was good but the thoughts and worries that filled my head kept interrupting my reading. So I just laid there staring up at the ceiling, listening to the rain pelt the window.

The door opened and Oz announced:

"Lunch is served." He paused. "Hey Buzz, I just want you to know that I believe you. If you say Keemo is innocent, then it must be true. I've never known you to be a liar. And, I want to let you know I discussed it with Jimbo and we agreed that we will help you try to prove Keemo is not guilty of stealing that ring."

"Thanks Oz," I felt a little better knowing that they believed in me. We walked downstairs together.

Jimbo was helping mom serve the soup and sandwiches. I was silent while the conversation went from the most interesting things at the Tsunami Museum to surfing, and then on to the next days' barbeque.

"Buzz, go upstairs and change into a collared shirt and slacks," mom shattered my calm. The lunch was over. "We are going to pick up your father and take you to the lawyer's office. Jimbo and Oz would you both please clean up the kitchen and watch Eric while he takes his nap?"

"No problem." Jimbo gave a fake salute with his left hand as mom walked upstairs with Eric on her arm. "Whew, now it's off to a lawyer. Buzz, you really got yourself into one this time!" He teased me. Oz was silently washing the dinnerware, while Jimbo whistled, as he dried and stacked the dishes next to the sink. I wondered whose side he was on.

Resigning myself to my fate, I put on a white short sleeve collared shirt and blue trousers. Mom had also put my black leather shoes out. They felt extremely uncomfortable and confining after having walked barefoot for so long. The ride to pick up my dad on the way to the lawyer's office was silent. Now, the surroundings we drove through were becoming more familiar. The lawyer's office was in town, past the pharmacy on the opposite side of the street. The large modern office building had a parking lot. Dad held a huge golf umbrella over us as we ran from the car to the entrance through the pelting rain. We entered the building. I followed my parents into the lawyer's office suite.

Dad spoke to the receptionist and she told him: "Mr. Delton is expecting you. Please have a seat for just a few moments and he'll be right with you."

The reception area was plain. There were only a few chairs and a coffee table with magazines. Behind the counter, there seemed to be a long hallway with single offices. We waited. I felt nervous, like having a bunch of butterflies in my stomach. Mom grabbed a women's magazine from the table and leafed through the pages nervously. Dad just stared at the wall and anxiously tapped the umbrella on the floor once in a while. He looked like he was deep in thought.

"Aloha, welcome," the silence was interrupted by a tall slender Hawaiian man wearing slacks and a red and orange floral Aloha shirt. "I am Duke Delton. And I suppose this is Buzz?" He walked up to me and gave me a firm handshake. I nodded. The lawyer shook both my parents' hands and said: "Since Buzz is going to be my client, I would like to speak with him alone first. There are some forms for you to fill out and a contract for my services. Of course, there is the matter of my retainer fee. It was discussed with you on the phone. A check will do just fine. Makani, could you please give them the forms while I speak with Buzz?"

"Of course," the receptionist got up and pulled several sheets of preprinted forms from a filing cabinet behind her desk.

I followed the lawyer down the hallway past closed office doors with beveled glass windows. He stopped at an open door and motioned me to enter.

"Please have a seat, Buzz." Mr. Delton told me while shutting the office door. The first thing I noticed was a blow up of a photo on the wall that looked like the lawyer riding a very big wave.

"Is that you?" I pointed to the photo.

"Yes, that was taken on the North Shore of Oahu, a few years ago." He answered looking through his desk. "Ah yes, here we go a pen and a notepad. Now, I am ready." He sat down behind the huge dark wooden desk. I sat in one of the comfortable red leather chairs in front of the massive wooden deck. "The reason I wanted to see you first Buzz, is that I am going to be your attorney and to make it clear that anything that you tell me is confidential. That means that I can only reveal stuff you tell me if you allow me to. You can trust me not to tell your secrets. That goes for everyone, your parents, too. They can't force me to tell them what you say to me. That's called attorney-client privilege. Do you understand?"

I nodded.

"You need to give me audible responses. Nods and uh-huhs and uh-uh's are not proper communication. Especially if we have to go to court and you testify. You must speak clearly."

"Yes," I answered.

"So, tell me what happened?" He narrowed his eyes and wrote on the yellow legal pad while I told him about the earring and Keemo at the pool.

"Keemo didn't steal anything." I concluded telling him the whole sordid series of events asking: "So, am I in big trouble? Can we help Keemo?"

"Well, Buzz my loyalty is to you so I cannot help your friend unless it also helps you. It seems like you are not a likely suspect. So I would say that you are not in trouble; however, the police could theoretically charge you as an accomplice." His words made me freeze.

"But, I didn't do anything!" I exclaimed.

"You were in the wrong place at the wrong time." Mr. Delton responded looking over his notes. "Okay, do not discuss this case with anyone. Now, I will talk to your parents. Do you have any questions for me, before I meet with them?"

"No," I reflected a moment before answering.

"Okay, we will be speaking, soon." He guided me out of the office and patted my shoulder when we returned to the reception area. My parents followed him to his office. After about half an hour they returned. For the first time since this mess began, my parents looked at me sympathetically.

That evening we went to a Chinese restaurant. The hostess that greeted us was very pretty, nice, and friendly, welcoming us all. For a moment, I didn't feel so alienated anymore. Oz, Jimbo, and I sat next to each other on one side of the booth, while Mom and Dad were on the other. Little Eric sat in a high chair at the head of the table like the great C.E.O. of a huge company. No one understood what he was babbling. It was nice that even Mom smiled again. On the way home, the windshield wipers seemed like they were working overtime in the heavy rain.

The next morning, we awoke to bright sunshine. I ran outside only to find myself in a sun shower. Even though the sun was shining on me, a cloud was sprinkling rain onto the ground. It wasn't long until I was soaking wet, but I didn't care and went inside to dry off. Mom served pancakes for breakfast. We all helped clean up, then my dad, friends and I left in the van. We dropped Jimbo and Oz off at the beach; I gazed longingly at the surf. It looked real fun, but instead of staying at the shoreline and watching my friends have a great time, I accompanied my dad shopping. Mom had made him a list of things to buy, so she could prepare dishes to bring to the barbeque that evening. It felt good to have one-on-one time with my father. I was able to buy postcards for Stephanie and Nana. The stores there were the same as the ones at home, with a few interesting differences. On The Big Island grocery store, the produce section had an immense crate of pineapples. Some of the other fruits and vegetables looked strange to me.

When we got back to the house with our huge load of groceries and supplies, I had a pleasant surprise.

"Hello, Buzz." Keemo's dad Hiro was working on the dishwasher.

"Hello sir."

He stood up, wiped his hands on a rag, which was sticking out of the side of his overalls and reached out to shake my dad's hand and then mine. "I'm very sorry for the trouble we have caused your family. Keemo is a good boy." Hiro sighed.

"Please sit down for a moment, would you like some iced tea?" Mom moved the grocery bags from the table to the counter.

"Well, yes thank you." Hiro sat down in the chair my dad pulled out for him. I sat down next to Hiro. Dad then seated himself. "Keemo is on house arrest. The judge let me bring him home. He says that he was just catching a gecko, which had climbed on the lady's wall."

"That's what our son told us happened." My dad commented: "We were naturally very disappointed at first, but now it seems clear that they have been the victims of an unfortunate set of circumstances. The mystery of it all is what really happened to that ring?"

Mom poured a glass of iced peppermint tea for each of us and sat down at the table. We sipped for a moment in an awkward silence. Then, Hiro exhaled and said: "He will be mistaken as a juvenile delinquent because he is unique. His behavior at the time of the arrest did not help Keemo's situation." He paused looking really, really sad, sighed and said: "My boy is unique. Keemo has autism. I realize that we have troubled you enough already, but Keemo's public defender said it would be helpful if Buzz could come to court and testify on his behalf. I apologize for any inconvenience."

He paused and looked down at the table. His eyes began to tear a little for a moment. "Keemo is a good boy. A drunk driver killed his mother when he was still very young. The doctors first thought that he was in shock from her death. Later they diagnosed him with autism. I am afraid that he will be mistaken as a delinquent and found guilty of this crime just because he is different." Hiro took a sip from his glass of iced tea. He paused and stared down at the table.

My parents looked at each other for a moment. Dad nodded and said: "Of course. Buzz will come and tell the truth in court." He got up pulled his wallet out of his back pocket and sat down. He pulled out one of Mr. Delton's business cards out and said: "Here is our lawyer's card. Have Keemo's attorney call him and make arrangements. We are very sorry for you and your son." I felt both relieved knowing that I was going to be able to help Keemo and tell the judge; and heartened, knowing that Dad was clearly behind me on this.

After we finished our tea, dad went to pick up Oz and Jimbo from the beach. I stayed home and helped mom in the kitchen, while chatting with Hiro. I was disappointed to learn that the judge had ordered Keemo not to have contact with Leilani or me as a condition of his house arrest. If he violated any one of them he could be sent back to juvenile hall. That's what they call the jail for kids. Hiro finished fixing the dishwasher and left before Dad came back with Oz and Jimbo.

We ate a light lunch, prior to getting ready for the barbeque that afternoon. Mom was the master director, organizing dad, Eric, Jimbo, Oz and me while preparing the dishes for us to bring to the gathering. Dad had driving directions written down on a piece of scrap paper, which mom handed him. He buckled his seatbelt and studied the sheet before starting the ignition. Then, finally we were off. Everyone seemed a little nervous in the van as we drove off. The passenger compartment was filled with a sickly sweet odor.

"What is that smell?" Mom voiced the common question as the strong scent wafted throughout the van's passenger compartment.

"Oh, you noticed my cologne." Jimbo replied in a suave tone: "I got a sample of this stuff at the department store back home. Actually, I grabbed a whole bunch of samples if you guys want some. 'It's the perfect scent for an interesting evening' was what the lady with the spray and the basket of samples said. I filled my pockets with these samples." Jimbo pulled a tiny bottle with an amber colored liquid out of his shirt pocket. "Go ahead take one." Jimbo tried to push his fancy cologne to us. Oz turned his nose up at first and then raised both arms to block his face when Jimbo continued to insist. He then stuck the bottle in front of my nose. The smell was noxious. "Here you go," Jimbo shook the tiny bottle and dropped some of the liquid on my shoulder.

"JIMBO! Put that away, NOW!" Mom commanded from the front of the van.

"OOPS!" Jimbo put the bottle away in a flash. "You really missed some fun waves this morning, Buzz." He cleverly changed the subject, but the noxious smell that filled the passenger compartment didn't disappear. The uncomfortable feeling in the van reached a maximum level. Silence loomed over the cabin for the entire ride. Even with all of the windows rolled down, the smell made me nauseous.

After about twenty-five minutes and a few wrong turns, dad finally announced: "This must be it!" Turning the van down a narrow driveway that widened in front of a large house. A few other cars were already parked in the driveway, but Dad managed to find a spot.

Mom unloaded Eric from his car seat as Oz, Jimbo, and then I slid out of the rear seat of the van. After jiggling with the keys and fixing his hair, dad went to the back of the van and handed us each our own little parcel of Mom's contributions to the barbeque. Our little troop marched to the front door with dad in the lead. The sound of his 'KNOCK, KNOCK, KNOCK' echoed from the gigantic brass pineapple doorknocker announcing our arrival.

"Aloha!" Doctor Hank answered the door in a bright orange and yellow floral Hawaiian shirt with a huge flower necklace around his neck.

"Aloha!" I was the first to instinctively greet our host, the rest followed.

"Welcome all of you! Hanna, our guests have arrived!" He gestured to a slender blond lady wearing a brightly colored floral dress. She was accompanied by a girl with long dark brown hair wearing a dress with a similar pattern. The girl had a floral headband and was carrying a basket full of flowers. Following her was a giant Golden Retriever with a bright, shiny coat.

"Aloha," the lady greeted us. We responded with our 'Aloha' almost in unison. "Welcome, here are leis for each of you."

The lady pulled yellow flowers from the basket, which turned out to be made into necklaces. She put it around Dad's neck and kissed him on the cheek. Jimbo and Oz giggled. Then, she handed another lei to Dr. Hank, who put it round Mom's neck and kissed her on the cheek. Next, the lady gave each of us guys a flower necklace and a kiss on the cheek. Eric refused looking afraid in Mom's arms. When she got to me, the fresh smell of the flowers was a welcome change to the nasty odor of the liquid Jimbo had dumped on me.

"I'm Hanna and this is our daughter, Alika." The woman gestured to the girl with the basket. She looked like both her dad and mom at the same time. Her eyes looked distinctly Asian, while the rest of her resembled a miniature version of her mother.

Dr. Hank smiled as he led us into a huge living room. It had long couches and a pool table. I felt something cold and wet touching my elbow. I turned and patted the head of a tall Golden Retriever.

"That's Magic. I almost forgot to introduce him, but I guess he already has introduced himself." Dr. Hank turned to my parents and said. "The boys can hang out in here and play pool while Hanna and I give you a tour of the house." Dad and mom followed them. Hanna carried little Eric.

"Cool, let's play!" Oz exclaimed while Jimbo rushed to the table in a flash, picking a cue stick off the wall rack. Oz wasted no time to begin pulling out the colorful balls and racking them up on the table.

"Do you want to play checkers?" Alika asked me.

"Sure," I was relieved. My pool skills were never that great and I had trouble hitting the white cue ball straight without leaving chalk marks on the felt table. She went to a huge wooden chest in the corner of the room and pulled out a box. "We can play over here." Alika set the box down on a large wooden coffee table that sat on a giant fluffy rug. She sat down on the corner of one side of the table. I sat on the other.

"Hey Buzz, you can take your flower necklace off now." Jimbo teased. When I didn't respond he added: "I guess you like flowers and not playing pool with the guys." Oz was focused on his next shot.

Alika laid the checkerboard down on the table. "Do you want to be black or red?" She asked, pulling the round pieces from the box.

"Black," I replied.

From the far end of the room we heard the loud CLACK, of Oz breaking; then the CLUNK, CLUNK, CLUNK, of several balls dropping into the pockets. My friends' leis were already hanging on the wall rack with the unused pool cues. I felt a little self-conscious wearing mine but didn't feel like taking it off, just yet. It actually felt really good to wear this bright yellow, fragrant gift. I couldn't understand why Jimbo was making such a big deal about it.

With the checkerboard set up, Alika asked: "Do you want to flip a coin to see who goes first?"

"Nope, red before black, fire before ash, it really doesn't matter to me. You go first." I replied.

Watching my new friend look down at the board and move one of her pieces to a safe square on the side of the board, I contemplated my first move.

"So how do you like it here on The Big Island?" Alika asked.

"It's great. I really wish I could surf here except for my stupid ear infection, but it's real nice. I don't know. I've had a lot happen to me, since I got here."

"So I've heard." Alika giggled moving another piece into the center of the board.

I felt my face turning slightly red. "Yeah, how do you know?"

"My parents talked to yours on the phone when they were looking for a lawyer for you. I know Keemo. His cousin Leilani is my girlfriend, too. We are in hula class together."

My spirits lifted. The only way to help Keemo was to get together with Leilani, since the judge had ordered him not to have contact with me. That didn't prevent me from talking to Leilani. I made another safe move pushing one of my checkers to a square on the side.

"Can you get a note to Leilani from me?" I asked.

"Sure no problem, I'm going to see her tomorrow at the hula festival." She moved another piece on the board. Alika paused for a moment looking at the board and then got up to pull a note pad and pencil out of the wooden chest. She handed them to me. "You can write on this."

After moving another checker piece, I picked up the pencil and began to write. "You know what? I don't know my phone number here."

"I think I know how to find it." She got up and walked into the kitchen and returned with our telephone number on a little yellow piece of paper. "Here you might want to keep this until you remember."

"Thanks."

Alika sat down on the plush rug and moved a piece. I stopped writing, jumped that piece and removed it from the board. Turning my attention back to the note I heard the CLICK, CLICK, CLICK, of her jumping three of my pieces. I finished the note and handed it to Alika. It read:

Dear Leilani,

Keemo is innocent. We need to help him. My telephone number is 555-9283. I'm staying in the white house, seven houses down from keemo on the same side of the street. Look for the white van in the driveway. Please call me.

Yours truly,
Buzz

Alika smiled, folded the note and put it in a small pocket inside her dress. "So, it's your turn Buzz."

"Thanks, Alika," I felt relieved for the first time since that horrible day when Keemo was arrested. We finished the game right before we heard someone blowing loudly into a conch shell announcing that dinner was ready. Alika's mom, Hanna, came into the living room and said: "We're eating outside, children." There was a hoot from over at the billiards table and we all followed her out to the yard where a picnic bench was set up for us. My parents were sitting at another table with our hosts. Eric was sitting in a high chair with a huge bib. His face and hands were smeared with barbeque sauce. He looked like he was covered in it. We all stuffed ourselves with the delicious food and had enjoyable conversations. When they were done eating, Jimbo and Oz spent a few minutes walking around the giant swimming pool and waterfalls in the yard.

"Next time we're bringing our swim trunks!" Jimbo exclaimed before returning to the house.

In the living room, Alika played some of her favorite music, mostly native Hawaiian songs and a few top 40 hits that I knew. Oz and Jimbo were getting competitive at the pool table, while Alika and I played Rummikub.

After a fun evening we exchanged hugs and said: "Mahalo and Aloha," to our host and hostesses and climbed into the van. On the way home I noticed that I still had my lei on and didn't take it off until I was back in our room, where I hung it on the windowsill.

CHAPTER EIGHT
A Reunion

The next morning after the barbeque, none of us were really hungry for breakfast. Mom announced we were going to a 'fête' that day. We had no clue what that meant, but Jimbo talked her into letting Oz and him go surfing instead. I was bummed that I hadn't asked Dr. Hank at the party if I could go surfing sooner and sat at the kitchen table sulking.

Meanwhile, my friends buzzed with excitement getting ready for their session. We loaded the van. Dad dropped Oz and Jimbo off at the usual beach. The parking area was crammed with cars and the water looked packed with a mob of surfers, so I didn't mind that much not being able to ride the fun looking waves with my friends. Neither one looked back once, as they headed hastily down to the beach. Dad turned the van around and we were on our way to the event.

After driving through town we only had a quick ride to the community center. It wasn't until reading the sign at the entrance to the parking lot that I realized we were going to the Hula Festival! The grounds were crowded with people in bright colorful costumes. When we got to the outdoor amphitheater dad spotted Dr. Hank who was sitting near the stage with his wife. Dad waved to them and led us there. He sat next to Dr. Hank. Mom handed Eric to Hanna, and then sat down beside her on the other side. I took the aisle seat next to dad. The adults were immediately locked in conversation with each other. Bright flowers decorated the outdoor stage. Looking around the seating area there were quite a few people in attendance under the huge sail shaped awning; however, the stage wasn't covered. I wondered what would happen if one of the frequent rain squalls hit. Just then, a single drumbeat began. A moment later, more drums joined in. I couldn't figure out where the music was coming from. A group of seven ladies wearing bright yellow grass skirts walked out on the stage. They wore tops made of citrine flowers, and headbands of the same canary colored blossoms. The audience applauded and hooted. On stage, the dancers moved in unison swaying their hips from side to side at a fluttering speed. It was hypnotizing. The drumming stopped and the dancers froze. The sound of a woman's soft voice began to fill the arena singing in Hawaiian, which sounded foreign and melodic. Soft string instruments accompanied her. The ladies in yellow began to sway in perfect unison again, moving their arms in wave like gestures while gyrating their hips.

"Look at their beautiful movements. They are telling a story with their hands." Dad whispered. "This is really beautiful hula. These ladies are synchronized." Looking up at my father, he seemed to be in a trance. At the end we applauded enthusiastically. For the first time since being driven home in a police car, I felt good. A giggle escaped me. Mom noticed it and turned her gaze to me and then to dad. She shot me a sharp glance. I straightened up and tried my best to look like the dancers were boring. Dad seemed to being doing the very same thing as the ladies walked off stage.

It took only two minutes for the next performance to begin. The audience fell silent. A distinguished man in native attire stepped onto the stage. He radiated charisma, generating whispers and gasps from the audience as he looked up holding

a giant gourd like instrument with a huge bulb on the top. The man was dressed in a kilt made of grass and was dark skinned with bulging muscles. He sat down on a small stool hidden behind several large stones, which were decorated with green chains of thick leaves. He interrupted the silence tapping a rapid rhythm with his finger while pounding the instrument on the stage floor. This created a deep bass drum beat that filled the arena. I even felt it vibrating in my chest. A large group of girls dressed in bright yellow hula dresses and matching floral headbands walked onto the stage. The young man began to chant in a deep mellow voice that sounded ancient, accompanying the graceful gyrations of the girls dancing.

Hanna pointed and mom nodded and smiled. Alika was on stage near the center of the group. Then, I noticed a taller girl to the left of her. It was Leilani. At first, I didn't recognize her. She was known to me as a tough 'tom boy' skater. Now, Leilani, looked beautiful wearing a headband of lemon yellow flowers waving her arms to the side. Their movements reminded me of gently flowing waves.

A nudge in my ribs woke me out of my daze.

"Nice dancing, eh Buzz!"

"UHHH, yeah dad," I gasped for air for a moment. "That looks like Alika. Is that her?" I knew it was and felt stupid after lying about not noticing her. "Yeah, they are doing some very nice dancing." Just then, the girls started chanting in unison. I tried to act casual as my face cooled off. The man changed the rhythm of the beat. Leilani, Alika and the rest of the girls changed their cadence and repeated the man's chant in sync. They moved in unison to the left of the stage and then moved to the right side before returning back to the center. The sound of the drumming faded after the man's voice stopped and the girls hustled off the stage. Over the loudspeakers a deep rich male voice announced a brief intermission. A few minutes later, a flash of yellow appeared to my left. It was Alika. Her hula skirt rustled as she stood next to me.

"Dad, can I take Buzz, back to meet my friends?"

"Sure honey, if it's okay with you." Doctor Hank looked at my father, who shrugged his shoulders.

"Sure, I don't see why not." Dad was interrupted by mom:

"We know our son. He seems to have a talent for attracting trouble." Mom's comment hurt my feelings. She paused. "But, okay go ahead." She finally relented.

"Come on," Alika waved for me to follow as she walked up the stairs out of the amphitheater. Once we were in the main entrance area she slowed down and turned to me. "Buzz, Leilani is going to meet us by the stage door. You can talk to her while I change out of my dance costume. We walked there side by side. "So what did you think of the hula dancing?"

"It was great. You are a real good dancer." I complimented.

"Too bad you weren't here for Easter, that's when we have the big hula festival. People come from all over the Pacific Islands to compete and watch the dancing. Here we are. Wait a minute. I'll go inside and tell Leilani that you are here."

Alika disappeared into the back stage area through the big metal door. I sat down on a low wall that bordered the pathway. The door opened. Three ladies walked out and looked at me a little surprised. "Aloha!" They exclaimed and then smiled.

"Aloha," I replied shyly.

A few minutes later, the door swung open and Leilani strutted out wearing jeans a pink t-shirt and matching flip-flop sandals.

"Hi Leilani," I stood up and approached her.

"Aloha," Her eyes narrowed as she looked at me. "I got your note. So you really want to help Keemo?"

"Yes, of course! Have you spoken to him lately?"

"Just on the phone, he's not allowed to have any visitors. My uncle is so worried he won't let us break the judge's order." Leilani's tone softened. "What do you think we can do?"

"Well, we can check the scene and retrace our steps for one thing. Maybe we'll find some clues that will help us figure out what happened to that ring." I hadn't come up with any brilliant ideas, but this was a start.

"Just like in a detective story, we look for clues and try to solve the problem." Leilani added approvingly. "At least we will be doing something, and not just sitting around while Keemo is stuck at home on house arrest. The only problem is that we're not allowed to go back to the vacant house either. It's off limits to us."

"That makes our job impossible." I was disheartened.

"No, that means we just have to figure out another way." Leilani had a determined look on her face.

The metal stage door swung open again. Alika and a group of girls, all wearing street clothes exited. "Have you made a plan?" She joined our conversation.

"Yeah, the problem is that my mom has me on such a tight leash. Since I got a ride home in a police car, she has been really ticked off at me. I don't know how I'm going to get away."

"I'll just ask if you can hang out with me, tomorrow. We can tell our parents we want to go collect shells or even fishing. Then we will have enough time to investigate." Alika had an answer to my dilemma. "I'll ask my dad if he can give us a ride to the beach tomorrow. He doesn't go to the office until later in the morning."

Lelani had to go home. I really enjoyed the rest of the show sitting in the back row with Alika giving me play by play about the performances we were watching: "Hula is not just a dance, it is story telling."

After the show was over Alika got her dad to agree to drive us to go fishing at the beach, the next day. My dad had no problem with me going and mom didn't raise a fuss about it.

We parted company with Alika and her parents and drove to the beach to pick up Oz and Jimbo. They were already sitting under a shady tree in the parking area. When we drove up Oz stood up immediately and picked up his surfboard and backpack. Jimbo picked up his backpack along with two pieces of his surfboard. It was broken in half!

"Hello gentlemen, ready for your ride home." Dad jumped out of the driver's seat, opened the side door and back hatch.

"Looks like your surfboard has seen better days," he patted Jimbo on the shoulder as he placed the broken stick into the van.

They jumped in and we drove off.

"What happened to your board?" I was anxious to know.

"Don't really know. I took off too late and wiped out on this gnarly wave. When I popped back up to the surface, my board was in two pieces." He sighed.

"So what are you going to do? Do you think you can fix it?" I asked. Oz shook his head.

"Well, I'm glad you asked that." Jimbo paused for a second. "Since you can't surf because of your ear, can I use your board buddy, old pal?"

The question hit me like a lightning bolt. The idea of taking turns with Jimbo waiting on the beach to use my surfboard was upsetting. "ERR, SHH-sure. But I'll be going to the doctor in a couple of days and then I'll be back in the water surfing again."

"Sure, Buzz," Jimbo retorted, as if he was humoring me. His sarcasm was annoying.

The rest of the ride home was quiet, except for my parents' conversation in the front of the van. Little Eric was sound asleep. I wasn't happy, brooding about the prospect of Jimbo possibly snapping my board in half, too.

My friends left for the beach early the next morning with my dad. At around ten thirty, Alika knocked on the screen door. My backpack was ready with a bottle of water, sunscreen, a beach towel and a sweatshirt.

"Are you ready?" She asked as I opened the front door. Mom was standing behind me holding Eric.

"Yes." I replied opening the door. We walked down to the large white station wagon. Dr. Hank was sitting in the driver's seat with his elbow resting on the open window.

"Aloha, we can all fit in the front." He motioned through the open passenger window for me to get in.

Alika slid next to her dad on the huge front bench and put her seatbelt on. I jumped in put my pack down at my feet before reaching for the seatbelt and buckling up.

Mom and Dr. Hank spoke for a few minutes before we drove off. The car radio played soft Hawaiian music.

"So Buzz, are you enjoying yourself on The Big Island?" Dr. Hank asked me.

"Yes very much, but it will be a lot better when I can surf again."

He chuckled: "In a few days we'll check you out again and see how it looks. You need to let it heal completely before you go back into the water. Your dad used to be the same way about scuba diving. He was always in the water. Like father like son." He looked at Alika. They smiled at each other.

Driving through town, we turned towards the ocean. The salty breeze patted my face through the open window. Palm trees lined the road on the open area. Dr. Hank pulled into a parking lot and drove up to the loading zone.

"Here we are fishermen, eh, and fisher-lady." He added after a sharp glance from Alika. Dr. Hank shifted the car into park with the handle on the steering wheel column. The door alarm sounded its 'BING, BING, BING, BING,' as he got out of the car. Alika slid out after him and I grabbed my backpack and followed. "Okay, here's your gear. He took two long fishing poles out of the open back gate window and leaned them against the back of the car. Then he pulled out a bucket with a tackle box and a net. He hugged Alika, kissed her on the cheek and patted me on the shoulder. He looked at his daughter and said: "Your mother will be here in two hours to pick you up. If you have any problems, use the pay phone over there to call me in the office. I can be here in fifteen minutes, but if it's an emergency don't hesitate to call 9-1-1, before you call me okay?" We both nodded. He handed each of us a fishing pole. Alika took the net and I grabbed the bucket. "Now go catch a nice papio. It will be great on the barbeque! Aloha!" Dr. Hank laughed heartily as he got into the car.

"Aloha," we responded and watched him drive off.

"Now what do you want to do?" I asked when the huge wood-paneled station wagon turned out of sight.

Looking at her watch, Alika said: "Leilani should be here by now."

We were silent. I felt awkward but couldn't think of anything to say. Apparently Alika didn't either, so we stood silently at the loading area holding our fishing poles. After a few tongue-tied minutes, I felt silly standing there.

"Maybe we should just fish close by so we can still see Leilani when she gets here." I suggested.

"Okay, we can fish on the inside of the breakwater." Alika pointed to the end of the parking lot. "The bigger fish are on the other side, but you can usually catch small bait fish over there."

We walked over to an empty bench by the edge of the sea wall. I leaned my pole against the armrest and put the bucket down on the cement. Alika pulled the tackle box out and opened it.

"We need to use small hooks over here." She said authoritatively. "This frozen squid is good bait."

Following, Alika's example I set up the rig for a small hook, no float and only a small sinker. Alika pulled out a plastic bag with frozen squid and took a small piece. She handed it to me. There was a metal railing with a lower cross bar at the edge of the walkway. Looking down at the calm water, I could see the bottom rocks and sand. A bunch of little crabs scurried down the vertical wall into the water. Tiny one-inch fish swam in a school just below the gray green surface.

"Just drop the bait near the bottom." Alika released the line from her reel and it slowly dropped into the water. I followed her example and watched my bait disappear from sight. The line stopped unwinding when it hit the bottom, so I wound up a few cranks on the reel to raise the bait a little. Resting her fishing pole on the top of the railing, Alika turned to me and said: "Looks like Leilani is running late, but we can at least talk about how we are going to prove Keemo didn't steal that ring."

"Good idea, while we are waiting we can formulate a plan. I have been trying to think about who could have taken the ring. Maybe it fell down the drain or out the window and is in the grass lying right under their noses." I started the discussion.

"The police must have searched for all of those obvious solutions. Leilani might know; she talked to Keemo's public defender." Alika placed the bottom of her pole on the ground and leaned it on the lower horizontal metal railing. "I packed a pen and notepad." She pulled them from the bottom compartment of the tackle box.

"What's a public defender?" It was a new word for me.

"Oh, that's a lawyer you get if your parents can't afford to pay for one." Alika opened the steno pad and took the cap off the pen. "I've already taken some notes from when I talked to Leilani on the telephone last night." She turned a few pages until she reached a blank one. "So, tell me what you remember about that morning."

The thought that my parents had to pay money to Mr. Delton had never occurred to me. Suddenly some things made sense. Mom was always worried about the budget and she frequently said she was concerned about us being able to afford living on The Big Island with Dad; she even stated, he should live in a dorm for the six weeks and we could have managed at home okay while he was gone. It was supposed to be a family vacation and I had cost our family a lot of money. No wonder Mom was mad at me!

"Hey are you here? Earth is calling, Buzz." Alika looked at me demandingly.

"Yeah, I was just thinking." Then, I told her everything I could remember about the fateful day when Keemo was accused of stealing the diamond ring.

"Are you guys trying to catch baby fish?" We were interrupted by Leilani. She was sitting on an old men's beach cruiser that had been spray-painted fluorescent pink. Naturally, her shirt and shorts matched the bike.

"We were waiting for you." Alika put the cap back on her pen. "Let's reel in." We clicked our reels. My hook was clean. The fish had been fed the bait. Alika spoke authoritatively: "I took notes. Both of your statements are consistent."

"Yes, Miss Marple." Leilani looked at her sarcastically as she leaned her bike against the railing. She clicked the strap off her pink helmet and plopped down on the bench. Stretching her legs she complained: "That was a long ride." Then, looking at her watch Leilani exclaimed: "I can only stay five minutes. My aunt wants me to help in her garden. Let's make this quick!"

"We can't solve this mystery in five minutes, Leilani." Alika looked dismayed.

"Well it took me a half hour to get here and it will take another to get back home. You could have planned this meeting closer to town. Let's just decide what we are going to do now and we can meet again and get started tomorrow."

"Okay," Alika sat down on one side of Leilani. I sat on the other. "Like I said, both of you told me basically the same events. Keemo went into the brush and Buzz followed. They came back a few minutes later with a gecko lizard." She leafed through her notes. "You didn't see anyone else except for the police and the lady next door after Keemo was arrested. So, I think that someone must have been there that you didn't see. Did you hear anything weird, like noises, maybe a motorcycle or other motor sound?"

Leilani was shaking her head and I did the same when Alika looked at me inquisitively. Frustrated I racked my brain trying to remember the exact events of that fateful day. If there had been another person at the scene, we would at least have a suspect. Then the real shocker came.

"So Buzz, did you plan on giving the stolen diamond ring to your mother or girlfriend on the mainland?" Alika looked at me with a laser-piercing stare from her golden eyes. I was flabbergasted. Looking over at Leilani, she gave me a charcoal cold stare. I felt both furious and betrayed at the same time.

"Wait a minute. Are you guys for real?" The accusation made me angry. "I don't have a girlfriend. Why would I care about saving Keemo if I stole that stupid ring?" I jumped up. "I'm out of here."

"Wait, wait," Alika stood up next to me, reached up and put her hand on my shoulder. "I was just making sure, you are not a suspect."

"Haha," Leilani chuckled and looked at me with a piercing glance and then smiled. "Relax. Sit down and let's talk." Her eyes changed to radiate warmth. I calmed down.

"Come on, Buzz. A detective must eliminate the obvious wrong answers to reach the final conclusion." Alika was apologetic while Leilani seemed to enjoy the discord between us. "I've read every Miss Marple novel and almost all of the rest of Agatha Christie's books and Alfred Hitchcock's: The Three Investigators and a lot of other stuff and I thought that my knowledge would help solve this mystery and get Keemo out of this trouble. You are not his only friend, you know. Just because you come to our island on vacation and Keemo makes friends with you doesn't mean you are the only person who cares about him. We want justice on The Big Island. He didn't steal that ring. We know that. So if you are finished feeling sorry for yourself, maybe we can figure out how to help Keemo."

"UHH, well umm, of course I want to help Keemo that's why I'm here. I mean, like you, but…" My face flushed for a moment.

"Okay." Alika interrupted my sputtering, paused for a moment brushed her long blond hair back with her right hand, pen and pad in her left. "We can solve this mystery, I just know it. The answer is right before our eyes but we can't see it! We really need to work together on this."

"I'm sorry, my time's up." Leilani interrupted our exchange. "Time for me to say 'Aloha' and pedal back home. You two work out your differences and we'll meet again, Aloha sister."

"Aloha!" Alika perked up as Leilani got up off the bench. They kissed each other on the cheek. Leilani snapped in the chinstrap of her pink helmet and jumped on her bike.

"Good luck fishing, and working out your differences. Aloha, Buzz." Leilani laughed and waved the thumb and pinky fingers of her right fist as she pedaled towards home through the parking lot, dwarfed by the giant boulders of the breakwater.

"So do you want to fish?" Alika looked at me.

"Yes, sure that's what we told our parents we are here for. So let's go fishing." I was not very enthusiastic, but the prospect of another hour of conflict before her mom picked us up was not very appealing.

"Okay, let's go over to the ocean side and fish." Alika pointed to the top of the stone jetty. We climbed over the huge rocks carrying our gear. The wind was stronger on the other side where the water was deeper and choppy. "You might want to use a lure for casting. There are bigger fish out there."

We settled on a large flat boulder at the water's edge. Alika opened the tackle box, pulled out a shiny blue and pink lure and handed it to me. The lure was about five inches long and had treble hooks in the middle and back. She grabbed a similar one. I removed the hook and sinker from my rig and attached the lure. My first cast only went out about ten feet, but the second and third traveled three or four times as far and I slowly reeled the lure in. On the fifth try I felt a strong jolt only a few seconds after the lure hit the water. "I think I got one. The reel is getting really hard to crank. It feels like it's a pretty big one!"

"Good job, I'll get the net!" Alika rushed over to the bucket.

The rod felt like it was vibrating and a couple of times the fish pulled so hard that the reel made a whining sound as it gained more ground against me taking back many yards of line. After about fifteen minutes of struggling back and forth there was a splash twenty feet away. The fish came to the surface and thrashed its tail. It looked big. The excitement was getting intense. A final pull signaled it was losing strength, which was a good thing. I was about to, too. As soon as it was at the edge of the rock, Alika swooped the net into the water and pulled the huge flapping fish out using all of her body weight. I could feel the strength of its tail pounding on the rock. Some on lookers clapped and hooted from the top of the jetty.

"Nice ulua!" I heard a male voice shout.

"Yeah, this is a nice big ulua, Buzz." Alika agreed, smiling. "I'm going to call Dad, he's going to want to see this. She ran over to the pay phone."

Dr. Hank's eyes almost popped out of his head when he returned ten minutes later.

"Nice one son, this fish must be at least thirty pounds!" He picked the fish up by its tail. "Now Buzz let me take a picture of you and your prize. You know for the ancient Hawaiians it was 'kapu,' forbidden for women to eat this fish." He pulled a small camera out of his pocket and took a few pictures of me holding the fish next to Alika.

That evening we were all invited by Dr. Hank to his house for an impromptu barbeque to honor, and fry up the catch.

CHAPTER NINE
The Eruption

"**A** toast for the fisherman!" one of the guests raised his white-rimmed red plastic cup. Everyone else in Dr. Hank's backyard followed his example. At Dr. Hank and Hanna's request, dad invited some of his colleagues from the university to enjoy the fish BBQ. There certainly was plenty for everyone. That was a huge fish. Some of our hosts' guests brought side dishes, while my dad's friends from the university mostly brought bottles for the adults to drink. Mom seemed to be having a good time and little Eric wandered around with two other toddlers entertaining the assembled adults. Alika was busy helping her mother prepare and serve drinks with the food. I walked over to look at the swimming pool in the backyard, again. It was amazing. There was a huge main pool that had three separate waterfalls with smaller pools and a rock which Oz and Jimbo jumped off of. It was rough not being able to plunge in myself, even though my ear felt a lot better.

After spending most of the time in the immense swimming pool, Jimbo and Oz were glued to the pool table again. I hung out watching them play for a little while before getting bored.

"So, I hear you are the big fisherman." A familiar voice came from behind me. It was Leilani.

"Yeah, I guess I was lucky today. How did you get here?"

"My cousin drove me. He just got his license. Alika invited me to the barbeque. I'm going to help her makuahine and her finish cleaning up and then we can play a board game and continue trying to figure out who stole that ring. Alika said you should pick a game from the chest in the living room."

Without further ado, Leilani turned around and walked back to the house. I paused for a moment and then followed her. On the way to the house, one of the adults stopped me.

"Nice catch. Is your name Buzz?" The man wore a light blue golf shirt and had a red cup in his hand. "Share your secret with me. How did you catch that fish?"

"Uh, thanks it wasn't that big a deal I guess." I didn't know what to say, but wanted to get back into the house to be with Alika and Leilani.

"Come on Buzz! Tell us about your catch." Dad prodded me proudly. Mom was sitting next to him and gave me a stern look that left no room to refuse.

"Well, it was real luck I guess." The adults laughed at my honesty. "I cast the lure out a couple of times and then 'POW,' there was this heavy weight wiggling at the other end of the line."

"What was the magic lure that you used?" Another adult posed a question.

"Um, I don't know it was blue and about five inches long. Alika gave it to me."

"Ah yes" Dr. Hank came to the rescue and provided me the opportunity to exit. "That particular lure is a mackerel squiggly wiggly. It has worked very well in the past. I remember when…"

Slipping away to the house, a burst of laughter from the adults sitting outside followed me into the living room. Sliding the screen behind me the CLACK of pool balls being whacked filled the air. Two young men were standing at the table with Oz and Jimbo. Apparently they had joined in the game. Their complexion was dark like Oz and they smiled brightly when I entered the room. One of them was slightly bigger, but they looked almost like twins.

"So, you are the guy, who caught the big ulua today." The taller of the two men walked across the room to greet me. "Aloha, I am Kala and that is my brother Kai." He was tall and lanky but his handshake was strong as a vice.

Kala leaned over the pool table and took a shot. "Oh, I missed. Oz it's your turn." The other man turned and walked towards me. "Aloha, Buzz. I'm Kai, Kala's big brother." He shook my hand. Oz took a shot and missed.

"You mean older brother, bra!" Kala chided him. "Age before beauty, it's your turn to shoot."

"Hey Buzz, Kala and Kai are going to show us some surf spots, too bad about your ear. Maybe if you get better before we leave this place, you can come with us." Jimbo bragged from across the pool table.

"Don't worry; you will be better. Of course you are invited too. I work at the university with your Pops. My brother is for the birds!" Kai slapped me on the shoulder before returning to the pool table.

"Haha, funny bra, I study native Hawaiian birds at the university." Kala corrected him.

The lid of the large wooden chest lifted remarkably easy on its hinges. Inside was a trove of board games. I studied the selection and decided on Clue. Since we were talking about solving a mystery, it seemed like a good game and it is actually quite fun to play. After setting up the board and leaving the pieces out for Alika and Leilani to choose their own, I walked over to the pool table to watch the competition.

"Do you want to play next?" Kai asked me.

"No thanks, we're going to play a board game when Leilani and Alika are done helping her mom."

"Buzz doesn't like pool. He'd rather play with girls." Jimbo smirked just seconds before, Alika and Leilani walked into the room. Leilani gave my friend a sinister look. Oz who was concentrating on the cue ball took his shot. He shook his head frowning at Jimbo, who sheepishly said: "Oh is it my turn?"

"You can play with your friends if you want." Leilani probed.

"Oh, don't mind Jimbo. He gets a little full of himself sometimes." My noble attitude surprised me.

"I gave him stink-eye." Leilani whispered to me looking over at Jimbo annoyed.

"Hey, that's a great choice of games, Buzz." Alika changed the subject. "Do you know how to play Clue?"

Leilani nodded. We sat down on the fluffy rug at the far end of the huge wooden coffee table where I had set up the board.

"I need to get my notes." Alika got up and pulled her steno pad out of the chest.

"First, let's get started playing. I don't think we need anyone to know that we are trying to help Keemo." Voicing my concern over how mom might react if she knew we were trying to get involved in Keemo's case. I shuffled the three stacks of cards and put them down on the table. Alika picked three, which she put in the envelope. That was the mystery.

"I'll be Mrs. Peacock and I assume you will want to be Miss. Scarlet. Who do you want to be, Buzz?" Alika looked at me.

"Colonel Mustard, I want to duel everybody. Too bad we can't just open an envelope and find out who stole that ring." I wished.

We began to play.

"I think we need to find out what the police have already done to investigate this case. Otherwise, we will be wasting our time. Buzz is the only one that can get it." Alika proposed. In response to my blank look, she continued: "Your lawyer should be able to get a copy of the police reports. I did some research and found out that he has to let you look at the reports and any other evidence. You have the attorney-client privilege, which means he can't tell your parents anything you don't want him to."

"But how am I going to get there? Right now my mom won't let me out of her sight."

"Maybe you can come to town with my mother and me when we go to the library. She volunteers there, tomorrow." Alika offered. At first, I didn't like the idea of sneaking around town.

"How is Keemo?" I asked Leilani, to change the subject.

"He's still stuck in his house. Uncle Hiro is really taking it hard. My Aunt Flossie has been over there with food and she says he can't eat because he is so sick with worry." She replied. "He is afraid that Keemo will be sent away to prison."

"Hiro doesn't think that Keemo stole the ring, does he? They never found it on him. There is no evidence! Just because he had the earring that we found in the gutter, and he was in that woman's yard means nothing." I interrupted.

"No, everybody knows that Keemo didn't take that ring." Leilani answered defiantly. "But, you know…"

"Actually, there is circumstantial evidence." Alika interjected. She added: "I suggest Mrs. White in the library with a rope. No? Okay. Anyways direct evidence is what you or someone else sees directly; like catching the criminal committing the crime on videotape. Circumstantial evidence on the other hand is like pieces of a puzzle that add up to point the finger at the guilty party.

"What…?" Leilani and I were looking at each other.

Alika paused, before continuing. "I did a little research."

"So what you are telling us is that they don't need to have the actual ring to accuse Keemo of stealing it?" I was annoyed.

"That is correct." Alika replied.

"That woman could have lost the ring or kept it and accused Keemo!"

"Hmmm, hmmm." Alika affirmed. "Well, the evidence needs to be strong enough to add up. Otherwise you could convict a Spam sandwich." She chuckled at her own joke. "We don't have any evidence that anyone other than the two of you and Keemo were at the scene of the crime that morning." She returned to a more serious tone.

I suggested: "Professor Plum with a candlestick in the Study."

"No," Leilani responded.

"We should go back to that place and look around. Maybe we can figure out who stole the ring."

"Remember that will be a problem because we're not allowed back there." Alika shattered that idea.

"That stinks!" I was disappointed.

"Well that just means we have to be sneaky about it." Leilani looked slyly. "We can always go there late at night."

"We can't break the law. That's trespassing and disobeying a court order." Alika cautioned.

"First, we have to get that police report and then we can figure out what we have to do next." Leilani turned to me. "Do you think you can handle that, Buzz?"

"Well, I guess."

"We can ask your mom if you can come to the library with my mom and me tomorrow." Alika came to my rescue. "Then we can take a break and walk over to Main Street where your lawyer's office is."

"Sure, if I can get away. That will work." I wasn't too comfortable about the prospect.

"Okay so we'll meet at the library tomorrow. Then Buzz can go and get the police report," Leilani declared. I felt better knowing that she would be there to back me up. "I accuse Mr. Wadsworth the butler of murdering Mr. Boddy with a gun in the ballroom." She placed her cards face up on the table and reached for the envelope.

Just then, the sound of shaking, rattling and clinking glass started, which became louder and louder. Then, the floor underneath us began to shake. Stunned, I looked at Alika and Leilani to see if it was my imagination.

"It's just an earthquake." Alika educated me matter-of-factly, before returning her attention to our friend, Leilani who was slowly opening the envelope to reveal the three cards, solving the game's mystery. She acted like a presenter at a Hollywood awards show. I felt scared after hearing the "WHOOOOAAAA!" from the grownups in the backyard. The wobbling floor and flickering lights didn't help much to calm my tremendous fear. Not to mention the sound of rumbling and clinking glass was loud. Then, Leilani and Alika nodded at each other and vanished underneath the table. Looking over at the billiards table, Jimbo and Oz were under the middle section of the four-legged pool table. Kai sat under the left edge and Kala waited crossed legged on the right side. A small hand reached out and grabbed my wrist. With a firm grip, Alika pulled me underneath the large wooden coffee table.

"What are you waiting for?" Alika questioned, kneeling hunched over under the giant table. Leilani was lying sideways and I was forced to assume the same prone body position. "Well what is in the envelope?" She looked impatiently. Leilani was still acting like she was presenting an award.

"The winner is…" Leilani announced as she pulled the flap of the envelope up and pulled the sides apart just far enough for her to peek in and check out the cards. "Yes, you know it's always the butler and a gun is an easy weapon and except during a ball, there are no witnesses in the ballroom. It's perfectly logical dear Watson. Yes, I win!!"

Alika's mouth was wide open. "How did you figure that out so fast?" She looked at Leilani suspiciously, who just grinned. The floor was still rumbling underneath.

I cleared my throat. "Ahem, what is going on? The house and everything is shaking and you are acting like nothing unusual is going on!"

"Oh it's Pele." Lelani laid on her back and answered looking up at the bottom side of the tabletop.

"What is Pele?" My response elicited giggling from my friends.

"You mean who is Pele. Didn't you know we are living on the edge of a volcano, silly? Pele is our Hawaiian legend for the spirit of the volcano. You better not make her mad. Sometimes she appears as an ancient lady in white clothes walking on the side of the road. If you help her you will have good fortune, if not 'tisk tisk.'"

"What do you mean 'tisk tisk'?" They looked at each other. First, Leilani and then Alika broke out into laughter at my comment.

"Well there are many stories of people who were rude or mean to Pele and afterwards, really bad things happened to them." Leilani explained.

The rumbling had stopped for a while when we heard three knocks on the table top and Dr. Hank's voice say: "What's going on under there?"

"Oh, we were just…" I stuck my head out from under the table to see most of the party guests standing around the table.

Leilani and Alika climbed out from different sides. My face felt red again.

"Telling the girls fish stories, eh Buzz?" one of the men heckled.

Most of the other adults were smiling, dad included. Mom holding Eric on her hip looked at me with an emotionless expression. She didn't seem pleased. It did not feel good. Hanna's interruption was greatly appreciated. She was holding a small battery operated radio, which sounded fuzzy. "Kiluea is erupting!" She exclaimed. "There was an announcement of the emergency broadcast service. We are fine, but there are some homes threatened farther down the coast. The lava is flowing towards them on its way to the ocean."

"Not to worry," Dr. Hank assured my parents. "We had a strong earthquake a week or two ago and that was an indicator that the volcano is venting built up pressure. Follow me. Let's go up to the observation deck five at a time." I was ushered away from my friends and up the stairs by my parents, Oz and Jimbo in tow.

Dr. Hank led us up the long spiral stairwell into a room that looked like a study. He pulled the curtains back, opened the large sliding glass door and walked out into a wooden deck. A telescope was positioned at the far edge, which looked over dizzying heights.

"Just let me adjust the angle of the telescope and you can all have a look. Ahh, yes there is definite activity to be seen this evening. It is beautiful! Please take a look." Dr. Hank yielded the eyepiece of the sizeable telescope to my dad.

"Wow, the red and orange lava is shooting out like three separate water fountains." Dad was excited. He grabbed Eric in his arms and pulled Mom over to look though the scope. Her body language was stiff. "It's really far away." He added and looked at Dr. Hank who jumped up as if Dad had nudged him in the ribs.

"Oh, yes! That's more than fifty miles away. There's no danger kaikuahini." Dr. Hank tried to reassure my mom, who had a strange expression on her face after moving away from the telescope. The adults moved into the room and off the deck.

Jimbo pushed in front of me to look through the viewer. "Wow, that's cool! It looks like three red water fountains. That's amazing!"

Oz didn't push ahead of me. I let him look through the scope when Jimbo was finally done, because I wanted to listen to my parents who seemed to be having a heated discussion on the other side of the patio screen door.

"I don't think we should discuss this now. Let's go home," was the last thing I heard my dad hiss in a low voice.

"Wow that is cool." Oz had one eye glued to the telescope.

When it was finally my turn, it took a few seconds for my right eye to get adjusted to seeing through the scope. It was dark and fuzzy at first but then a most fascinating and beautiful sight came into focus. Three tiny bright red and orange spouts of fire glowed. Small specks of molten lava broke off the stream and flew aside from the arched flow. It was captivating.

"Boys we are leaving." Dad interrupted my view of the earth's spectacle.

"Awwww."

"No, let's go." He commanded firmly.

We walked down the stairs. Mom was already giving her thanks to Hanna. Dr. Hank bade farewell Alohas to the other guests. Alika and Leilani were in the hallway. Mom gave them both hugs.

"Can Buzz come with us to the library tomorrow?" Alika asked mom. "I already asked my mom. She said it is okay. We can pick him up on our way to town." She spoke authoritatively.

"Well, I don't know. Uh, I guess it will be okay for just a few hours." Mom looked frazzled.

"See you at ten tomorrow morning. Aloha!" Alika gave me a hug and Leilani surprised me with a tight squeeze, too.

Jimbo announced: "Kala and Kai see you guys tomorrow!"

"We'll get you at seven and don't forget your wetsuits. The water is cold where we are surfing tomorrow. The break is at the mouth of a river that flows cold water into the ocean." Kai informed them and said: "Aloha."

Mom and dad hardly spoke on the ride home. When we got there they put Eric to bed and went into their room.

I overheard my dad saying: "We can't leave. We signed a lease. The house back home is rented out. We can't back out, now;" and "it's safe here."

"Mom wants to leave The Big Island already?" I thought. That was bad news.

CHAPTER TEN
Back To Surfing

The next morning, Jimbo and Oz left before I got up. I heard them stirring, but decided to stay in bed and snooze for a while longer. When I finally got dressed and made it downstairs, Mom seemed stressed out. She was on the phone in the kitchen talking to someone about reservations and leaving early. I didn't like the sound of it. Alika and her mother, Hanna, picked me up at ten. We drove to the library and arrived in ten minutes.

"I'll be at the circulation desk for the next three hours. So have fun, let me know if you need anything." Hanna told us as we got out of the car in the library parking lot. Pointing over to a giant boulder and a smaller one she told me: "Those two big rocks are famous monoliths. The larger is called the Naha stone it is from the island of Kauai. The smaller of the two is from Heiau. Enough of the history lessons, I hope you kids have fun. What are your plans?"

"Well Mom, I'm going to show Buzz around and then we are going to walk into town." Alika informed her.

"Okay, be back here before noon. Then we'll get some lunch, so don't spoil your appetite eating too much candy." Hanna warned as we walked through the main doors of the library.

"Let's go in and see if Leilani is here yet." Alika looked around at the bike rack. "I don't see her bike here. Let's go inside and wait for her."

We entered the library. It looked like just about every other library I had ever been in. Hanna walked over to the circulation desk. Alika and I checked out the biology section. There was a large selection of books about animals and plants. She grabbed a book about tropical birds and I reached for one with large glossy photographs of marine life. We sat down at the nearest table. The book I picked had bright photos of colorful coral and amazingly patterned fish. On the glossy full color cover was a picture of a brown black and white triggerfish. I gazed at the glossy photo.

"That is our official Hawaiian State fish, Humuhumun-ukunukuapua'a." Alika informed me.

"How long have you been here?" Leilani interrupted my gaze with a punch on the upper arm. She pulled a chair up to the table and sat down.

"Not long, Aloha Leilani."

"Aloha Alika, hey Buzz, so what's the plan?" Leilani asked.

"We should go over to the lawyer's office and look at the police report." Alika opined.

"Lets go, then." Leilani confirmed our plans.

Shutting the big book, I took a deep breath, grabbed Alika's closed book and put them both on the cart for books to be returned.

"Okay let's go." I summoned courage against my fears, while trying to figure out what to say when we got to the lawyer's office.

Hanna was occupied with an elderly gentleman at the circulation desk, so she didn't notice the three of us walking out of the library. After a few minutes outside, I noticed a funny sulfuric odor in the air and asked:

"What's that smell?"

"Vog." Alika replied.

"What's vog?"

"It's what happens when oxygen and moisture in the air combine with toxic sulfur dioxide and acid rain that have spewed from the active Kilauea volcano. It's kind of like smog, except it's not created by car exhaust." Alika answered authoritatively. "We only have about an hour and a half, so we better get to the lawyer's office right away. We don't know how long it will take to read all of the reports."

Heading towards town, the thought of walking into the lawyer's office and demanding to see the police reports in my file seemed even more daunting. I did not feel comfortable about the prospect and was afraid I'd make a fool of myself. The girls were talking about something. I didn't hear what they were saying, because my mind was focused on the impending task. Alika and Leilani giggled. As we walked closer to the ocean, I could feel the fresh sea breeze in my face. It gave me a sense of courage like a strong gust filling the sails of a ship.

"How is Keemo?" I asked Leilani during a brief interlude in their conversation.

"Oh, he's okay, I guess. Keemo doesn't know this, but a social worker came by and they think that they may want him to live with another family after they saw the house and yard full of junk. The social worker said Uncle Hiro is unfit. He is beside himself. Everyone is really worried about him. Keemo seems unfazed by all of this. He just hangs out at home and fixes stuff." She looked down with a deep sadness in her beautiful dark brown eyes. It made me sad, seeing her pain.

That was all I needed to spark my enthusiasm. "Here we are at Mr. Delton's law office." I held the door open as my friends entered the waiting area. I walked up to the receptionist and announced myself: "Hi I'm Buzz, and I want to look at my file."

The lady at the reception desk had a bright red hibiscus flower in her hair, which matched her lipstick. She smiled warmly. "Yes, Buzz I remember you. Please have a seat for a moment while I let Mr. Delton know that you are here. She picked up the telephone and pushed a button. "Young master Buzz is here to see you." She listened intently. "Yes Sir, I will tell him." They looked up at me from her desk. "Mr. Delton will be with you in just a moment."

Amazed by the accommodation I was receiving, I sat down on the maroon winged back chair in the reception area. Alika and Leilani sat down on the armrests on either side of me. I felt a little more confident. They each had a fancy fashion magazine on their laps. Searching the coffee table before us, I spied a surfing magazine. Before I could grab it and get situated, the door with the beveled glass opened and Mr. Delton walked out wearing a bright red and yellow aloha shirt.

"Well, what a pleasant surprise! I just got off the phone with your mother. What can I do for you?" He shook my hand. "Please sit down."

"I would like to read the police reports in my file, please." My request did not come out as confident as I had planned. "Oh and I don't want you to tell my parents I'm here because of attorney privilege."

"Attorney-client privilege." Alika whispered in my ear.

"Attorney-client privilege." I corrected myself.

"Well, okay," he chuckled, "and I assume that you would like to have your two lady friends view the file with you?"

"Yes, of course." I looked over at Alika and Leilani who were both nodding in unison.

"Okay, please follow me." He took us to a conference room with a huge table and twelve chairs at the end of the hall. "Have a seat. I'll go and get your file."

We sat down at the large wooden executive meeting table. Alika's chin barely reached the edge. "Here you are. Please don't remove anything or make any marks on the file." Mr. Delton plopped the long manila folder down in front of me. "Oh, and by the way, I just got a subpoena for you to appear in court in a couple of weeks. When I called your mother, she said that she was thinking of leaving The Big Island with you boys earlier than planned. Now, it's clear you are not leaving so soon. Let me know if you have any questions. I will be in my office down the hall." He shut the door.

"What was that about?" Alika asked.

"Oh, I think my mom got scared and wanted to leave after this problem and then the earthquake and volcano." I was relieved by the news of this new development. We were not leaving sooner!

"See, I told you. She's already got island fever." Leilani declared.

"Let's see what's in this file." I opened the folder. There was a subpoena for me to appear in court on the top of the right side. On the left side was the police report. "Here it is." Alika and Leilani got up and stood close to me leaning on my shoulder. We read in silence. The report was five pages long and included a lot of repetitive information. Leilani was referred to as the 'female juvenile' over and over again. I was 'juvenile suspect number two.' The contract and my parents' receipt for payment were at the bottom of that side of the file. "It looks like the police did everything. The entire property and neighboring yards were searched inch by inch with a police dog. They even sent a plumber to check the pipe under the sink to make sure the ring didn't fall down the drain."

"Yes, Buzz it looks like the police did everything." Alika agreed.

"They did everything except find out who really stole the ring." Leilani corrected her friend. "If they had done everything, they would have found the ring.

"How are you doing?" Mr. Delton stood in the doorway.

"We're done." I informed him, confidently.

"Well, since the District Attorney is going to go forward with Keemo's case, I'll need you back here in my office before the trial, to prepare you for your testimony." Mr. Delton patted me on the shoulder as we walked out of the conference room. "You don't think that I would put you up on the stand at trial without preparation? Remember the 'Five P's': Prior Preparation Prevents Poor Performance. And if you are thinking about playing little detectives, forget it." He gave me a stern look before turning to walk back to his office. I shrugged my shoulders.

"That was great." Leilani commented sarcastically as we stepped back out of the law office onto the sidewalk heading back to the library. The vog smell was hardly noticeable anymore. A few light sprinkles of rain glazed the pavement. The mist felt good on my face, with Leilani on my left, Alika to the right, we walked closely together. I felt proud of myself for walking into my lawyer's office and asserting my right to be informed about my case. It was better to know the facts than to assume what was going on. Even though all their facts pointed at Keemo, I knew that he was innocent. It felt good in my heart knowing this to be the truth. We walked quietly for quite a while.

"I thought you were great, Buzz." Alika finally broke the silence grabbed my right arm, squeezing it she declared: "Now, that we know what the police did. We can launch our own investigation. This is so exciting. Now, we have a true mystery!"

The drizzle was short lived and the sun burst through the clouds, as we walked back to the library. When we walked into the building, Hanna spotted us and waved.

"I'm glad you are back early. We are going to pick up Alika's dad and then we'll all go to lunch."

Food was a very welcome suggestion. Hanna drove the station wagon to the hospital, parked and the three of us went inside to get Dr. Hank. Walking through the empty reception area, we followed Hanna back to the examination room.

"Well, look who's here." Dr. Hank looked up from a chart and smiled. He stood up to hug Hanna, Alika and Leilani, then, reached out and I felt his firm handshake. "I think you are scheduled for an exam tomorrow. Why don't you sit down real quick and I'll take a look at your ear. How is it feeling?" He patted me on the shoulder.

"Great!" I wasn't exaggerating as I sat down in the examination chair.

He grabbed a black plastic cap and snapped it on the scope in his hand. I felt it in my right ear. "That looks good, now the other one," Dr. Hank rolled his stool around to my left side. "Yes, this ear looks good too."

My spirits rose. "So, can I surf again?"

"Yes, I don't see why not. As a precaution, it would be a good idea for you to wear ear plugs in the water." He put the scope away. "Now, let's go and get some lunch."

Dr. Hank drove us to a nice restaurant. I had a tuna sandwich. We talked about a lot of things. After the server cleared our dishes, Hanna said: "We were thinking of going to the beach this afternoon, Buzz, would you like to join us?"

"Sure," I could never resist that invitation. "Is there any surfing where we are going?"

"Yes, there is." She answered. "Would you like to stop by your house and pick up your surfboard on the way? We can ask your mom if it's okay too."

"Oh, Jimbo has my surfboard. He broke his in half. I lent him mine, so I'll just have to sit at the shore and watch."

"You can borrow one of my boards. I store my two surfboards over in Keemo's shed. Can we go by there?" Leilani stretched over to the front seat and leaned on Dr. Hank's shoulder.

"Of course," Dr. Hank looked at us through the rear view mirror. "I hope it's on this side of The Big Island though, hee hee."

"No worries Doctor, Keemo lives a couple houses down from Buzz." Leilani replied, her long black hair flapped wildly in the wind out of the open window. "The surfboards are in the shed in the back. I can grab them real quickly. I have the combo for the padlock. Keemo gave it to me." She looked very sad, and blurted: "Those people think that there is something wrong with him, but there isn't!!" Leilani's voice rose. "Keemo is innocent!" A tear dropped down her cheek. "He is a good guy! They don't know him! He is just a little different."

'I know,' I thought and blurted: "I'm sorry I found that stupid earring in the gutter and showed him. It is all my fault! I know." The guilt burst out of me. "Keemo is in this problem because of me. There was no hiding the fact…. Jimbo was right. 'If Buzz finds something, you better run for the hills, it is only going to mean trouble for you.' If only Keemo had run away from me, up that steep hill, instead of looking at the earring I found and putting it in his pocket. He only wanted to return it to its proper owner." My sprits sank as fast as they had risen. Now, I was embarrassed by my outburst on top of everything. Alika's parents had both been silent.

"No Buzz," Hanna corrected me: "You cannot blame yourself for these events. Don't be so hard on yourself."

"She's right Buzz." Leilani agreed. "It's not your fault. I know you care about Keemo, too. Otherwise you wouldn't be trying to find out where that ring really went."

Dr. Hank pulled the huge station wagon into the driveway of the house where we were staying. "Here we are Buzz, do you want to ask your mom for permission to go and grab your beach stuff?"

"I'll go in with him and say hello." Hanna opened the car door, stepped out and followed me into the house. Mom looked terrible, her eyes were red and it seemed that she had been crying. I really wondered how much fun she was having on this vacation. Hanna recognized the situation immediately and said: "I'm going to stay here and we're going to have a girls' chat. We'll make some tea. You go and grab your things and run along. I'll run out and tell Hank to get me when he drops you off."

It seemed so long since I had surfed, it took me a little while to find my things. Luckily, I had brought a bunch of surf wax and grabbed a new bar from the stack on the shelf. After giving Mom a quick hug I was outside and hopping in the huge back seat.

"How's your mother, Buzz?" Alika asked sympathetically.

"She's kind of sad, I think."

"Island fever." Leilani diagnosed my mom's condition authoritatively.

The drive to Keemo and Hiro's house took less than a minute. As the judge forbade me from having contact with Keemo, it was decided that Dr. Hank and Leilani would grab the surfboards from the shack in the back yard. Keemo was standing inside the front window motionlessly. He looked like a statue, and only moved away when Leilani knocked on the door. He led them around the outside to the backyard, and out of sight. Alika and I sat in the car quietly waiting. The three emerged from the side of the house with Leilani carrying a bright pink surfboard and Dr. Hank the neon green one. It was exciting just to think I would be surfing on it soon. Keemo did not walk up to the car. Instead, he turned the corner of the house and walked to the front door. Leilani dropped her board in the tall grass and ran after him. She caught up at the front steps and gave him a hug. Keemo's arms hung limply at his sides while she squeezed him. She turned and walked over to Dr. Hank, who was already putting the green board into the back of the wagon through the open rear window.

When we stopped at Leilani's house she ran in and returned back to the station wagon within minutes, wearing pink baggies and a matching pink t-shirt. Under her arm she had tucked a big colorful beach towel. A portly lady in a one-piece floral mu'u mu'u dress walked out with her.

"This is my Aunt Flossie." Leilani introduced her to me.

"Aloha Doctor, Alika, and Buzz, I have heard so much about you." She reached into the car window and patted me on the shoulder. "Are you enjoying yourself here?" I nodded.

Aunt Flossie smiled and waved as we drove off. After a half-hour stop at Alika and Dr. Hank's, which felt like forever, we were on our way to the beach! It was already mid afternoon when we arrived there, so the parking lot was almost empty. "Here we are kids!" Dr. Hank proclaimed while he shifted the wagon into park and turned off the ignition. We unloaded the car and walked to the black sand beach. The wind was blowing sideways to the shore and the waves looked mushy, but I didn't care. There were only a few surfers in the water. Dr. Hank had a rolled up newspaper and some medical journals in one hand and a couple of folding beach chairs in the other. Alika walked behind him with her inflatable raft and a beach bag. We followed them to a spot in the sand and dropped our stuff. I just wanted to get into the water as fast as possible and waited for the cue, which was Dr. Hank saying: "Okay this is a good place. Have fun."

The fluorescent green board didn't have much wax on it so I pulled the bar out of my backpack, pealed the plastic wrapper back and began to rub it onto the deck in small circles. The smell of coconut filled my nose. I handed the wax to Leilani. She rubbed it on the deck of her bright pink surfboard in a quick zigzag motion. We walked down to the shoreline. Looking back, Alika and her father were sitting in their beach chairs reading.

Finally, after almost ten days restricted from surfing, the water felt warm and comforting on my toes. We waded out a few feet, jumped on our surfboards and began to paddle side by side towards the breaking waves. There were three separate surf spots at that beach. We passed through the small shore break where little kids rode their rafts or body surfed. The board Leilani lent me felt thinner than mine and a little less stable, but made for faster paddling. My arms got tired and I had to take a short break, while she got ahead of me. Resuming with harder arm strokes, I caught up with her after a little while.

The middle surfing area was another seventy-five yards further offshore. Only two surfers were sitting there waiting for waves. Farther out where the breakers were bigger, there was quite a crowd. A set came through and I sat up and watched three surfers take off on the outside. The two riding farthest from the curl quickly steered their boards up and over the lip to let the surfer in position ride the wave.

A smaller surge reached the two surfers at the middle break. One of them caught the first wave, just as outside another was cresting. My heart was beginning to pump. The other guy dropped in too late on a larger breaker. His surfboard shot up in the air while its rider tumbled over as the water crumbled over him. We paddled closer. By the time we got to the take off spot, the set had passed and there was a lull in the action. I followed Leilani to a spot just a little farther out than the foamy water from the previous set. The two guys who were there before were heading into the shore, so we had it all to ourselves. Looking at the beach, I could see Alika and her dad sitting in their folding chairs. The sky was cloudy but the air and water felt warm.

"Here comes another set." Leilani announced.

The outside riders had already caught rides, when a waist high wave rose up before us. My friend turned around and began to paddle. I felt my surfboard rise over the peak, as Leilani jumped up on her feet. She rode gracefully towards the shore. The next wave was mine! I watched it rise a little higher than the previous one and SPLASH, the white water of the breaking crest pounded me. My body was flipped off the deck. For the small size of the wave I was surprised how much force it produced, tumbling me under the water for quite a few seconds. Reaching the surface and collecting my surfboard, the takeoff spot wasn't too far. Leilani's wave had deposited her about thirty meters away. I sat enjoying the peacefulness of floating in the water between sets. The wind was blowing so strongly from my right that I had drifted from the takeoff spot. Realizing this when Leilani returned from her wave, I had to paddle back to adjust my position.

The next set came just a few minutes later. As before, Leilani was the first to catch one. The next was funky and escaped me, but the wave after that rose in perfect position for me to catch it. Two arm strokes later, I felt it yank my board into its grip, and pull me towards the shore. Jumping to my feet, my bottom turn was not quick enough and the face was out of reach. Disappointed, I rode the white water from the crumbled wave. It was faster than the breakers we rode at home. Looking towards shore, the beach chairs were empty. I wondered where Alika and her dad had gone.

"One more wave to warm up here and then let's go out to the outer reef." Leilani glided towards me.

"Okay!" I gulped and looked nervously out to sea where the other surfers were sitting and that guy had wiped out. She didn't hear me because she had already caught another ride.

My next wave was a little better, but the wind was blowing straight offshore, causing the spray of brine to blind me. By the time I could see and try to turn on the wave, it had faded into nothing. Leilani was already paddling out again. I followed.

As we made our way back out, another set passed through. We were unaffected, moving through deep water along the side of the reef. A group of five guys who had been surfing the outer reef paddled towards us on their way to shore: "Aloha Leilani!" one of the dark tanned men greeted her. He gave me a probing look, then nodded. He turned to his friends and said something I couldn't hear. They roared with laughter as they paddled past us. We progressed. The distance to the outer break seemed a lot farther than it looked. My upper back and shoulders began to ache from the long paddle. The gap between Leilani and me was widening. The strong force of a wall of white water hit me. I continued on. Another wave pushed through and three more followed. My strength was waning.

Leilani made it out more quickly, caught a wave and rode by me. Plopping down on the deck of her board, she turned to me and asked: "Do you like paddling? Why are you going straight into the break? You need to go around in the deep

water." She turned her board and paddled sideways out of the foamy soup, into glassier water over a darker sea floor. "Why fight the white water when you can have an easier paddle just a few feet away."

"Oh!" was my only response following her into the calmer water.

When we got away from the shallow area Leilani stopped, sat up on her board and waited for me. Finally reaching her, the rest period was welcome. We sat silently with only the sound of the wind whipping against the ocean surface.

"Okay, Buzz. Let's go catch some waves!" came far too soon for my liking, but I followed. My arms felt less sour after that short break. From somewhere, I don't know where, I felt more energy to paddle further.

The wave faces were a solid six feet, two of the surfers caught set waves as we approached. They both gracefully maneuvered up and down the shoulders and one even got covered in a tube before being deposited in the channel. They headed to shore about the time we reached the take off zone. My heart was pounding.

The first wave of the next set came but didn't have the height or steepness to ride. The one that followed rose behind it made me gulp.

"Okay Buzz, go for it!" Leilani hooted.

My arms pushed the water back and the surfboard gained momentum. Within a few strokes I was on my feet. The wind blew stinging spray into my eyes. It took a few seconds for my vision to return, dropping down from the top of the face of the wave. Bottom turning, the neon green surfboard accelerated like a rocket and I just stood on it racing through each section of the wave. It was so fast that turns weren't an option. All I could do was dig my toes into the deck and hang on. The speed and power of the ride made my jaw drop. Before I knew it the thrill was over as the board slowed in the calmer water of the deep channel.

Exhilarated from catching my first real Hawaiian wave, I returned to catch five more powerful ones. After that we headed back to shore, exhausted. Alika and her Dad were already starting to pack up their stuff. Leilani stuck the tail of her surfboard into the sand. I followed her example. They looked like sculptures standing next to each other. After toweling off, I put my t-shirt on. I was amazed that my baggies were already almost dry. We grabbed our things and went back to the car.

Dr. Hank drove Leilani home from the beach first. She got out with him and grabbed her pink board from the back of the station wagon, but when he reached in to grab the neon green board, Leilani said: "No, Buzz can use that one for a while. Take good care of it and don't let anyone else ride it, okay?" She punched my upper arm through the open window, flicked her long ebony black hair back over her shoulder, and walked around the car.

"OH WOW, okay thanks." I was stunned by her generosity. Now I wouldn't have to share a surfboard with Jimbo, I thought happily.

"Aloha girlfriend," Leilani walked up to the front passenger window. "Aloha and Mahalo Doc."

"Aloha Leilani," Alika and her dad responded in sync. He waited for her to drop her surfboard on the front porch and walk into the house before driving off.

Back at the house Mom and Hanna were sitting in the living room. Eric was playing with his blocks on the floor. For the first time in a while, Mom smiled at me when Dr. Hank, Alika and I walked into the room.

"That settles it, you and the boys will spend a couple of days at our condo on the west side of The Big Island." Hanna got up kissed Alika on the cheek and hugged her husband. "The sunny Kona Coast will do you all a world of good. We go there on weekends sometimes to get away from the rain here on this side of The Big Island."

"You'll like it there, Buzz." Alika added. "There's a beach you can snorkel at with coral and colorful fish and you can surf at a spot to the north, too."

"Yes the beaches have the light colored sand you are used to, but it's a little bit more 'touristy' there than it is here." Doctor Hank elaborated. "You will have fun. Consider it doctor's orders!"

CHAPTER ELEVEN
The Other Side Of The Island

And so two days after Dr. Hank cleared me for surfing, we loaded up the van and headed to the other side of The Big Island. On the way we drove through lava fields that looked more like the lunar landscape than a tropical island. A desert like area followed, before we entered a lush jungle. As you might expect, "are we there yet?" was a frequent question, which seemed to annoy my parents to no end.

After countless hours in the car, we finally drove into a town where the street was lined with a three-foot high wall made of melon sized lava rocks followed by tall buildings and a lot of people walking on the sidewalk. The sun was bright in the clear sky and the beach looked inviting with yellow sand and turquoise blue water. We drove through what seemed to be a downtown area. Traffic was heavy. For the first time since we got to The Big Island, I heard honking car horns. There were more people walking on the sidewalk here than back on the other side. The crowd looked bright, colorful and multi-cultural. Dad turned the van right onto a side street. A few blocks further, and he pulled into the driveway of a bright white three-story building. He reviewed the paper on which he had written the directions.

"Here's number thirty-four, our parking space." Dad pulled in stopped, and turned off the engine. He got out and opened the sliding door to let us out. My legs were stiff after the long drive and stretching them felt good. We unloaded the bags and left our surfboards and snorkel gear for the second or third trip up the stairs to the top floor. The condo had two bedrooms a small living room and a kitchen.

While we were unloading, Mom went to a shop and got pulled pork sandwiches. She unwrapped them from the white paper and put the sandwiches on a large serving plate. We all huddled around the small dining table in the corner kitchen window. It had an amazing view to the beach. We gazed with messy hands and mouths out at the deep blue sea.

"When can we go snorkeling?" Jimbo asked with a mouth full of food.

"When we are done unpacking, you boys can go down to the beach together." Mom shook her head and frowned at his horrible table manners.

The view from the kitchen window was amazing. We could observe most of the beach. Dad stood up and pulled the curtains back. "Do you see those rocks over there? I do not want you to go past them." Dad elaborated pointing. "There is a lifeguard tower over there and I want you to stay within that area. You are on The Big Island boys and no matter how great you think you might be in the water, you are totally outclassed here. Sometimes rogue waves will appear out of nowhere, or a giant roaming tiger shark hungry after months without food. Do you understand?" We nodded and then gulped down our sandwiches.

Unpacking seemed like a breeze, since we hadn't brought much stuff. There was a dresser and two trundle beds. Each of us put our clothes in a separate drawer and placed our bags into the closet. The diving gear and surfboards were safely stored on the living room balcony. After that, we were forced to listen to another lengthy lecture from Dad, which included the admonition: "Don't stand on the coral it is made up of millions of tiny organisms. They take a very long time to grow. Make sure that you tread water. Avoid stepping on the polyps." We were on our way down the stairs.

"This is going to be cool, the coral reef fish should be bright and colorful compared to the ones we have back home." I was enthused.

"Yeah, this is the first time we are going snorkeling since we got to the Island." Oz added.

Jimbo was ahead of us opening the stairwell door out onto the street. Oz and I followed a few feet behind him.

"Boy he is in a hurry." Oz commented. "You'd think the ocean is going to close soon."

It felt good to have some time to hang out alone with Oz. We walked at a casual pace and talked while Jimbo forged ahead further, clearing more space between us. By the time we got to the main street, Jimbo had already begun crossing. The traffic was still pretty heavy. He began to run. The cars were beginning to approach him. Jimbo was almost at the other side of the busy street, when he dropped one of his swim fins, stopped to pick it up and sprinted to the safety of the other side. A car horn honked as a driver slammed on his brakes to avoid hitting him. He sprinted across the lane to the adjacent sidewalk. Looking to his right at the car that stopped to avoid hitting him, he missed seeing an elderly lady with long gray white hair, who was pushing her cart full of pineapples. We watched in shock as a car almost hit Jimbo, and then plowed into the cart knocking it over, sending pineapples flying onto the sidewalk. He almost pushed the lady over too.

"What has gotten into him?" Oz was stunned by our friend's reckless behavior. "Look at that poor lady. He's not even helping pick up the mess!"

Jimbo ran off towards the beach as the elderly lady in a red floral dress stood there aghast, with her hands on her cheeks. The heavy traffic passed, Oz and I hurried across the street. Without speaking we tossed our masks, fins and snorkels on the bordering grass lawn and began to help the gray haired lady pick up pineapples and stack them back on her pushcart. The first one I grabbed pricked my finger, so I learned real fast how to pick them up carefully. Oz and I had all the fruit back on the cart in no time.

"Mahalo Nui Loa." The lady smiled at us. "You are good boys. Here is a nice pineapple for you to share." She handed us one of the fruits.

"Thank you, errr, I mean Mahalo." I thanked the lady holding our reward. We turned our attention to the lawn and retrieving our belongings.

"Where did she go?" Oz poked me in the back as I was picking up my gear in one hand.

Turning around, she was gone in a flash! "I don't know Oz. How could she just vanish so fast with that big cart full of pineapples? That's weird!" I shrugged my shoulders. We both looked up and down the sidewalk and across the street. There was no sign of her. "What are we going to do with this?" I lifted the pineapple.

"Eat it of course. We'll put it on the beach while we snorkel. Have you ever had fresh pineapple? It's the best!" Oz explained.

"My mom cuts one up sometimes. It's way better than canned and a lot healthier."

Looking around one more time to try to see the lady, who had vanished, we walked on the grass to the shore. Approaching the lifeguard tower, there was a commotion. Jimbo was standing there holding his left arm. Oz started to run and I followed as fast as I could with my gear and the pineapple.

"What happened?" Oz was concerned.

"I dove into the water and broke my arm." Jimbo exhaled sharply. "Diving into the water, I guess my hand hit a rock or something and bent my wrist back. OUUUCHH!" Jimbo's face was red and contorted from the pain. He repeated himself: "I broke my arm."

"We've called for the ambulance to take you to the hospital. It should be here shortly. Are your parents here on the beach?" The dark tanned lifeguard asked Jimbo while applying a large ice pack to his injured wrist.

"OWWW, I'm with his parents." Jimbo nodded to me.

"My parents are back at the condo, a couple of blocks that way." I answered pointing in the general direction.

The lifeguard handed me a card with an address and telephone number printed on it. "The ambulance will take your friend to this emergency room. Your parents can pick him up there."

"Grab my gear. It's over there." Jimbo's face was cringing. For the first time since we got to The Big Island, I felt like he was my friend again. At least now, he was not acting like a pompous jerk!

The ambulance came and picked up Jimbo. He tried to resist getting on the gurney, but was told that was the only way that they were going to take him to the hospital. When he continued to argue the medics just lifted Jimbo up and put him on it. Oz and I watched the ambulance drive away. I looked at the card in my hand and turned to Oz feeling uneasy.

"My parents are going to freak out."

"It's not your fault, I wouldn't worry. If you want, I'll tell them. They'll just pick Jimbo up from the hospital when the cast is finished." Oz tried to calm me. "We should probably let your mom and dad, know right away. If we go in the water before telling them, they may have good reason to be mad about that. He picked up Jimbo's gear and we walked back to inform my parents.

Mom and dad weren't mad at all. I was surprised. Oz and I stayed with mom, while dad drove to the hospital. She put Eric into the stroller and we mingled among the other tourists in town. We had shaved ice and went from one little store to another. After a while I recognized the same merchandise was available in each shop. This part of the island felt different from Hilo. I already felt a little homesick for my friends and the familiar rainy life on the other side of The Big Island. Wondering what Keemo, Alika and Leilani were doing, I looked into a glass case at one store and saw a necklace on one of the shelves made from small white shells. Oz was tired and wanted to stay outside with Eric who was sound asleep in his stroller. The pretty petit Asian lady, who had greeted us at the door, asked me: "Is there something in particular you would like to look at young man?"

"Uh, ummm," I thought of my promise to bring Stephanie a souvenir and of course wanted to bring something back for Nana, too. "Oh, no thank you." I lost my courage.

"Come on, we'll take a look at this display." Mom put her arm around my shoulder and studied the shelves intently. The lady pulled up a stool, sat down and unlocked the glass case with a key that hung on her wrist. "We need to bring presents back. What were you looking at Buzz?"

"Well now that you mention it, I promised Stephanie a present as trade for her doing Nana's lawn while we are here."

"Okay, let's look then." Mom smiled supportively. "Could you please show us that piece, please?" She pointed at the pink necklace. "That's sweet, Buzz. Would you like to give that to Stephanie?"

"Uh sure, but do you think that she will like it?" I felt uncertain. "I don't know if I have enough money, mom." The lady smiled at me, warmly.

"Okay, we will take that and do you have a matching bracelet and earrings?" It was as if mom and that lady were instant friends communicating in secret code. "Oh, it looks like you do. We'll take them, too."

"These are puka shells. I assume that this is for a young lady, then?" I nodded. "Would you like gift wrapping?" Mom and the lady got into a deep conversation about jewelry, while I looked at the other items in the display. My eyes focused on a shiny golden pineapple broche on the bottom shelf that reminded me of the prickly fruit the lady had given us that afternoon.

"Do you see anything else, Buzz?" Mom looked as if she already knew the answer.

"Well, I was thinking that we should probably bring something back for Nana." I answered. "That pineapple looks cool, what do you think?"

"Nice Buzz, that's really cute. You have great taste." She turned to the lady. Could you please show that piece to us?" Mom looked intrigued as she examined the intricate design of the golden broche. "Do you gift wrap?"

"Of course I will do that for you." The lady smiled.

By the time we got back to the apartment, Jimbo was already in the living room watching TV, with a cast on his left arm and wrist. He looked paler than usual, which made his freckles stand out even more.

"If I get a water proof cast, I can surf again in a couple of days." Jimbo tried to convince himself.

Dad walked into the room to greet us and chuckled at Jimbo: "I think you may be out of the water for a little longer than that, but let's see what the doctor says when you go for the permanent cast. By the way, we have a baby sitter coming to stay with you boys this evening. Mom and I are going out to dinner. The lady comes highly recommended."

"What, we're getting a babysitter? I AM A BABYSITTER, we don't need someone to sit for us!" Jimbo exclaimed, indignantly. Oz and I nodded in support from the couch. Dad looked at Jimbo, who was sitting in the reclining chair. He glanced down at his cast and then looked up at Jimbo again and replied: "In view of recent developments, I think my wife and I will feel far more relaxed on our date knowing that you are all being supervised by an adult."

Checkmate - that ended the discussion. Mom was feeding my little brother Eric in his high chair. Her hair was wrapped in a towel and she had a bathrobe on. Dad took over the feeding so that she could finish getting ready. Jimbo, Oz and I sat in the living room and watched TV, for a while.

"I am bummed that I can't go into the water." Jimbo broke our silence complaining.

"Well, I know how you feel." I offered my sympathy with a touch of sarcasm.

Just then, there was a loud banging on the front door. Before any of us could get up, dad opened it. He was wearing a bright new floral Aloha shirt that mom had bought him earlier that day.

"Aloha, I am the babysitter, Madam Kanani." The voice sang from the doorway.

"Aloha, please come in." Dad motioned an open welcome with his arm.

A stout figure in a blue and gold mu'u mu'u dress stood in the doorframe. She wore a straw hat and carried a large handbag woven out of palm fronds. Dad escorted the lady into the kitchen where Eric was still sitting in his high chair. Mom came into the kitchen and gave our babysitter instructions. A tray of lasagna was baking in the oven, which she had prepared back at the house and brought it in a cooler. The delicious aroma was wafting through the living room, where we were still watching TV.

"Aloha boys!" Madam Kanani walked into the room.

"Aloha." Oz and I greeted her in unison.

Jimbo was acting a little weird said: "Alohahaha."

Madam Kanani ignored him and said: "I see. Dinner is ready, and young man…" She gave Jimbo a hard glance. "Aloha is a word that has mana, or what you might call energy or power. So don't mock it!" Jimbo froze and sank into his chair. I was really beginning to like this lady!

Mom served us the lasagna in the kitchen before she and Dad left on their date. We ate, while Madam Kanani sat with little Eric who was contently dozing off on her lap. His platinum blond hair contrasted with her long jet-black locks. In her free hand she held an ancient looking picture book.

"This book is about the Menehune. They are little people who have been living on the Islands since before our ancestors arrived. They are a very secretive people, very short, but ten times stronger than the strongest chief."

Reading the book's title I was a little puzzled: "It looks like you should pronounce the word 'Men-eh-hewn'?"

Madam Kanani chuckled and explained: "The Hawaiian language is very simple. The vowels all have either short or long sounds. The important thing is that you pronounce each and every vowel distinctly. 'Meh-Neh-Whoo-Neh'." She used her index finger to emphasize the syllables in the word 'Menehune' by tapping on the front cover of the tattered book. "The Menehune live in the remote areas like mountains and secluded valleys, where they might find shelter in a cave or hollow log. They are small people who have a serious almost scary expression on their faces."

"They sound like Leprechauns." Jimbo was intrigued.

"Are they like the Musuis in the mountains of Peru?" Oz added.

"Yes, and the Kobolds of Germany too," Madam Kanani turned another page of the picture book. "These dwarf-like people are magical creatures, they complete amazing works. The Menehune Fish Pond at Nawililwili, the Menehune Ditch at Waimea and the Poliahu Heiau, are all credited to them. The Menehune are especially fond of children, and they have some human friends but most of the time they stay out of sight of people."

We listened captivated while Madam Kanani read the rest of the book. Eric had his thumb firmly planted in his mouth and was sound asleep before she finished reading. His head rested on her ebony curls. She quietly closed the book and put it on the kitchen table and rose to her feet with my little brother in her arms.

"I'm going to put this little keiki to bed. Wash off your dishes in the sink, Mahalo."

"Yeah Buzz and Oz you guys will have to take over. I really would love to help out and do my part. You must understand it pains me, but I can't get my arm wet right now." Jimbo popped out of his seat and plopped down on the couch in the living room in front of the TV.

"I'll wash if you dry." Oz proposed.

"Deal!" I accepted enthusiastically.

Madam Kanani returned, put the book back into her woven bag and pulled out a folded piece of white cloth with blue thread and a needle stuck in the embroidered portion. She began to silently work on the quilt. Meanwhile, Oz handed me the first clean plate. After drying it, I looked through the cabinets to find its place.

"You boys are doing a good job." Madam Kanani complemented our efforts. "What's wrong with him?" She pointed to Jimbo whose attention was locked on the TV set in the living room.

"Oh, Jimbo broke his arm today. He dove into the water and hit a rock, which bent his hand back at the wrist." Oz informed her.

"Diving into shallow water is foolish. Did the two of you do that too?" Madam Kanani asked.

"No, we were picking up pineapples. Jimbo ran ahead of us to the shore after he knocked an elderly lady's pineapple cart over. Oz and I picked them up for her and she gave us that pineapple as a gift." I pointed to the welcoming fruit sitting on the counter.

"What did this lady look like?" She inquired further. Oz described her. Madam Kanani chuckled and said: "It sounds like you had a meeting with Pele. She smiled on the two of you, but had a message for your rude friend over there. Madam Pele came to these islands from Tahiti with her seven brothers and six sisters. Each was a Kahuna in their own right, each was an expert in the hula."

"My friend Alika does hula, do you mean like dancing wiggling their hips? Guys do that too?" I was puzzled.

"Ah you know Alika?" Madam Kanani said: "I have spent quite a bit of time with her. She is smart and pretty, a lovely girl. Hula is dance that tells a story. Yes, Buzz; men perform the hula, too. They don't emphasize the same body motions, but they can tell a story by moving their bodies rhythmically, just like the girls." Madam Kanani continued. "Pele lives in the crater of the volcano and appears in many forms. Sometimes she appears as a beautiful young woman, sometimes as an elderly lady in need of help. People who have seen her have later said that she miraculously disappeared without a trace, sometimes from the back seats of moving cars. You must respect Pele boys, or else..."

"Are you guys talking about soccer?" Jimbo entered the room as I was putting the last plate into the cupboard.

"What do you mean?" I asked him surprised, never having heard of the famous soccer player. Alika and Leilani had already told me about the Hawaiian Pele during the earthquake.

Oz laughed and answered Jimbo: "Pele is the nickname of a famous South American soccer player. He is actually from Brazil." He slapped Jimbo on the shoulder and bent over laughing. "Madam Kanani was telling us about the Hawaiian Pele, it's a lady who lives in the volcano and I don't think that she plays soccer."

"She is a very powerful being, who punishes bad people and rewards those who are good and kind. You, young man, must learn about kapu." She gave Jimbo a stern look. "It is the ancient system of law of these Islands. We all must obey Kapu in order to survive on these small specks of land in the middle of this giant ocean, or face the consequences." Madam Kalani poked her right index finger into Jimbo's chest. He stared at her with eyes as large as saucers. "Terrible horrible things have happened to people who have been foolish enough to disrespect Pele," our sitter added. "Now who wants some of that pineapple?" Madam Kanani got up, grabbed a sharp knife from a drawer and swiftly sliced it. "Here you go." She placed the plate on the table in front of us and took a piece herself. "Umm this is good, perfectly ripe and sweet."

"What's an auma, auma…?" I couldn't remember the word Leilani told me about the gecko, which led Keemo to the lady's property.

Madam Kanani looked at me with a puzzled expression and then her face lit up. "Do you mean aumakua?"

"Yes, that's it. What does aumakua mean?"

"Aumakua is very important to us Hawaiians." She explained: "Aumakua are spirits that take the task of helping the living people that they love. Most often the families select the shark family, the owl, Hawaiian crow, which is vanishing, or a reptile species. How do you know about the aumakua young one?" I felt a little uncomfortable. She was suddenly studying me with an intense look that felt like it went through me.

"Oh, don't worry that's just crazy Buzz." Jimbo interrupted. Madam Kanani gave him a sour look. "He met this weird kid Keemo on the other side of the Island, and man when I tell you this kid is weird, he really is… he creeps me out. He's like Frankenstein. He has no expression on his face and just stands there like 'Duh.' His dad, Hiro, is the fixer guy at the rental we stay in." Jimbo slurped on a huge piece of pineapple while he had another two pieces in his other hand. "They told my friend here that a gecko was his spiritual protector. Buzz is a little slow, if you know what I mean. He had an ear infection and it went to his head. As far as I'm concerned all this stuff is bull." Jimbo blabbered, while I just balled my fists listening.

"Ah ha, I see this makes everything clear to me." Madame Kanani gave me a reassuring look. "Let me tell you young men about the aumakua. But first, let me ask you boys a question. What is the thing that you great young surfers fear in the ocean? I mean, you brave big waves and feel like great heroes but what is the thing you are afraid of the most? Breaking your neck on a shallow reef or sand bar to get the perfect barrel or drowning in an avalanche of water of giant waves; not being able to tell your family and friends that you love them unconditionally for one last time, while you struggle against forces no other human being could withstand… Well?" She looked at us all inquisitively.

"Uh, I don't want to get chewed on by a shark." Jimbo was the first one to volunteer his opinion, chewing on a piece of pineapple. Juice was dripping down his chin.

Madame Kanani continued: "Ah yes, there are many families for whom a shark species is their aumakua. In the past, the bodies of deceased family members were fed to the animals to appease them. The mighty King Kamehameha who conquered and united the Hawaiian Islands did so in the name of the mo'o-woman Kiha-Wahine. The King was deeply committed to his belief in the powers of his aumakua. He set up her a statue in her honor cloaked in yellow and tapa, in Kohala. The King demanded that all who passed by her likeness, including ocean bound vessels must show respect."

We all sat stunned by the story with sweet pineapple juice dripping down our chins. I looked at my friends, who were speechless for a moment.

"Okay, why are you so afraid of sharks? Once, a shark grabbed a lady's ankle while she was wading in the water collecting shellfish. Her name was `Ala and the shark was her family guardian, when she screamed out the name of the animal it released her from its grip and apologized."

"Sharks can't apologize." Jimbo commented sarcastically.

Ignoring him, Madame Kanani continued. "It sounds like your friend Keemo's family aumakua is the mo'o. Legend tells that the mo'o can take many shapes from a huge dangerous reptile that lives deep under water in a fishpond to the small cute gecko. It is also part of our mythology that the mo'o can take up many shapes and forms, anywhere from a monster to beautiful lady to a gecko." Madame Kanani told the bewildering tale.

"That sounds like a load of bull." Jimbo interrupted.

Our sitter continued: "Kapu is the ancient law of these islands. It is a system that has kept order for over a thousand years before Captain Cook first brought Europeans to the islands. It was the law that respected the power of the Kahunas, who were later declared outlaws by the missionaries. Young rude one, you could use a kahuna La'au lapa'au, right now. They can heal a broken arm in just a few days."

"Yeah, right. The doctor at the hospital said three weeks in a permanent cast and then three weeks no sports... Oh never mind." Red faced, Jimbo resigned slamming his body back into the recliner next to me.

"Yes you cannot even follow the advice your doctor gives you that are in your best interests to help you heal better. You had better beware with that attitude! The marching dead are full of spirits like you that could not obey kapu." She lowered her voice. It gave me the chills up and down my spine.

"March of the dead. I read about that." Oz dropped another slice of pineapple on his plate. "People out walking at night have seen strange lights and heard voices and soft laughter and have reported seeing a line of beings walking by like a platoon of soldiers. They laid down face first in the dirt and it is said that, that saved their lives."

"Yes, kama kane you are right. The army of the dead also known as the 'night marchers' can be seen on dark moonless nights. They have displeased the gods and cannot enter Po, so they must march until eternity. Some say they are armed spirit warriors on their way to or from battle, holding their weapons wearing decorated helmets and cloaks. Others say that they are high-ranking alii spirits traveling to places of high importance, or to welcome new warriors to the battlefield. Some say that they are the restless souls of the army of death, looking to reclaim rightful territory, replaying a battle gone awry and avenging their own deaths. Some say they are searching for an entrance into the next world..."

We huddled next to each other on the couch listening mesmerized to Madam Kanani talk about the folklore of the Hawaiian Islands while stitching her quilt with nimble hands. We never interrupted her again. Finally, all six of our eyelids stared drooping. Jimbo fell asleep first, sitting in the huge chair with his broken arm leaning on the armrest, snoring softly. Madam Kanani woke him with a tap on the shoulder and managed to command us all to brush our teeth before jumping into bed. I instantly fell sound asleep, dreaming about Kahunas, aumakuas and surfing huge beautiful, light blue, cylindrical waves, carving turns deep in the tube.

The next morning I awoke to bright sunshine and the smell of bacon. Mom was cheery. Soft Hawaiian music was playing on the small, white clock radio on the grey Formica counter next to the stove. The room was bright and cheery.

"Good morning sweetie," Mom gave me a hug for the first time since before we got to The Big Island. "What are your friends doing?"

"Oz is getting dressed and Jimbo is still snoozing." I felt Mom's warmth radiating a feeling of security from her tight embrace.

"Your dad took Eric in the stroller down to the beach. They will be back in about ten minutes." Just then, Oz came into the kitchen. "Oz honey, could you please wake Jimbo and tell him that we will be having breakfast in about ten minutes, so please get him to hurry!" She gave Oz a big hug.

"Good morning, of course I'll get that lazy lump out of bed." Oz had a touch of sadism in his voice. "Yeah, Jimboooooo, wakey-wakey, wiki-wiki," we heard him in the next room.

Mom grabbed a bunch of bacon out of the frying pan and put it on a paper towel to drain the grease. She pulled more strips from the package and laid them into the hot frying pan, then turned to me and said: "I think that I have to apologize." She grabbed a few more strips of bacon and placed them into the pan. The hot oil sizzled as she laid each piece down. Mom wiped her hands on a dishtowel that she had hanging on the oven handle. "Buzz, I'm sorry. I feel that I was too hard on you. I think now I understand a little better what you were trying to tell me about your friend Keemo. Madame Kanani explained why that gecko was so important to him; it is his family's totem. I believe that you and your friend are the victims of unfortunate circumstance. It all seemed so weird to me I thought you were not telling the truth and honestly didn't trust you. It wasn't your fault, Buzz. Your father and I admire you for standing by your friend, Keemo, even when it seemed everyone was against you and no one believed you. It shows strength and maturity to stand by your principles like you have done. Buzz, we are very proud of you."

"Gee thanks!" Jimbo walked into the room. Oz followed closely behind him.

"I hope you boys are hungry," Mom ignored Jimbo's attempt at humor. "We'll eat as soon as Dad and Eric get back."

Just seconds later, the front lock clicked open. The stroller with little Eric appeared first from behind the open door, and then dad entered the condo.

"There you are. Come on everybody, wash up, breakfast is ready!" Mom cheerily commanded. Dad pulled Eric out of the stroller and took him into the bathroom attached to the master bedroom, while the three of us huddled over the sink in the main bathroom.

"Squirt some soap in my hand, Oz." Jimbo demanded with a whine.

"Get it yourself. Don't boss me around." Oz shook his hands out in the sink basin, walked over to the towel rack, dried his hands and walked out of the bathroom.

"Looks like we touched a nerve there, could you please oblige a handicapped friend?" Jimbo put on his used car salesman voice.

"Sure Jimbo, you know I always oblige a friend in need, just like my friend Keemo, who you say is weird and really creeps you out, remember? By the way he is innocent." I squirted a huge gob of the soap into Jimbo's hand, walked over to the towel rack, dried my hands and left.

"Geez, what's gotten into everybody?" Jimbo muttered as I walked out of the door.

Eating at the crowded table, breakfast was a feast. Mom made bacon, scrambled eggs and hot biscuits from the oven. We had the biscuits with butter. "Have some of the guava jelly." Mom pushed the jar of caramel colored jam towards me.

"Thank you for breakfast." Oz expressed his gratitude.

"This is awesome!" Jimbo was chewing on a bite of the biscuit. Guava jelly was dripping from the corner of his mouth. He was right it was delicious! We devoured the breakfast and at the end dad announced: "I have a surprise for two of you. Unfortunately Jimbo, because of your broken arm you cannot go into the water, so you will be staying with my wife and Eric here in town. Buzz, Oz, and I will board a boat after lunch to go skin diving."

"Oh." was Jimbo's sullen response. He was clearly fighting back a pout.

"We'll go shopping and have dinner, it will be fun." Mom attempted to cheer him up.

Jimbo, Oz, and I spent the morning hanging out at the beach. We took turns in the water and sitting on the sand listening to Jimbo complain. After a light lunch, we collected our gear and piled into the van. Mom drove us to the dock. Jimbo jumped into the front seat after dad got out. He sat there while we pulled our gear out of the back. After a hug from mom, we followed dad down the dock to a big white ship.

"This is it." Dad walked up the narrow aluminum gangplank and was greeted by a crewmember with a clipboard. He checked us in and showed us a compartment in the main cabin to put our gear. Another group walked up the plank and he turned his attention to them. "Okay boys, let's sit over there." Dad pointed to empty seats. There were rows of benches in the main cabin. Quite a few were already occupied by other passengers. The area was open and there were no glass windows. A nice breeze blew through. Just seconds after we sat down the deep loud 'VVRROOOMM' of the diesel ship engines started up. Deck hands appeared on the dock outside and untied the ropes from the moorings.

The crewmember that checked us in picked up a microphone, tapped it to make sure it was on and addressed us: "Aloha and welcome to the Devil's Corral Reef. We are about to depart from the dock on our diving cruise. Those of you who will be SCUBA diving please check in with Mac." A young man wearing a blue crew shirt with a bushy yellow beard raised his hand and bowed to the passengers. He was missing a few teeth. Some applauded and one of the ladies hooted. "Well don't let him get too full of himself." The crewman with the microphone bantered. "Those of you who will be snorkel diving are with me. My name is Roy and I will be your guide." He continued to lecture us on the rules and safety. Once he finished his speech, he put the microphone away.

It only took about ten minutes for the vessel to clear the harbor and enter the open ocean. The captain set us at full speed along the shoreline. We stood at the bow and felt the strong sea breeze in our faces. After only twenty minutes, the boat slowed and turned into a cove. Roy reappeared from below deck and grabbed the microphone in the main cabin. "Attention divers, we have reached our first destination of the day. SCUBA divers will enter the water first with Mac. Snorkelers please wait until I give you the okay to jump into the water. We are at a very famous location, which has an under water arch. Some of you more advanced skin divers may be able to hold your breath long enough to dive underneath it."

It took the five SCUBA divers about twenty minutes to put the tanks on their backs and get the other gear ready. Watching them was fascinating. They looked like astronauts preparing for a moon landing. Finally, we had our turn to jump into the water. Dad went first, then, Oz splashed into the clear turquoise sea. After a moment hesitating, I joined them.

The water was warm. When the tiny bubbles cleared from my mask, I was amazed at over one hundred feet of clear visibility underwater. It was like being suspended high over the sea floor, I felt the 'heebie-jeebies' for a moment. It was like nothing I had ever experienced before. I could see more than fifty feet down to the bottom with such clarity. It felt like I was hanging above the ground. After getting over the momentary uneasy feeling, I followed Oz and my dad as they swam towards the shallow reef into the cove. An immense school of thousands of bright yellow fish with black vertical stripes stayed a safe distance away from our splashing troop. I caught up within about ten feet of my dad and Oz, who were now kicking through the water next to each other. Most of the others from our cruise remained behind. Dad stopped and pointed and then looked back at me nodding towards the bottom. It took a few seconds before I recognized the shape of a shark, patrolling the ocean floor beneath us. It was black with white tips on its fins and must have been about five feet long. Since it was so far away the shark didn't seem terrifying at all. The predator looked beautiful moving gracefully, swaying its serpentine tail beneath us before abruptly turning back into the blue void of deeper water.

We swam further towards the shore. A canary yellow clarinet fish floated erect with its snout, pointing straight up to the water surface. The strange fish looked like a cross between a sea horse and a snake, standing perfectly still with its tail touching the reef, as if we couldn't see it swimming by overhead. I noticed that they were already far ahead. It took a minute for me to catch up with my father and friend, reaching the trail of fine bubbles spiraling off their kicking fins. The reef was healthy with multitudes of different colorful fish. As we got over the coral, Oz pointed out a spotted eel and an octopus. The highlight of the dive for me was when I drifted a few yards away from the group. Swimming over a coral head into shallower water I noticed a big boulder move, froze for a second before realizing it was actually a sea turtle grazing on the reef. Its carapace was the size of a manhole cover. The slow moving terrapin looked up at me for a moment and then resumed eating. Remembering that the crew members had warned us several times not to touch sea turtles because it causes their shells to ulcerate, I resisted the urge to pet the beautiful creature. There was almost no current in the water, so floating above was effortless. Looking more closely, the huge shell was covered with a fine layer of green algae. Munching away, unbothered by my presence, the huge turtle kept on ripping algae off the reef with its parrot like beak chewing, swallowing and then repeating the process. Oz and then dad came over and we floated side by side watching this living remnant of prehistoric times, before it suddenly darted away flapping its front flippers gracefully like wings, disappearing into the murky depths.

Dad pointed to his watch and then made a fist with his thumb sticking out and motioning us back to the boat.

"That was awesome!" Oz was the first to speak when we got back on deck. "Thanks a lot for taking me on this trip." Oz shook my dad's hand.

"Yeah, my favorite was the turtle. It looked at me and stopped for a minute before it started eating again. And then, how amazing was it when the turtle just flew away!" I felt great after the dive.

"Attention passengers," the voice of the captain came through an intercom system. "We are going to head back to the harbor, and let some of you off, pick up a few other divers. Then, we'll head out again for our night dive. Those of you, who are staying, will have half an hour for you to stretch your legs on the dock. But, don't make the mistake of going too far. This ship will leave on time at 6:30 p.m. If you are a second late you can wave good bye because we'll be off the mooring and on our way."

"Are we getting off or staying for the night dive?" I asked Dad handing him my gear to put into our compartment.

"Yes, we are staying for the night dive son. Tonight is going to be real fun." He smiled as Oz handed him his equipment.

"Cool, I've never dived after sunset." Oz was excited, too.

The boat trip back to the harbor seemed to go by a lot quicker than the ride out to the cove. We said Aloha to the departing divers and Aloha, to our new diving companions, mostly college students and a few couples who were being checked in. Oz and I were the two youngest divers on board.

Like clockwork, the captain pulled the boat away from the dock at exactly 6:30 p.m., the designated time. The sun had already begun to set. In the tropics, the sun seems to set a lot faster than at home. The lights in the cabin were turned on. Outside the sky was igniting with a final fiery red, pink and golden display. Within minutes, the boat was cruising through the dark sea.

Roy came back into the main cabin, grabbed the microphone and gave us a lecture on the night dive. We were going to a place to see giant manta rays feeding. "They are harmless," we were assured. The fact that they were called devilfish by ancient mariners made me feel just a little uneasy.

Finally, Mac came out and lectured the SCUBA divers of the group. They went into the water first again, but this time I didn't mind at all. The thought of jumping into the water with devilfish in the dark, gave me the creeps. There were several other boats in the area when the engines were shut off and the anchor chain rattled as it sunk into the deep.

"Yeah, Buzz this is going to be fun. Why are you looking so glum? What's the matter?" My friend could tell I was nervous. "It's got to be safe or they wouldn't allow us to dive here." He said reassuringly and slapped me on the back.

The loudspeaker crackled and Roy announced: "Okay snorkelers let's have a head count. Remember we all need to stay together in a group and do not touch the manta rays, or any other sea life for that matter."

Then the time finally came. We put our gear on. A few others jumped into the dark black sea first then Dad, Oz and I experienced the feeling of diving at night. It was a dream world. The bright lights made the area look like an underwater arena. Underneath, the SCUBA divers were split up into groups in the fifteen-foot deep water. Their bubbles trailed up to the surface like aeration in an aquarium. A school of foot long fish swam around them feeding on tiny fry and shrimp that were attracted to the lights.

Our group huddled at the surface surrounded by the darkness of the nighttime ocean. We were floating, looking down on the scene. It was eerie. I took comfort in getting kicked on the arm by someone's fin. Suddenly the first majestic creature appeared flying towards us slowly through the water. Three more giants appeared soaring out of the dark behind it. The first manta ray swam within ten feet of our group, then turned up towards the water surface showing us its white spotted underside and swam upside down in a loop. It swam back into the other direction and performed another loop and returned. Other huge rays joined the underwater arena.

At one point I counted sixteen animals swimming around, under the lights encircling the divers. Occasionally, one of the manta rays would come close and loop in front of us or bank a turn and glide back to the center of the group. The whole scene was dreamlike.

After about forty minutes, I started to get cold. I broke away from what was left of the group and swam back to the boat. Oz and Dad followed shortly thereafter. By then, most of the scuba divers had boarded. The rest of the skin divers were returning, too. After a thorough roll call and double-checking that all of the divers from both groups were back on the boat, the captain powered up the engines. The anchor chain rattled as it was pulled up from the deep. We were on our way back to the harbor through the darkness, after a great diving trip!

THE GROMMETS:

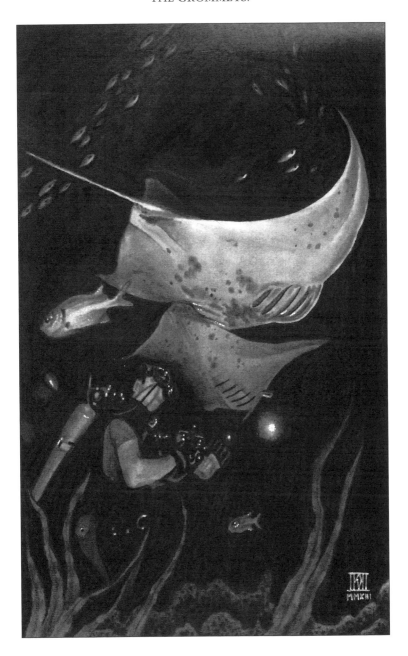

CHAPTER TWELVE
The Paniolo Trail

The next day was our last in the condo on the west side of The Island. We had cereal for breakfast. Then, each of us had a cleaning project assigned, while Mom went down to the laundromat to wash the linens and towels. Before she left, we used three straws of different lengths to decide who could have first and second choice on the cleaning projects. Unfortunately for me, my straw was the shortest, so I had to clean the bathroom.

After about half an hour I happily announced: "Finished!" Mom inspected my work and made me go back to rinse the residue around the faucet and toilet. When my job finally passed her inspection, I scrubbed my hands. The van was already loaded and we headed out just minutes later. It was still early, so the beach town seemed abandoned as we headed north to the highway.

"We're going to a famous surfing beach, first. After that we are going to drive up the coast a little further and then head into the center of The Big Island and visit some old friends of mine, before we head back home." Dad announced our itinerary. After about half an hour later he pulled the car to the side of the road and turned off the engine. "We are here!"

"Where's the beach?" Oz asked looking out his window.

"Just a short walk down there," Dad pointed to a narrow path.

Jimbo darted ahead down the dusty path. Oz and I unloaded our things from the van. I decided to take Leilani's neon lime green surfboard, Oz grabbed his, too. Once mom was finished strapping little Eric into the backpack and helping Dad put it on, we were on our way. The path looked like it belonged on the moon and not a tropical island. Only few plants were able to survive in the hot and dry desert like conditions on this part of the island.

After a while, sweat began to sting my eyes. Mom passed around a big bottle of water. We each took a swig, then, the march continued. About twenty minutes later, a welcome breeze cooled my forehead and the sea came into view. Unfortunately, the surf was so flat the ocean looked like a lake.

"Bummer!" Oz voiced our mutual discontentment.

"Oh, come on boys! This is a beautiful beach. Not everything in life is about surfing." Mom corrected our negative attitude. So much for her knowing everything!?

Jimbo smirked, shaking his cast at the two of us. "Yeah guys, all you think about is surfing. Can't you just enjoy the beauty of nature?"

We did. Exploring the shoreline and tidal zone with my Dad explaining the various creatures was a really fun experience. I was amazed by his knowledge of every creature and shell that we found and left there. Even though it is very tempting to keep a souvenir as a keepsake from this beautiful place, we did not. It is kapu, and morally wrong. Not to mention that it is bad for the environment.

After about an hour enjoying the beach, we packed up. Climbing back into the van, we were again on the highway, heading north in no time. It seemed like we were driving through a lunar landscape. The black tar lanes with the two yellow stripes in the middle wound through the gray stony terrain. Alongside the road, people had stacked oval rocks in little vertical columns.

"Hey look, an ass!" Jimbo broke the silence a few minutes in.

"I beg your pardon, James, your language!" Mom turned around and gave my friend a disapproving look. Dad began laughing. She turned her gaze to him.

"No, look there are donkeys out there." Jimbo defended himself.

Sure enough, there were wild donkeys grazing a few yards away from the highway. Their gray fur blended in well with the surrounding terrain and could have been mistaken for rocks, if they didn't occasionally raise their heads.

We devoured the sandwiches mom passed back to us. Afterwards, I fell asleep. When I awoke, it seemed as though I was still dreaming. Looking out the window, we were coasting through a green grassy meadow. There were horses and cows in the pasture and dad was driving on a gravel road which lead to what looked like a farm house in the countryside back home. The overwhelming smell of cow dung made it clear; I was awake. But had we left The Big Island?

"Where are we?"

"We are at a ranch visiting some old paniolo friends of mine, son."

"What's a paniolo?" Oz asked.

"Oh they are Hawaiian cowboys. When I was going to college, I would come up here and earn extra money during the roundup or if they were shorthanded on weekends. My farm experience growing up in the mid-west helped me work my way through college. I would drive my old truck up here and stay in the bunkhouse."

"Wow, I didn't know you were a cowboy." Jimbo admired cowboys. Normally, Jimbo would visit his grandparents' farm every summer. Oz seemed equally impressed. As for me, I once heard about this cool part of my father's past, but never had given it much thought since then. Dad pulled the van up to a red barn and honked the horn before switching the engine off.

"This looks just like the barn on my grandparents' farm." Jimbo was enthralled.

Just then, a slim dark skinned man wearing cowboy boots, a blue and white palaka shirt and dusty blue jeans walked around the corner. He approached dad with open arms.

"Aloha Haole son," the man hugged may father. "Ipo has been so excited she has been cooking since yesterday. "We have a real paniolo pa'ina prepared. Go ahead and wash up in the house and say 'Aloha.'" He turned to us and introduced himself: "Aloha, I'm Chet." He hugged Mom gave each of us a firm handshake, then motioned us to follow Dad to a large white house up on the emerald green grassy hill. The gravel made crunching sounds as we walked up the driveway.

We were on the steps of the porch when the screen door slammed open. "Aloha, it's been a long time. And look at the beautiful family you have." A petit lady with a large white flower in her hair wearing a cream colored blouse and snug fitting blue jeans came out onto the porch. She gave Dad a hug and kisses on the cheeks. "Aloha I'm Ipo, you have already met my husband Chet. We run this ranch together." she introduced herself and put a yellow flower lei necklace on Mom. Before long, we each got a squeeze and she was carrying little Eric into the house. "Komo mai, please come in and wash up, the picnic table is set in the back, and we'll eat in just a little while."

Eating is what we did. Ipo had prepared a real paniolo feast. Among the treats served were chunks of loko and pipikaula or salted and dried beef. The golden crispy fried fish looked delicious. There was also smoked pork and laulaum, which is made with taro leaves wrapped around meat, and then steamed.

During the meal Chet told us stories about the Paniolo cowboy life. He had a look of strength in his squinting eyes. Ipo would correct and say: "You know the actual correct way to say it is Paniola," emphasizing the final letter "A."

"The first Paniol'Os," Chet shot a teasing look at Ipo emphasizing the "o." She shrugged and ignored him." They would use the Po'Waiu method to catch cattle. They would herd the 'pipi' from the mountains. A Paniolo would rope a wild bull and tie him to a tree or stump. Once the animal was completely tied up the Paniolo would leave and come back the next morning with tame steers. Then they would be used to herd the captured bull back to the corral. There were no cows in Hawaii until a small herd of cattle was given to one of the Hawaiian Kings as a gift. Over time, they went wild overpopulating The Island. Then, the pipi became a nuisance, destroying forests and farm crops. That's how the first Paniolos got their jobs, capturing wild cattle. Later longhorn bulls were brought in and the style of ranching we have today was introduced here." Chet captivated us with his vast knowledge and storytelling skills.

Ipo got up and began clearing the table. Mom followed suit. "Sit down honey, I can handle this." Mom didn't heed and smiled as she stacked our plates and followed her to the house. Little Eric was happy, sitting in his high chair with his face and bib full of barbeque sauce, contently chewing on a rib bone.

"After our food settles a little, we'll go for a ride. I'll have the ranch hand saddle up some horses. Speaking of saddles, ours are different than those you have on the mainland, eh son?" Chet slapped my Dad on the shoulder and they both laughed.

We listened intently to the stories of the Paniolo until Mom came back to pull Eric out of his high chair and clean him off. Then he stayed with Ipo, while Chet took us on a ride to 'tuck in the herd' as he called it.

He led us over to the corral, where five brown horses stood hitched in a row to a horizontal post. Outside the enclosure stood a beautiful black and white mare, tied to a hitching post. Chet motioned us over to our rides. He looked at Dad. "This nag is for you son. I think you may know which end is the front and which is the back." We all laughed. I did nervously. Even though Dad was supposedly this great cowboy, my experience was limited to time spent on a saddle at the county fair strapped down on a small pony. These animals looked big and intimidating. Chet helped Mom up unto the saddle next to Dad. He motioned each of us to a horse. Despite his cast, Jimbo was the first to scramble up on his saddle. Oz was up in no time too. My first mistake was putting my right foot into the stirrup standing on the left side of the horse. I plopped back down and stuck my left foot into the stirrup. At that point it was obvious to my friends that I was having trouble.

"Need help?" Jimbo offered patronizingly.

"No," I stubbornly swung my right leg up. The saddle tipped me back down. I took a deep breath and tried again. My friends chuckled. This time Chet came up from behind me grabbed my left foot and pushed me up. It was a relief finally making it up on my mount.

"Okay riders, let's go." Chet opened the corral gate and untied the black and white horse. "Come on Molly, let's go." He patted the beautiful mare on her neck, then, mounted up. Molly turned and headed at a slow trot to a dirt packed road. As if on command our horses followed. Dad galloped his horse around the corral a few times before joining us. Catching up to me he suggested: "Loosen up on your reins, Buzz. You're pulling too hard. Your ride is stopping and you are falling behind the group." He was right. When I let the reins hang down a little, my horse seemed to relax and riding was much easier. "These horses are originally from South America and not the type we are used to on the mainland. They don't jolt the rider up and down as much as a quarter horse. It's a much smoother ride." Dad and I caught up with the rest of the group.

Chet led us through a small patch of trees. On the other side the view was amazing! As far as you could see there were meadows of green grass. Far below down the hill, were the dark specks of the grazing herd.

"This is it. The ranch land runs as far as the eye can see." Chet pointed off into the distance. Let's go and sing a little lullaby to the cows before they go to sleep." Chet chuckled and took off in a gallop. Jimbo joined with Oz behind him. Mom followed suit.

"Come on let's go Buzz." Dad urged me on. I preferred my horse walking, but WWHHACCKK, he made a snapping sound behind my horse and it took off! All I could do was grab hold of the saddle horn and squeeze my legs into the animal's sides to keep from sliding off sideways. Dad passed me with a burst of speed, hooting, which made my horse seem to want to go faster. It scared me. The sounds of the wind against my face and the pounding of the hooves on the dirt filled my ears. I held on, tightly. Then, I began to relax and started to giggle. This is fun! My mare seemed like she was enjoying the ride, too.

As much as I didn't enjoy the gallop at first, it seemed too soon when it ended. My horse slowed to a canter as we approached the rest of the group who were letting their horses rest.

"That was fun!" Oz was smiling.

"Yeah, that was a blast." I agreed wholeheartedly.

Jimbo rode next to Chet. Mom and Dad were riding side by side. We were getting closer to the herd of cows. Chet stopped and looked around.

"I need to take a closer look at the herd. You can stay here and relax. Dismount if you like." Chet hollered. Jimbo rode with him. We waited behind. Dad jumped off his saddle and helped Mom dismount. As if on command, both of their horses went off to eat grass in the rich meadow.

"I never would have believed there are cowboys in Hawaii." Oz exclaimed.

"Yeah, I remember my Dad mentioned something once, but I really didn't know he worked here. I thought he just milked cows in a barn. Riding fast was fun. It was a little scary at first, but then it got easier."

"We should ride back up to where we started. That way we can go fast again." Oz suggested, pointing up the path. "Ask your Dad if it's okay."

"HEY DAD, CAN WE RIDE BACK AND FORTH?" I shouted over to my parents, who were sitting in the grass. Dad flashed an, 'OKAY' sign with his right hand.

"Let's go!" Oz made a clicking sound and his horse galloped off. Mine was slow to start at first, but then we picked up speed. The thrill of galloping was exhilarating, like riding a wave. I was starting to get the hang of it and having a blast! Oz slowed and stopped riding about a hundred yards back up the dirt road. "Yeah, Buzz that was fun." My horse slowed and stopped in front of my friend. "Who would have thought that there are cowboys and ranches here on The Big Island. We should go riding when the surf is flat back home." Oz shared my newfound enthusiasm for horseback riding.

"That would be cool!" I agreed. "I wonder if there are any places near where we live?"

"There must be. Want to head back?" Oz smiled and made another 'CLICK' with his tongue. His horse dashed off as if on cue. I copied him and followed. We were soon galloping back to the group. "YAHOOOO!" I hooted.

We took two more fast rides, before Chet and Jimbo returned. Mom and Dad were already back in their saddles, waiting.

"You boys like exercising the horses." Chet laughed.

Jimbo wasn't so humorous. "While you guys were horsing around, we were tending to a sick calf." Just then his horse lifted its tail and began to poop. It seemed never ending. Oz and I began to laugh immediately, after a few seconds the adults joined in. Jimbo looked around at us dumbfounded. He turned around to look behind and then saw his horse's pile on the ground. Without missing a beat our friend said: "All in a day's work on the ranch, right Chet?" Chet was laughing so hard; he could only nod.

As the sun was setting, we rode the horses into the corral. After dismounting, then over to Chet's horse Molly and patted her on the shoulder. I followed the group back to the house. Turning around to take one more look, the ranch hand was already leading Chet's horse to the stable. She snorted her farewell.

Ipo had sandwiches and iced ginger tea prepared for us when we got to the house. After a short snack, we exchanged hugs and farewell Alohas, loaded up the van and headed back home to the other side of The Big Island.

The day after we got back my Mom went through the accumulated mail and opened a letter from my lawyer, Mr. Delton, informing me that I would be testifying in a few days. My mood suddenly soured with the thought of the whole situation, involving my innocent friend, Keemo. I was overwhelmed with fear, guilt and worries about his fate. We had tried to help but didn't find any evidence to help him. It was frustrating!

CHAPTER THIRTEEN
The Investigation

T he morning after we returned, mom was in a sour mood again. It seemed as if the letter from the lawyer informing us of Keemo's upcoming trial, and my necessary appearance washed away the joy of the last few days traveling around The Big Island.

We were sitting in the kitchen eating breakfast when the phone rang. "Top of the morning, James speaking," Jimbo answered. "Oh, I am not sure if that is possible, miss." The person at the other end sounded agitated, but I could only make out that the voice was female. "Now, that's not being very nice, Lady please." Jimbo was smirking.

I got up, rinsed off my dishes and loaded them into the dishwasher. Just as I was walking out of the kitchen, Jimbo said: "Ah, Buzz it's for you." He threw the receiver at me. It hit me in the chest. The long phone cord stretched and recoiled. My feeble attempts at catching were useless. The hard plastic piece hit the linoleum floor. It bounced back to the wall where the base was attached. I chased it and grabbed the receiver just in time for Mom to walk into the kitchen with a questioning glare. I froze and stuttered: "H-H-Hello."

"Aloha Buzz," Leilani's voice sounded distant.

"Hi Leilani." I couldn't think of anything to say with mom's glare sending shivers down my spine.

"What are you up to?" She asked.

"Uh, nothing, I guess."

"Your friend thinks he is real funny, eh? Tell him my cousin Maleko says: Wazzup!"

I relayed Leilani's message. Jimbo looked at me with a look of fear and ran out of the kitchen. I had forgotten that Mom was still in the room and felt her sudden tight grip on my right shoulder.

"Buzz, are you still there?" Leilani sounded concerned.

"Yup, I am still here."

"What did you mean about Maleko to scare James and who are you talking to?" Mom commanded answers.

"Oh, it's Leilani."

"Is your mom freaking out again? Island Fever, it hits all of these Haole wahines. Do you want me to call you back?"

At the same time mom asked: "Are you ignoring me?"

I answered: "Yes," to Leilani and got the wrath of not paying attention.

"How dare you. Hang up the phone young man and you are restricted to your room, immediately!"

"I heard." Leilani responded before, Mom grabbed the receiver from my ear and slammed it on the base. The call was over and I was on my way up to the bedroom. Luckily, I was reading a great book about Hawaii. Nana gave me the fat paperback before we left on our trip, the hours between meals just melted, as I was captivated reading. Dinner was dismal. Dad had to work late and Mom made frozen dinners in the less than hot oven. It didn't matter. I just wanted to get back to my book, and was enjoying the time reading alone. Oz and Jimbo watched TV. I must have dozed off because when I awoke the room was dark. My friends were fast asleep. Then, I heard a 'TAPP.' It came from the window and caused me to jump up on my bed. The porch lights barely lit that side of the house; nothing unusual was visible. Another slightly louder 'TAPP,' hit the pane. I opened the window, stuck my head out and 'WHACK,' a small pebble hit me on my head.

"Ouch," I was barely able to maintain a whisper. Below me there was a soft giggle. "Leilani, is that you?" I spoke softly.

"Yes, meet me on your back porch." She responded. It was only when she tip toed away around the side of the house, that I recognized her outline. With all the finesse I could muster, I shut the window and snuck down the stairs to the living room. The large sliding glass door made a loud CLICK. I froze for a few moments to make sure that no one upstairs was awoken. Then, I quietly slid the huge metal framed door open just enough for me to slip out sideways, with curtains drawn so the gap was not visible from the inside. The deck felt cold under the soles of my bare feet.

"PSSST," Leilani motioned to me from the lawn below the corner of the porch, "over here." I walked over and stood at the railing. "You are tough to wake up. I was throwing pebbles at your window for five minutes."

"I'm glad you didn't wake my parents."

"Yeah listen, I wanted to tell you that Alika's Mom is going to call your Mom to ask if you want to come to a hula practice with us. Say 'yes,' and Dr. Hank will drive us around afterwards to investigate."

I froze.

"BUZZ... What are you doing out there?" Mom's voice boomed as the glass door slammed open. Leilani vanished silently into the darkness below. "What are you doing?" I felt paralyzed.

"Just leave him be. Maybe he's sleepwalking." Dad was up too! "We should leave him. You know what they say, don't wake a sleepwalker. Poor kid has been under a lot of stress with all that's been happening, not to mention all of this ridiculous court stuff. I tell you, you've been too hard on him."

Turning around, I was blinded by the porch floodlight and momentarily startled. With my hand cupped over my eyes I stuttered: "I-I-I didn't…"

"It's okay son, go back to bed. We'll come in and check up on you in a minute." Dad rubbed the top of my head, while Mom was leaning over the porch railing, and peering around the yard. I walked back upstairs and climbed into bed feeling very, very relieved.

The next morning Jimbo and Oz had already left to go to the beach with Kai and Kala, when I awoke. Mom told me that she was going out with Hanna and that she wanted me to hang around with Dr. Hank and the girls. She was worried after my 'sleep walking' incident, and found comfort in the fact that I would be with the doctor. I felt glad that we would finally be able to investigate Keemo's case. Afterwards we were invited to Leilani's house. Her Mom called my Mom and Hanna and invited both of our families to a luau at their home.

At ten o'clock the white station wagon roared up to our curb and I ran out and jumped in. Alika and Leilani were sitting in the front seat with Dr. Hank. "Aloha!" I bounced onto the huge bench back seat.

"Aloha!" the girls replied almost in unison.

"Aloha, Buzz! Don't forget to fasten your seatbelt." Dr. Hank looked at me through the rear view mirror. "Okay, we are off to the hula performance." He clicked on the car radio. Hawaiian slide guitar blasted through the speakers. It felt great listening to the relaxing sounds and feeling the breeze through the open windows. Judging by the nods of their heads, Leilani and Alika were locked in conversation. Dr. Hank pulled a pipe out of the ashtray, stuffed it and lit it with a lighter.

Alika and Leilani pinched their noses and turned to me. I could barely hear them shout: "EEWWW! That stinks!" Their dark long hair fluttered up and around them. They laughed, turned around to face the front and were again deeply locked in conversation. Alika peered over the front seat. She looked me in the eye, smiled and then turned. The ride was fun. The station wagon slowed and I sat up awoken from my daydream. We passed a very distinctive masonry sign announcing the entrance to Volcano National Park. Dr. Hank parked the behemoth. We walked to an area in which at least twenty ladies and girls were wearing the same outfit as Alika and Leilani. They disappeared into the crowd. A guy wearing a headset with a clipboard commanded the group.

"It's time for us to get out of here." Dr. Hank motioned me away. "Let's go over there and get a newspaper and some candy; unless, you don't like candy."

"No, I like candy." I blurted.

"Good for you, Buzz. My dear wife and daughter frown on the stuff. Something about processed sugar. But I personally think that it's a great thing." Dr. Hank and I walked next to each other. "We'll just go over to this shop and then, hunker down. It's going to be a long wait. I used to like Gobstoppers do you kids still have them.

"Oh yes!" I answered authoritatively.

"Your mom tells me you were sleep walking last night. Has your ear been bothering you?"

"No."

"Were you having a bad dream?" He peered at me through his glasses.

"No."

"You are a young man of few words. It's like the way I remember your dad when we were first year college roommates together." We walked without talking up to the concessions. "Hello Sally, this young man is with me. Give him whatever he wants and I'll have my usual."

"Okay Doctor Hank, your secretary called us. We have your juice already squeezed here and the paper, too. Would you like any snacks?" The tiny lady behind the register smiled warmly. "Aloha young man, what is your name?"

"Buzz," I responded, "Oh Aloha, too." I had momentarily forgotten my manners.

"We have candy over there and comic books on the wall. Doctor, please make yourself at home at the executive bench outside our establishment." The lady looked even smaller as she walked out from behind the counter.

Dr. Hank let out a belly laugh and said: "I will be outside on the executive bench, Buzz. Please meet me there when you have finished with your selection. Help yourself to your choice of this establishment's fine wares." He nodded at Sally as he left the shop with a large Styrofoam cup in one hand and a folded newspaper under his other arm. "Just put it on my tab, Sally."

The store was full of stuff that I could have bought, but I really only wanted some gum, so I grabbed a pack. "Is that all you want?" Sally looked at me disappointedly. "Don't you want anything else? There's lots of other candy and stuff, even souvenirs for you to give your momma and girlfriends. The doctor said you can have anything you want."

"No thank you, Ma'am. I would just like this pack of gum."

Dr. Hank was sitting on the bench outside the shop. Notably, it was the only bench in the vicinity. "What did you get, anything good?"

"Yeah I got a pack of gum, do you want a piece?" I handed the pack to him.

Dr. Hank snorted. "No thanks! I'm trying to quit." He handed me the cartoon section of the newspaper. "Here are the funny pages."

"Thanks," I unfolded the grey paper. A mini bus pulled up and the door opened. A herd of people with funny hats, bags and cameras suddenly flooded the parking lot. They had all disbursed into the surrounding area, before their driver took his cap off and sped off to a far corner of the lot. He parked and blasted the music from his radio after he was a safe distance away. The comics were not really that funny, but I mused at the many different people wandering about the place in their multitude of outfits.

Dr. Hank looked at his watch and said: "It's time to head over to the performance." I walked next to him back to the area where we had left the girls. People from the mini bus were already seated to see the show. Dr. Hank walked over to two empty seats in the back of the small area. The outdoor stage was made of a wall of lava rocks. The grass covered performance area was lined with tall reed like plants, which created a screen surrounding it. The doctor unfolded his newspaper and resumed reading. Looking around, the audience was made up of different people from all over the world. Within a few minutes, the familiar sound of pounding on the large hollow gourd began. The male voice that chanted in accompaniment was different. It sounded a little softer and raspier than that of the man who had performed with Alika and Leilani the last time. A large group of ladies walked out from behind the wall of plants. They all wore the same black dresses with green leaf-leis. I looked at Dr. Hank. His focus was locked on his newspaper.

"How are they doing?" He asked me.

"I can't see them." I scanned the performers.

Without looking up from his paper, he replied: "Alika and Leilani are on the right towards the back." He was correct.

Leilani was dancing behind a really tall lady and Alika was next to her at the edge of the group. It looked like Alika was totally copying Leilani. It was neat to watch them. They looked great! The audience applauded loudly when the chanting and the hula dancing stopped. The dancers left the stage's natural setting.

A cheesy announcer appeared and advertised the concessions stands with their imported souvenirs and sugary treats. He rambled on and on before announcing the two final acts. "Next before the Grand Finale, we have the cutest little hula girls for your entertainment!"

Two other girls entered the stage before Leilani and Alika walked up behind them. The chanting and pounding resumed. The four girls began to gyrate and move their arms in a snake like fashion. They appeared to move almost in unison. At closer observation, it was clear that Alika was copying Leilani. It was uncanny. Alika seemed to anticipate her best friend's motions. They were almost totally in sync, except instead of looking forward, Alika was looking to her left at Leilani. Both had big smiles on their faces.

The dance ended. I watched as a few of the audience left their seats and walked to the exit. Several minutes passed. Dr. Hank finished his paper. Another group of ladies entered the stage and the accompaniment began. Carefully folding the newspaper, he asked me: "So, how did you like the dancing?"

"It was good."

"Only good? You did not think we were excellent?" Leilani knuckle punched my shoulder while Alika gave her dad a hug.

"Uh, no I think you are excellent." I stammered.

"Okay then," Leilani had a satisfied look on her face, "Alika we are excellent. Buzz agrees!"

We walked back to the car. The girls chattered with excitement about dancing on stage with adults. Alika admitted that she didn't really know the dance that well yet, but was able to copy Leilani. We returned to our original seats in the giant white imitation wood paneled station wagon. The engine started to rumble and Dr. Hank revved it a few times. "Okay, where to next?" Suddenly, Dr. Hank, Alika and Leilani turned around from the front seat and looked me in the eye.

"Uh, weren't we going to investigate?" I was surprised.

They all turned back around. Dr. Hank blasted the radio and stepped on the accelerator. I was lost in the breeze and the calming sounds of the music. Along the way, I looked out the window, as familiar sights passed by like a blur. We reached the top of the long hill in minutes, which had taken what seemed like hours for Keemo and me to reach on foot. The jungle looked like a familiar friend. Before I knew it, the station wagon stopped in front of the house. The 'For Sale' sign had unfastened on one corner and was hanging lopsided. Dr. Hank got out of the car. We followed. I was beyond nervous, scared beyond belief, worried that the evil woman in the red car would suddenly appear. I blurted: "I don't think this is such a good idea."

"Nonsense," Dr. Hank announced reassuringly. "This place is up for sale and my family has been looking for an investment house like this for a while now. Besides, I am on the Land Use Commission and this property has come before us on more than one occasion. Personally, I would like to look around. You kids can stay in the wagon, or come with me. But, don't you dare bring your skateboards!" He turned and winked at us. We jumped out and followed him closely into the backyard.

The little black crow immediately greeted us. I got angry at it. 'Why do you have to be so noisy right now?' I thought. Dr. Hank stopped. Alika and Leilani halted too. I was looking at the bird and didn't. Colliding into Leilani's back, she was pushed into Alika who stumbled into her Dad's back. "OOOPPS, I'm sorry," I felt really silly. Leilani looked a little annoyed and shrugged her shoulders. Alika and her Dad looked at each other and giggled. They turned around and we walked into the yard. The pool looked inviting for a skate session.

Alika stopped and turned around. She pulled the notebook out of her handbag and flipped the pages and said: "It's time to work. We have very little time. Dad knows that we are here on a fact-finding mission to help save Keemo. He is also on the Land Use Commission and is here on official business. The lady next door, who thinks that Keemo stole her ring, has complained about this place at many public meetings." Alika studied her notes. "Okay Buzz, you have to check the border by the scene of the missing ring. You were there with Keemo, so you are best suited to examine that area." Alika looked back down at her notebook. I was in shock. Back over to that mean lady's house? I wanted to disappear. Then, I thought of Keemo sitting locked up alone at his home, accused of stealing a stupid ring. I took a deep breath to conquer my fear and broke away from the group. Walking over to the side of the pool, I retraced Keemo's steps next door. Looking around for clues the entire time, there was nothing. I looked real hard, but there was nothing.

The little crow came back and strutted around on the cement in front of me. It sounded like a cat meowing. My courage waned. A firm hand gripped my right shoulder. "Well Buzz, the lady living next to this property has made many complaints. Let's see if there really are a bunch of rats invading her property."

We walked along the side of the empty pool to the stairs. "This is where Keemo saw the gecko and went over to the lady's window." Dr. Hank followed me with the girls close in tow. I squatted to avoid being seen until I glanced behind me and saw the others standing up in plain view and felt a little foolish. Luckily, the woman didn't seem to be at home. "That window over there was open." I pointed. "Underneath it is where Keemo picked the gecko off of the wall. He came straight back here, and never even looked at the window."

The little black crow returned and strutted around as if examining the scene by itself. "Ah, that is a Hawaiian Crow. You don't see many of them anymore." Dr. Hank pushed his eyeglasses up on the bridge of his nose.

Alika interjected: "I think we've seen enough, here. Let's look around the yard. We spent a half hour inspecting the yard. I went through the dense jungle in the back. The vines that grew up the huge Banyan tree were so thick that they supported my body weight. I took a moment to try to swing on one, but it didn't go anywhere. The girls walked the perimeter. Alika took notes while Leilani scanned the area. After about ten minutes, Dr. Hank sat down on the step in the pool and stretched his legs. We continued. I thought it was bold of Leilani and Alika to walk in the street in front of the mean woman's house. They even went up to the lady in the house next door, who allowed them to walk on her property along the opposite side to the scene of the alleged crime. They returned and found me in the back of the huge tree struggling to make it through the undergrowth.

"Did you find anything?" I asked them.

"No," Leilani and Alika answered almost in unison.

"Too bad! It's tough when we really don't even know what we are looking for." I felt hopeless.

Finally, Dr. Hank announced: "It's time to go. We have gone over and over these grounds. If you haven't found anything by now, there probably is nothing. Besides, I have completed my observations as a member of the Land Use and Planning Commission. We need to leave. It's time to go to the luau at Leliani's house. I am getting hungry!"

We returned to the wagon. We were all disappointed that we hadn't found some kind of clue at the house that could have led us to something, anything!

CHAPTER FOURTEEN
The Luau

After the beach, we drove to Leilani's house for the luau. Cars and trucks filled the street, so we had to park further away. We passed the van, so I knew my friends and family were already there as our group walked closer to her house. The sound of laughter and ukuleles became louder as we walked silently about 100 yards before finally arriving at Leilani's front porch. Dr. Hank led our group. "Aloha, Doc!"

"Aloha, Bella!" A lady in a brightly colored mu'mu reached up and squeezed Alika's Dad with a hug with before turning to Leilani and me with the force of a boa constrictor. Dr. Hank returned the enthusiastic hug and disappeared into a large group of adults, who were standing on the porch.

Leilani walked through the front door, first. We were squished by the lady's loving hugs before entering the home clouded by Aloha Spirit and the overwhelming smell of fresh flowers and blossoms. The intoxicating sweetness filled my head. Mom came up to me and gave me a hug. The crowd of smiling grownups parted as I made my way into the house, which was filled with a delicious aroma. Not really knowing where I was going, I followed closely behind Leilani. Alika was walking close to my right. The atmosphere was festive.

"Aloha, Buzz!" was the mantra of the crowd of smiling faces.

We walked out of the house through the covered porch to the outside. Leilani's yard looked like it was surrounded by a lush tropical rainforest. "Wow, this looks like a jungle! This is amazing." I exclaimed.

"My Uncle Lolo has a landscaping business and plants are his hobby, so he stores his collection of native Hawaiian plants here." Leilani surveyed the crowd and smiled. "It looks like almost everyone is here. Let me introduce you to my cousins." She walked over to a large group of young people sitting at two picnic benches that were lined up together under a thatched roof cabana. "This is my cousin Ilima," she put her arm around a girl that looked a lot like her. She was a little shorter and stouter. "Say Aloha to Buzz and Oz; Mikala, Luka, Kiliwia and Lekili." A group of girls of various ages, who all looked very much alike, smiled and giggled. Each nodded as I met their eyes and said: "Aloha." Then, Leilani turned her attention to the guys. "This is Kaleo, there is Nikko and that's Hanu, and Makelo."

Suddenly, I went stiff at the sight of Leliani's cousin, who had punched Jimbo and given him the black eye. I had seen him around a few times and he seemed tough and mean. My jaw dropped while Maleko gave me a hearty handshake and a slap on the back. I cringed when Jimbo came around a row of banana trees with tiny green bunches of fruit hanging on them.

"Oh good, you guys finally made it. We are about to take the pig out of the imu. You gotta come and see this." As if answering my blank stare, Jimbo explained: "Maleko and I are bros, now. At first, when I got here things were pretty tense. I thought I would be in another fight, but then the elders held a ho'o pono pono with us. We talked about why we had been in a fight. We told each other our differences and worked them out. Don't worry; I guess I was a jerk dropping in on his waves a little too much that day. I apologized."

"What are you talking about, Jimbo, you drop in on everyone, every time you surf. You are a menace in the lineup.

If you weren't one of my best friends, I would never talk to you for being such a selfish jerk in the water." Oz approached us, but Jimbo had already walked back around behind the dense row of plants. A couple of the guys got up and followed him.

Leilani introduced me to the rest of the group and then said: "Go ahead and check out the pig. I'm going to put my stuff away in my room and get changed. Leilani turned back towards the house.

"If you guys want to check out the imu, follow me." Maleko waved for us to follow him as he walked around the row of banana trees. A row of guava trees of various sizes lined the path to the rear of the yard. Several men stood around what looked like a round sand box with a crude foot high wall of lava rocks surrounding it.

Jimbo was standing between them, looking up and chattering: "Okay, Uncle Lolo." A huge man in a blue and white Aloha shirt stepped over the low retaining wall. With the tip of a shovel he began to gently scrape away at the sides of a sand pile in the center of the circle of rocks. He worked in silent concentration. His forehead was covered with beads of sweat. It took several minutes until Leilani's Uncle Lolo stopped, and wiped his forehead with a blue bandana, which he pulled out of his pocket. Nodding his head slowly, he stepped out of the circle. Two younger, slightly smaller giants stepped in and pulled back a big sheet of cloth that revealed a pile of steamed seaweed and banana leaves. They grabbed the opposite ends of a huge metal basket and lifted the pile of seaweed away, like a patient on a stretcher.

The delicious aroma of cooked pork filled the air. I was really hungry. It smelled really good. My mouth was watering. Judging by the silent anticipation, everyone else was too. Underneath, was a cooked whole Kalua pig surrounded by melon sized round rocks and several round objects wrapped in aluminum foil. The two men returned and lifted the pig, which was wrapped in chicken wire. They carried it over to a battered old picnic table that was covered with banana leaves. Uncle Lolo unfolded the top of the wire mesh basket. We crowed around him. I looked straight at the closed eyes of the animal. The meat was so well prepared that it fell off the bones.

My glance fell on the bones sticking out from the pile of succulent meat. The sight of them made me instantly nauseous. Suddenly, I felt a flash of dizziness and a cold sweat. The sight was almost too much for me to handle. Needless to say, my dream of becoming a veterinarian ended that day. No one noticed me slipping away because everyone's gaze was fixated on Uncle Lolo, the Kahuna, handing out small pieces of meat to the group.

Walking by the guava trees and around the row of bananas, my nausea waned. I wiped my forehead and saw Alika who had joined a girl our age who was sitting at the side of the yard. The girl had my little brother, Eric, on her lap.

"Buzz, you look pale as a ghost." Alika giggled.

"I ERR, UH," was all that I could get out of my mouth.

"That pig stuff is gross, isn't it? I am mostly a vegetarian, myself." She smiled sympathetically patting my back. "This is my cousin Savanna." Eric gave me a brief glance and then focused his attention back on the girl reaching her hand out to me. I wiped my sweaty right palm on my shorts before shaking her hand. "Aloha Savanna, it's nice to meet you."

"Aloha, nice to meet you Buzz, and you know who this little boy is." Savanna smiled.

"Yes, but he doesn't seem to know me." I joked, feeling much better. "I think I saw you at the hula dance with Alika and Leilani."

"We are going to perform later too. But, now I hope you are hungry." Alika sat in one of the lawn chairs and motioned me to sit down between Savanna and her. She was wearing a yellow dress with a green and orange bird of paradise flower print, and a headband and lei made of yellow flowers.

The men who had tended the imu walked past with giant metal trays full of Kalua pork. One of them had a turkey and a couple of chickens in it, which had been cooked and wrapped in foil. They were followed by the rest of the guys, who spread out into the lawn area around the cabana.

Aunt Flossie and Leilani's mom Tweetie, my Mom and a couple of other ladies brought trays and bowls of food out to the crowd in the yard single file and placed them on the picnic tables under the cabana. Mom was dressed in a bright green Hawaiian dress and had a flower in her ear. She came over, kissed me on the cheek and thanked Savanna and Alika for watching Eric while she helped in the kitchen. She grabbed his hand and they slowly walked over to join a group of adults talking with Dad. He smiled and waved at me.

"Let me get you some poi to start, just sit and relax Buzz." Alika jumped up and in a minute came back with three little wooden bowls. "Have you ever had poi before?" She handed me one.

"Uh no, I don't even know what poi is."

"It's ground taro root." Savanna informed me before dipping two fingers into her bowl, scooping some out and eating it.

Looking down at the gray purplish paste, I hesitated for a moment but after looking at pig knuckle joints sticking out of the animal, this was far more appetizing. With the bowl in my left hand I scooped some of the gooey paste into my mouth. "It tastes like potatoes." I remarked enjoying this new treat.

The three men that had worked the imu came out with platters of meat. The crowd standing around the picnic tables applauded.

"Let us get some food. Stay here. Just save our chairs for us." Alika and Savanna went over to the spread of food.

"Hey buddy, aren't you going to eat." Jimbo approached with a plate piled high with mostly Kalua pork and sat in Savanna's chair.

"That seat is taken."

"What, nobody is sitting there." He pointed at Alika's chair next to me.

"Sorry, that's Alika's seat." I insisted.

"Yeah, you are." Jimbo plopped himself down in the grass in front of me. Oz sat down cross-legged beside him.

"Here Buzz!" Alika handed me a plate of food and sat down to my right. Savanna handed me forks and napkins. I passed Alika hers.

"Thanks, this looks great." Looking down at the huge plate on my lap, I was famished. There were little red spare ribs, which were delicious. For some reason those bones didn't bother me.

"That is Char Siu you are eating Buzz, and that is Chicken Katsu, Chicken Adobo, Chicken Lu'au, Huli Huli Chicken. That is Lomi Lomi Salmon, Kim Chee and Lau Lau." Alika identified all of the small portions on the giant plate before me.

Jimbo whispered something into Oz's ear and laughed alone at whatever he had said. Oz gave Jimbo a frown. I ignored him. Then, there was a sudden silence over the yard. We ate and ate. Each different dish was delicious. After surfing you get really hungry and good food feeds not just your body, but your soul as well. The good company and good spirit in the air made the food taste even better! The sun was setting while we were eating. Two young men began lighting bamboo Tiki torches all around the yard. After about twenty minutes, the chatter began anew. Some people went back under the cabana for seconds.

Naturally, Jimbo was the first to jump back on his feet and head back to the buffet for round two.

"How did you like it?" Savanna asked Oz.

"Very tasty." He looked up and smiled.

"What was your favorite?" She followed up.

"Oh, well." My friend paused for a moment to think. "Yes, the Lomi Lomi Salmon was most excellent. I must say normally I don't eat pork but the Kalua pig was excellent, too. It's like nothing I've ever tasted. But, everything here tastes great."

I leaned over to Alika and whispered: "Thanks for not putting any of that pig on my plate."

She winked and nodded. "I have to go into the house and get changed for the performance. I'll see you later, Buzz." Alika jumped up, picked up her empty plate and ran up to the house.

Leilani came out on the porch dressed in the same yellow outfit and flower headband Savanna was wearing. She hugged a few of the adults and slowly made her way over to us. In the meantime, Jimbo had returned with another plate piled just as full as the last one. He rested it on his bent broken arm while holding the rim with the other hand and plopped down next to Oz, who was relaxing on the lawn. As he did, the plate tipped sideways precariously, but Jimbo was able to tip it back in time and save his load of food.

"This is quite a feast. Too bad your buddy, Keemo isn't here. This could be his last meal before he goes away for a long time." Jimbo looked down at the pile of food in front of him. He stuffed his mouth full of pork. He chewed his food a few times and swallowed. "You really are green. That kid took you for a ride, for sure! Don't you get it? Keemo stole that ring. Get with it. He is poor and needed the money. I mean he has gotten criminal written all over him. He just stands around and doesn't say anything. Then, when you talk to him it's not like he can catch a clue. If he finally speaks all he can talk about are skateboards and appliances. That guy has 'guilty' written all over him!" Jimbo took another huge gulp of food.

Enraged, I could not speak for a moment. "What do you mean?" I stammered. Oz looked alarmed. Leilani gave Jimbo a sinister look.

"Well," Jimbo chewed with obvious slow deliberateness. He swallowed and looked around. "Man, I could sure use some liquid refreshment." His pleading looks were ignored, so he continued: "You know, do I have to spell it out? You're lucky you are not staying here in a little cell with your friend Keemo."

"Are you talking about me?" Jimbo suddenly froze when he turned and saw Keemo standing behind him.

"The judge gave Keemo special permission to attend the family luau. Go get some food son." Hiro popped up next to him carrying a handful of brightly wrapped packages.

"I'll take him Uncle." Leilani hugged Hiro before putting her arm around Keemo and walking over to the food table with him. Jimbo's silence was refreshing.

"Sorry, we are a little late because we had a little trouble wrapping these gifts that we got for you out of gratitude for what you are doing for Keemo. You have been a friend to my son." Hiro looked at me and smiled. "It is hard for him to make friends. I appreciate your efforts to help him. This was supposed to be your summer vacation. Instead, I am afraid that we have been quite an imposition." Hiro handed us each a crudely wrapped gift. It felt like there was something soft and a hard object inside. "Go ahead and open them now, if you like." He urged.

We ripped the packages open. Each of us got a blue and white Aloha shirt. "You all can look alike. Like triplets." Hiro mused.

Inside my package was a hand carved wooden sculpture. A figure with a huge head and a grimacing mouth looked up at me through large squinting eyes. A V-shaped headband adorned the forehead, from which a zig-zag cloak hung shielding the back.

"Oh, you got a Tiki statute." Savanna identified the small wooden sculpture. "They used to stand at ancient Hawaiian temples."

"That's right, Savanna. Buzz, your Tiki is a figure of Kuka the Hawaiian god of protection. Yours is Ku the god of strength, Oz. And Jimbo, yours is the Big Kahuna." Hiro smiled kindly.

"Of course, the Big Kahuna is for me. Thank you Hiro" Jimbo looked elated. He got up and shook his hand. Jimbo took his t-shirt off struggling to pull the sleeve over the cast. He then slipped the loosely fit buttoned Aloha shirt over his head and was able to maneuver his injured arm through the sleeve. Keemo and Leilani returned each holding a plateful of food. "See, the Big Kahuna." Jimbo raised his wooden figure like a trophy. Leilani rolled her eyes as he walked up with Keemo. Each were holding a plate of food.

"Sit, Uncle Hiro. I brought you some food." She handed him the plate she was carrying. Keemo sat down on my other side.

"Thank you my dear niece." Hiro thanked her. "But what about you, aren't you going to have something to eat?"

"I had a snack before, in the kitchen. You know I can't eat before dancing." She replied. "We need to get ready. It's almost time. Enjoy, I'll see you later." Leilani looked at Savanna, who sprang to her feet and grabbed our empty plates. They both turned and waved, before entering the house.

Oz stood up, unbuttoned his Aloha shirt and put it on over his t-shirt. I followed his example.

"Grab that chair over there and sit Oz." Hiro motioned him to grab an empty chair at the end of the yard.

"No thanks, I'm okay sitting here in the grass." He sat down cross-legged in front of Hiro's chair.

"This is delicious. Have you boys enjoyed your stay on The Big Island?" Hiro took a bite of banana bread.

"Yes, the surf has been great." Oz answered. "It's nice to have warm water. The color is so turquoise blue, just like you see in the magazines sometimes. But, I didn't think it would rain so much here."

Hiro smiled and turned to me: "Well, I know you have had an eventful trip Buzz. Do you think you will ever want to come back?" He looked into my eyes through his thick round spectacles. I felt as though he could see right into me.

"I never thought of leaving." I blurted out, looking around me. "But, I will come back to see my friends here."

"Ah yes," Hiro chuckled. "That's what happened to me. I came here from the mainland, didn't plan on staying long; but then I met Keemo's mother and never left."

"Why did you leave the mainland?" Oz looked intrigued and leaning over to his side closer to Keemo's dad, in the grass.

"Well, that is a long story. During the war, World War Two, my family was sent to a camp because we are Japanese. I grew up not knowing I was different until I watched my parents have everything they worked for taken away. We were forced to live in a camp like prisoners. Both of my parents died there. I think it was out of shame for what they felt was their disgrace." He paused for a moment, with a distant melancholy look in his eyes. "When the war ended and we were released from the camp, I had nowhere to go to. So, I decided to travel far away from my homeland, which had rejected my family. My uncle lived here and always invited me to visit."

"You came to visit and never left?" I asked, surprised.

"Now, don't get any ideas young man. You have a family and school and obligations back on the mainland. I was already eighteen years old when I first came here. You have quite a few years to go." Hiro spoke with a mild strictness. "Since Keemo was charged with stealing that lady's ring, I have been afraid that he would be convicted just because he is different."

His words surprised me. "How is Keemo different? I mean he is pretty big and doesn't say much, but that doesn't make him different."

Keemo continued to eat. He sat next to me in his usual quiet manner.

Hiro peered at me for a moment and then smiled. "I guess you really don't know. Keemo has autism."

"What is AUTISN?" Oz asked. "I heard about it on TV."

"Autismmm," Hiro emphasized the "m," "is a condition of the brain, some people argue it is a disorder. It makes it tough for people like Keemo to interact socially. They seem different. My son has Aspberger's Syndrome, which is the mildest form of Autism." Hiro paused, looking down at the plate on his lap.

"I thought he just didn't talk a lot." Oz commented.

Hiro smiled. "Yes Oz, Keemo does not talk a lot."

Keemo seemed unphased by our conversation. We were interrupted by the sound of drumbeats coming from the front of the house. Maleko ran over and said: "Bring your chairs around along the side of the house to the front, the show is about to begin." He collected a few folding chairs and walked to the side of the house. Applause and cheering could be heard coming from the front yard. "Go ahead boys, we will be there in a minute when we finish eating." Hiro motioned for us to join the fun.

Most of the guests in the yard had already made their way to the front. I collapsed my chair and followed Oz. A row of tiki torches lit the way. When we turned the corner there was a crowd of people on Leilani's front lawn. The front porch had been converted into a stage. Young men were playing the drums wearing traditional sarongs and green leafy leis. The neighborhood was alive. Across the street, people were assembled on the lawn watching, some stood on the sidewalk looking on.

The drummers concluded their performance and walked off the porch to join the folks on the lawn. I gave my chair to an elderly lady who didn't have one and joined Oz, who was standing at the side of the yard. A man came out from the front door of the house onto the porch. He was wearing a matching floral shirt and shorts made out of the same material as the girls' dresses. I recognized him. He was the man who accompanied Alika and Leilani's hula group at the last performance. He sat down and began to beat on the giant gourd-like instrument, looking up at the sky.

Leilani was the first to walk out on stage, followed by Savanna, three other girls from the group and then Alika. They had their hands on their hips while they swayed them from side to side to the beat. The dance they performed was different than the last one I had watched. They moved their bodies a lot more like grownup ladies, than girls our age. At the conclusion the girls filed back into the house through the front door. The man stayed and two men with bright aloha shorts and ukuleles came out and began to sing and play to a slow beat. The audience applauded and hooted loudly when they appeared. After about three songs, one of the men grabbed a microphone from a stand and announced: "The girls are going to come out again, for the last dance of the evening. We would like to thank you all for coming, and a big Mahalo to our guests from the mainland!" The girls came back out and the guys came back up with their drums and joined the group. Their arms were undulating when I noticed Leilani waving for me to come up to the stage. Oz nudged me with his elbow and then pushed me towards the stage. I felt beet red when I got up there. The applause, hoots and laughter didn't help. Leilani and Alika waved their hips back and forth and urged me to copy. I felt frozen until Jimbo jumped on the stage and began to make exaggerated dance motions.

'Oh come on Buzz, don't be a chicken,' I thought to myself and tried very awkwardly to imitate the graceful moves of the girls. Someone pushed Oz on stage. He looked much more coordinated than I felt. The song ended, and applause filled the air. The luau was over. Someone turned the lights on and the front yard returned to its old self.

"Nice dancing, Buzz. Maybe you should join our troupe." Alika teased me. Leilani came from behind and put her arm around her shoulder.

"That was fun. Now, I have to help clean up. Aloha, you guys have a good night." Leilani gave a hug to each of the girls. She turned to me and squeezed me real hard and said: "Ohana," before walking back into the house.

Everyone said "Aloha," and wished each other a "Good Night" as Dad stepped on the porch to take us back home. We grabbed our tiki statues and headed down the street to the van. Mom was already strapping Eric into his car seat.

When we got back to the house, mom put him to bed. Then, she had to tend to Jimbo who had a stomachache. He got really sick and threw up from eating too much. Oz wanted to watch TV.

My dad invited me to sit out on the balcony with him. He brought a glass of brown liquid in a weird looking wine glass and we sat down on the wicker chairs and looked out over the neighborhood. "Your mom will not be too happy, but someone gave me this." Dad pulled out a cigar and lit it. I had never seen him smoke before and never have myself, to this day.

"How did you like the luau, Buzz?" He asked me after blowing a smoke ring up into the air.

"Oh it was great, except for seeing a whole pig with its bones sticking out. That was kind of gross."

Dad laughed. "I guess that takes some of us a little getting used to son."

"The other food was real good. I got this shirt and the tiki, was cool. We spoke with Hiro about Keemo's autism. Did you know Hiro was put into a camp when he was a kid because his parents were from Japan; even though, he was born in our country?" I babbled.

"I see." Dad took a long moment before he spoke again. That evening my father told me about some of the dark parts of human history. He explained what had happened to Hiro and his family. I was shocked about the holocaust, and other horrible injustices wielded against many innocent people. My father told me of Queen Lydia Liliuokalani and her failed attempts at preserving the Hawaiian Islands for the native people. "But when the missionaries came to the Hawaiian Islands, they outlawed many native practices, even surfing!" He concluded. That made me feel angry.

Mom came to the sliding glass door and gave him a grin. She gazed at me for a moment and said: "Okay son, it's time for you to go to sleep."

Later lying in bed, I stared up at the ceiling glowing and processing the day's events. That was when I first made my decision to become a lawyer and fight for the rights of innocent people and battle against injustice.

First, I had to testify in Court and tell the judge that Keemo was innocent!

CHAPTER FIFTEEN
The Trial

The days after the luau at Leilani's house flew by and the morning of Keemo's trial arrived way too soon. The day before was spent preparing for my testimony at Mr. Delton's law office. After a mostly sleepless night, I rose out of bed to get dressed for court. Mom had gone out and bought me a new collared shirt. I felt a sharp pricking pain on my left shoulder blade.

"Hey, Buzz there's a pin in your shirt." Oz relieved my plight and handed the oval pearl end to me. "So are you ready for court today, Buzz?" He asked. "You must be nervous about testifying?"

"Not really." I couldn't even admit the truth to my friends. My stomach, however, was far more honest and ready to betray me. I looked at the trashcan in the corner, ready to stick my head into it feeling like I had to throw up.

"Let's go over the facts again. I saw this on a TV show. Didn't your lawyer prepare you for your testimony today?" Without giving me a chance to say 'yes' Jimbo continued. "Gee what a quack! This guy sounds like a 'V6,' that's a violation of the Sixth Amendment, the right to competent counsel!" Jimbo jeered. He was obviously parroting something he had read somewhere, or seen on TV. Oz finished the last spoonful of his cereal, got up and slyly ducked into the living room to avoid the inevitable lecture. I didn't have the strength to leave. "Okay, relax for a second and close your eyes and retell the events of the day." He insisted. I rolled my eyes. Jimbo persisted. "No, come on; this is serious."

Looking down at my now soggy cereal, I took a deep breath closed my eyes, and began to recall the events of that fateful day:"Keemo and I walked uphill away from town for a long time until we got to this house, where Leiani's uncle was doing construction. When we first got there Keemo and I skated in the dry swimming pool. Then, Leilani arrived and dropped into the bowl. I rested for a while and watched this little crow collect stuff and fly up into this huge tree at the back of the yard. It made really weird cat like sounds and then…"

"Okay Buzz, it's time to go." Mom interrupted. "We are going to drive your father to the lab and then meet your attorney at his office. Oz and Jimbo are you going to go to the beach?" I got up from the table and walked into the living room. Oz who had been listening to everything, nodded and said: "Kai and Kala are going to pick us up." I ran upstairs.

Nervously brushing my teeth and then washing my face, water splashed everywhere making a huge mess. The parental units were waiting for me when I rushed through heavy rain to the van. Eric was already strapped in his seat and the engine was running. We took off as soon as my seatbelt was clicked. The familiar ride to the University was quiet. My parents were silent most of the way. When we arrived Dad got out. Mom slid over into the driver's seat reached down and moved it closer to the steering wheel. Normally I would have switched seats to move up to the front, but my nervousness was almost paralyzing. The new shirt felt stiff and was sticking to my rain soaked, sweaty skin. Mom turned the van around and we were off to Mr. Delton's law office.

My lawyer was ready for us when we arrived. He was wearing a dark pin stripped suit with a white shirt and a red striped tie. "Let's walk over to the court. Your friend's trial is going more quickly than expected. I think his attorney wants to put you on the stand to testify, this morning. We must hurry!" He put a trench coat on grabbed his brief case off the counter and escorted us out the door. "AWWW, shucks it's still raining. Let's take my car so we don't get wet. We jumped into his large grey sedan parked in front of the office and rode the short distance to the courthouse. The sky matched the color of the car. The ground was glazed by the rain. "Aloha," Mr. Delton greeted the officers keeping guard at the entrance.

We walked up the stairs to the hallway. Outside the courtroom my lawyer said: "Wait here, I'll check in with the bailiff. Go ahead and have a seat." He pointed to a wooden bench in the hallway and disappeared behind the double doors of the courtroom. Mom dropped her large purse on the bench and then sat down with Eric on her lap. I went to the nearby water fountain for a cool drink before joining her. There were a lot of other people in the hallway waiting too. Attorneys in suits would walk in and out of the various courtrooms up and down the hall. Mom dug through her bag and pulled out a container with crackers and gave one to Eric.

The courtroom door opened and Mr. Delton came out. "There has been a delay. You won't be testifying for another hour. I'm going to drive back to my office. The court has promised to call me and take a break before your testimony so that I will have time to get back here. There are vending machines down the hall if you would like some refreshments." He disappeared; walking away at a swift pace. I really did not want him to go, but there he went.

Eric was being fussy so Mom tried to keep him quiet. "Your brother is being fidgety. I'm going to walk him around a little bit."

"Okay," I replied dismally. At that point I felt nervous and wanted my Mom close to me, as she walked away. So, there I was alone in this strange place, staring at the walls and the ceiling.

The door to the courtroom opened again and Leilani walked out. "Aloha, Buzz how've you been." She confidently strutted over to me. "They are taking a break in there, so I came out here. Come over and see my Mom and Auntie Flossie." She pointed at them sitting on a bench across the hall. In all the excitement, we hadn't noticed them. They were both wearing bright floral muu'muu' dresses.

They both smiled and said: "Aloha," almost in unison. They got up and gave us all big hugs.

"Aloha Buzz!" Auntie Flossie giggled.

"Aloha!" I approached her with my hand outstretched.

"Oh you are going to get a squeeze from Auntie Flossie, too!" She got up and gave me a hug so tight I thought I couldn't breathe. Then, with her arm around my shoulders, she asked Leilani: "How is our nephew doing in there?"

"He is doing okay. Uncle Hiro doesn't look so good though."

Auntie Flossie turned to my mom and said: "Oh our poor Keiko'iki, he's such a good man it is hard to see him going through this. He loves Keemo, and after our sister passed, he never remarried raising our nephew all by himself. Not that there weren't a mob of wahines that would have gladly filled that space. He was so handsome when he was a kane male hau and our sister was such a beautiful bride. They were so happy together."

Leilani's mom, Tweetie interrupted: "Let's sit down. You are going to have us all crying in a minute."

The door to the courtroom popped open. A young petit Asian lady in a dark blue skirt and jacket with a white blouse stepped out and approached us. "We are in recess. Honestly, I have to tell you it's not going well in there. The prosecution witness was very effective and I think that the judge believes her. I will put your daughter on the stand first, when the judge reconvenes the trial." She looked at Flossie who was blotting her teary eyes with a balled up tissue. "Are you ready, Leilani?" She nodded solemnly. "Okay, you have about a half hour before I put you back on the stand. Alright then, I'm going into the courtroom to work on a few things during the break." She turned and disappeared behind the huge doors.

"That lady, Keemo's lawyer, bugs me." Leilani crossed her arms. "She is too bossy."

"She's the only hope our Keemo has, right now," her mom, spoke in a soft and soothing tone. "You have to be patient and focus when you are on the stand. The truth will set you free."

"I'm not the one who needs to be set free!" Leilani protested.

"How've you been Leilani?" We finally had a moment to ourselves.

"I'm okay Buzz, but I don't like this place very much." She flicked her hair back, looked me in the eye and said: "You've got to do a good job in there to convince the judge that Keemo is innocent."

"Thanks for putting the pressure on me." I protested.

"You know what I mean, just do a good job." She responded. "Between you and me, we are Keemo's only hope. He is acting his usual self and that is not helping things much. You know how he is always quiet and emotionless, but he can get really emotional if he is stressed out. The prosecutors are saying that that means he is guilty! They don't know that's just the way Keemo always acts!" She was on the verge of tears.

"I'll do a good job." I attempted to reassure my friend. "My lawyer prepared me for this yesterday and he thinks that there isn't enough evidence, because the ring was never found."

"But, the prosecutor is saying that it was a vicious prank and that Keemo threw the ring away so no one can find it." She responded.

Just then, we were interrupted. Keemo's young lawyer popped her head out from the doorway. "Are you ready Leilani?" Without waiting for an answer she said: "Let's go, wiki wiki."

Leilani glanced at her mom, who nodded and then looked at me as she walked by before disappearing behind the doors.

"Come over here and sit with us, Buzz." Flossie motioned me over to her side of the bench. Little Eric was relaxed sitting on her lap as if she was his new favorite aunt. Mom was locked in conversation with the two ladies. I felt anxious again. A bag of chips made its way over to me. I reached in. Even though I had no appetite, I bit into a chip. It was really good and tasted different than a potato chip. Looking on the bag I read they were 'taro chips.' After grabbing a couple more I handed it back. Chewing nervously I tried to listen to the adults' conversation, but couldn't follow along. My mind was racing. Looking around, the hallway was deserted except for us. The last chip went from my hand to my mouth. I got up and strolled over to the water fountain at the end of the hall. The cool water quenched my thirst and washed away the salty taste from my mouth. I looked out the window and wondered if Oz was catching good waves with Kai and Kala. At least now I wasn't the only one who was not surfing since Jimbo had to stay out of the water and watch. A firm hand squeezing my left shoulder interrupted my thoughts.

"Are you ready Buzz? You'll be on in a few minutes." Mr. Delton had returned. "I'll check in and let the court know that we are ready." He walked tall and confidently, swung one of the doors open disappearing inside.

Waiting for his return, I stood by the window. Just minutes later, the door swung open again and Mr. Delton walked out smiling. He spoke to my mom for a second and walked back over to me. "Okay, as soon as your friend Leilani is finished, Keemo's attorney is going to come out and get us. Remember what we talked about yesterday. The most important thing is that you tell the truth. Now Buzz, do you have any final questions before we go into the courtroom?"

"Yeah, I was wondering. Leilani said that the police are saying this was a vicious prank and that Keemo threw the ring away so no one can find it. The reason that they can't find the ring is that Keemo didn't steal it. It's that easy."

"Circumstantial evidence is used when there is no direct evidence of the commission of the crime." Mr. Delton took a deep breath and elaborated: "If one or more people had seen Keemo take the ring, or if the police had found it in his pocket when they arrested him there would be direct evidence against him. Since there is not such evidence the prosecution is relying on circumstantial evidence to back their theory that Keemo passed on or otherwise disposed of the ring before he was arrested. Does that make sense, Buzz?"

"I understand the difference, but it doesn't make sense and certainly doesn't sound fair."

"Well Buzz, that reminds me of one of my law school professors that said: Fair is only in the dictionary." He smiled and when I didn't seem amused changed to a serious tone. "The prosecutor still has to convince the judge to believe beyond a reasonable doubt that Keemo stole the ring. Circumstantial evidence is weaker proof than direct evidence, but it is still admissible at trial. Just tell the truth. That's all you need to do."

The courtroom doors opened and Leilani walked out. She had tears in her eyes and a solemn expression. "Okay, is your client ready Mr. Delton?" Keemo's attorney smiled wearily. That wasn't very encouraging.

"I'm ready." My voice crackled under the stress as I answered and walked through the doors into the courtroom. Keemo was sitting at a table next to his lawyer. The police officer who had arrested him was sitting at another table with a man in a suit. There were several people in the audience. Hiro was sitting behind Keemo's chair. He smiled and nodded at me. I spotted the mean lady, Mrs. Van Der Snoot, in the row behind the prosecution's table.

"Follow me Buzz, you need to be sworn in by the clerk first." The public defender motioned me to walk through the swinging gate to the table where Keemo was sitting. He was emotionless.

"Are you ready with your next witness, Miss Kim?" The judge asked her from the bench.

"Yes, Your Honor." She replied.

"Okay, Madam Clerk please swear the witness in." The judge commanded.

A lady who was seated at a desk below the judge's bench stood up raised her right hand and read from a white index card: "Do you solemnly promise to tell the truth and nothing but the truth, so help you God?"

I raised my right hand and said: "Yes, I do."

The clerk then said: "Please state your name and spell your last name."

I complied.

"Please sit down, young man. I am judge Zen. You have your lawyer here, good morning Mr. Delton. Mr. Delton is one of our finest local attorneys. If you have any questions or want to take a break to speak to him just let us know." Judge Zen had a handle bar mustache and spoke in a low deep calming tone. "The most important thing is that you tell the truth. The second most important thing is that you speak clearly and only when it is your turn. The lady sitting there is, Ms. Tanaka, the court reporter. She is taking down everything we say. That will be typed up into book form and will serve as the record of this trial. Ms. Tanaka is great at her job, but even she can only take down what one person is saying at a time. If we don't wait our turn to speak, we'll be in trouble with her." An Asian lady in a gray skirt and a white ruffled blouse sitting on the judge's other side was feverishly tapping the black keys on a small shiny gray box. She smiled at the judge and nodded without missing a beat on the keys. "Do you have any questions before we get started?" He looked at me with a kind expression. I shook my head. "I forgot to add that you have to answer with words like 'yes' or 'no' we can't expect Ms. Tanaka to write down gestures. So, young Buzz I will ask you again: Do you have any questions?"

At first I shook my head again, but answered "NO!" loudly into the microphone when I realized my error.

"Very well, Miss Kim he is your witness. It is the defense's case, now." Judge Zen put on a pair of reading spectacles and looked down at a piece of paper. Ms. Kim was sitting at the table next to Keemo, who was wearing a light blue dress shirt. He was staring ahead expressionlessly while his lawyer shuffled through some papers on the desk in front of her.

"Ahem, okay so Buzz, you know why we are here, don't you? My client, Keemo here is accused of stealing a ring."

"He didn't. I was there. He just found this gecko. It is his family aumakua. Keemo is innocent." My answer was cut off.

"Objection!" The portly man in a blue suit, who was sitting next to the uniformed officer stood up from the other table. "Non responsive, move to strike."

"Thank you Mr. Prosecutor. That objection is sustained. The answer is stricken." The judge didn't even look up.

"Okay, Buzz let's try that again, and this time please..." Ms. Kim was interrupted by a bang.

The courtroom doors slammed opened and a crowd of people stormed in, led by Jimbo with Oz, Maleko, Kala and Kai right behind him. Uncle Lolo and the rest of the family piled in. "STOP THE TRIAL!" Jimbo shouted authoritatively.

"What is going on here, Order in the Court!" Judge Zen pulled off his spectacles and looked angrily at the disturbance. The bailiff, who had been sitting at his desk dropped the telephone, jumped up and spoke into a walkie-talkie. "What is going on here?" Judge Zen barked. "No one is stopping this trial until I say so."

"Let Keemo go free. We found the ring! It was stolen by a bird. Maleko here, climbed up the tree and pulled this out of a crow's nest!" Jimbo held the ring up over his head with his good arm like a trophy.

"ORDER IN THE COURT! Bailiff, bring me the ring." Judge Zen bellowed.

The bailiff's gun belt and keys clinked as he approached Jimbo, who proudly handed him the ring, then walked over to the bench and handed the ring to the judge, who put his spectacles back on to examine it. He cleared his throat. "Mrs. Van Der Snoot is this, your diamond ring?"

"Well, it might be... but I really can't tell without my glasses. It could be, but maybe it isn't." She answered.

It wasn't until that moment that I realized that the woman who had accused Keemo of stealing her ring was in court sitting across the isle from Hiro. Judge Zen handed the ring back to the bailiff. He walked over to the lady who examined the ring and nodded, handing it to the prosecutor. The large man in the blue suit took a minute to examine it before jumping out of his chair.

"This is highly irregular, Your Honor." The prosecutor complained: "This is a farce; the minor planted the ring somewhere so that his friends would conveniently find it and bring it to court to exonerate him. This evidence is untimely and irrelevant." He looked flushed. "Your Honor, this is an outrage. We have produced the necessary evidence to convict this minor. Look at the fact that he has consistently behaved in a suspicious manner since police first contacted him. Oh come on, Your Honor, this kid hid the ring and now the ring suddenly pops up. This defendant is devious. He is smart. Now, that we caught him red handed, the evidence of his theft conveniently appears. This boy cleverly hid the ring as an insurance policy in case he was caught. Now, that he is on trial he called his friends to suddenly act like they found the stolen property. His friends should be charged as co-conspirators!"

Ms. Kim sighed and slowly rose from her chair to address Judge Zen.

"Just one minute," Mr. Delton bellowed in his deep loud voice. "This miscarriage of justice has gone on long enough."

"Your Honor, this is obviously exculpating evidence proving, my client is innocent." Ms. Kim had a quiver in her voice and was looking pale. "Your Honor, I have been pleading with you from the beginning of this case, to understand that my client has…" She paused and sighed for a second time. "AUTISM, everything the prosecutor is saying about Keemo's 'character' is due to his brain syndrome." She looked at the judge with a sudden rage. "This IS a miscarriage of justice! My client is not capable of such a despicable theft plot! I mean, come on…" The entire courtroom was focused on her thin frame. Even though the men in suits dwarfed her, Ms.

Kim stood her ground. She took a deep breath and concluded: "Keemo is one of the sweetest young men I have ever met. His large stature for his age, combined with his extreme excitability in stressful situations have caused the prosecution to find him guilty based on no credible evidence. The State is relying on his behavior and is bootstrapping their argument to claim that proves the case against my client. He has autism. In preparation for this trial, I spent many hours with this young man and his father Hiro, at their home. Keemo is innocent. He is the victim of unfortunate circumstances. The ring was found in the nest of a Hawaiian crow, the bird stole the ring, not Keemo. I have nothing more to say." In the back of the courtroom clapping erupted, which was quickly stopped by the judge who glared at them hanging over the bench with his gavel in the air as if ready to strike; not to mention the bailiff's intimidating approach.

"Okay Your Honor…" Mr. Delton attempted to speak.

"Thank you counsel." Judge Zen interrupted him. "I have a good idea what is going on here. Just because I have been sitting on this bench for many years doesn't mean I have cobwebs in my brain. By the way Kai and Kala how is your kuku kane?" He leaned over the bench. "Tell him I will be over soon for a little lama ho'ohuihui'ia." Judge Zen chuckled.

"Oh hey, Aloha Uncle Dan, we didn't recognize you in that black muu' muu'." Kai smirked.

"Your brother has always been a smart-alec hasn't he?" The judge looked at the brothers with a probing squint.

Kala nodded at the judge grinning and replied: "Our grandfather was just telling us that he hasn't seen you for a while."

"I move to dismiss this case, Your Honor!" Ms. Kim pounded her fist on the table.

"Okay, let's not get too far ahead of ourselves. I need to hear a little more evidence before I make my final determination." Judge Zen raised his voice and immediately the room was quiet. A tall pale man in a trench coat, who appeared to be sweating profusely walked up to the bench. "And who might you be?" He looked down at the man from the bench with an exasperated look. He looked out over his courtroom sighed and said: "If there are any other people out in the audience with surprises, please step forward now or forever hold your peace. I don't know how much more I can stand, here."

A tall pale man with a dark suit and black-rimmed glasses stood up.

"And who might you be?" The judge repeated his question before exhaling sharply.

"I am Special Agent Crunch from the F.B.I.'s Insurance Fraud Division. I am investigating insurance fraud involving a diamond ring, which was reported as a loss here." The F.B.I. special agent continued. "May I please see the evidence?" The judge looked at him blankly. "Your Honor, may I please see the diamond ring, which was just admitted into evidence?"

"Oh, of course, here you go." Judge Zen handed the ring to the agent. "Just don't lose it!" he chuckled at his own joke. Then, in a serious tone, he turned to the attorneys and asked: "I don't think that we need to swear this gentleman in as a witness, do we?" He looked at each of them probingly without a response. "Good, let the record reflect there was no response. Okay, please let us know about the new and separate criminal action, which I assume will be filed against Mrs. Van Der Snoot.

Special Agent Crunch put the ring down on the court clerk's desk, opened his attaché case and pulled out a manila envelope. He opened the envelope and pulled out an 8 ½ x 11 inch black and white photo of a ring.

"Your Honor, this is a photo of a ring which Mrs. Van Der Snoot reported as a theft loss five years ago in Key Biscayne, Florida. Mrs. Van Der Snoot accused a young bellhop at the hotel she was staying, but luckily for him, he had alibi evidence that he was away from the hotel the entire weekend the ring was allegedly claimed stolen. The young man spent a few weeks in jail before we were able to clear him. But now, the ring was again listed on an F.B.I. computer database as stolen. Before that she has claimed this very ring lost or stolen at least five times. That is why I am here. Lucius Van Der Snoot is a notorious jewel thief and I am here to find this woman and her husband to arrest them for insurance fraud and the theft of this ring from the Estate of the Duke of Burryberry in England, ten years ago. The suspect, Mr. Lucius Van Der Snoot disappeared, along with this ring and quite a few other valuables which he has sold or pawned on his travels around the world." We have been chasing him for years. The man reached into his jacket pocket and pulled out a pair of handcuffs. "Ludmilla Van Der Snoot, you are under arrest for theft, receiving stolen property, insurance fraud and numerous other charges which will be presented at your arraignment on Friday, in Federal Court in Honolulu, on the island of Oahu. You have the right to remain silent, any thing you say can and will be held against you. You have the right to an attorney. If you cannot afford one, one will be appointed for you." The rapid clicking sound of the handcuffs tightening around the woman's wrists and her shrieks and sobs, filled the silent chamber. A roar of the crowd that had pushed its way into the courtroom suddenly replaced the quiet.

"ORDER in my courtroom, everybody zip your lips!" Judge Zen shouted, banging his gavel. The decorum was reinstituted; he calmly looked at my friend and declared: "Keemo, I am sorry that you have been the victim in all of this. Especially, since it appears that the authorities mistook the outward symptoms of your autism for signs of consciousness of guilt. Mr. Prosecutor, your boss, the district attorney will be getting a call from me tomorrow morning."

"Of course Miss Kim, I am almost done here, please humor an old curmudgeon." Judge Zen nodded at the young attorney who stood up as if about to speak. He then chuckled and turned to me. "Go ahead and sit down, Buzz. I don't think we will need your testimony anymore. Bailiff, please have these young gentlemen approach the bench." Jimbo, Oz, Kala and Kai were escorted by the bailiff and sworn in by the clerk. "Okay, young man how did you figure out who took the ring?" The judge was leaning on his folded arms looking down at them.

"You see, judge," Jimbo took a deep breath: "This morning I interviewed Buzz about the crime scene and one thing he said struck me." Jimbo again paused, obviously enjoying the spotlight. "Buzz revealed he had 'watched this little crow collect stuff.' I remember my Grandpa on the farm telling me how crows collect shiny stuff and use it to decorate their nests to attract females. When I told Kala about that, he told me that Hawaiian crows are not attracted to shiny stuff, but will collect unusual things, or at least stuff they think will attract females, to put in their nests."

"That's right Your Honor. As you know, I study birds at the University. The Hawaiian crow has the habit of collecting objects that are unusual in their environment." Kala was interrupted by Jimbo, who looked down at him nodding with a smile.

"So, we figured out where the place was by calling Leilani's house. Her Uncle Lolo took us there. The crow was at the property when we got there. It was making funny sounds. We watched it a while and found the nest in this big tree. I would have climbed it, but…" Jimbo pointed to the cast on his forearm. "So, Uncle Lolo here brought one of his tree service ladders that is really tall and set it up against the tree, but it wasn't tall enough. So then, my buddy Maleko here climbed up and found the ring in the nest. That bird wasn't too happy though."

"Is that true?" The judge peered at the group.

"Yes sir, it is. That nest was on a branch 50 feet from the ground. No person planted it there. Only someone with my nephew's extraordinary climbing abilities could have done it." Uncle Lolo piped in. Oz and the others nodded in support.

The Judge chuckled. "Well, the Hawaiian crow, eh. That is my family's totem. I remember watching them with fascination when I was a young boy growing up on The Big Island. It is sad that you don't see that many of these wonderful birds anymore."

"Yes your Honor, unfortunately the species is suffering a rapid decline in numbers. If things don't change they may be facing extinction." Kala became solemn. "The Hawaiian crow is the aumakua for many families, here. That is why it is so sad and surprising that we are losing them."

"Well, speaking of LOSING THINGS, whether or not on purpose." Judge Zen turned his attention to the prosecutor and then glared at the lady who was sobbing, sitting handcuffed in the chair by the bailiff's desk, with the F.B.I. agent standing next to her. "Mrs. Van Der Snoot, I think you owe Keemo and his family an apology. The missing item has been returned, there is no evidence in this Court's opinion of theft, therefore: CASE DISMISSED!" He picked up his gavel and banged it down.

"YEAAAAAAAAAAAAAAAAAAHHHHHHHH!!!!!!!!!!!!!!!!!!!" The room erupted with cheers. Leilani, her mom Tweetie and aunt Flossie stormed in and hugged Hiro, who stood there in shock. From the witness stand, I had a perfect vantage point to watch the proceedings. The bailiff asked the judge if he should enforce order in the court.

Judge Zen smiled and shook his head and said: "No." He turned to me and said: "Well, young man, I am retiring to my chambers, I don't believe that I am needed anymore." He stood up and left through a door behind the clerk's desk.

"Are you going to stay up there?" Oz came up to the witness stand and asked me before joining the cheering crowd.

"This is true OHANA! Our family got together to help one of our own. Nobody gets left behind, alone!" Flossie announced over the cheers. Keemo, still expressionless in the center of the cantankerous mob, was being escorted out of the room. Uncle Lolo and another cousin had Hiro on their shoulders and he almost hit his head on the light hanging from the ceiling. I was speechless.

"Come on Buzz, let's go." Mom was the only person left in the courtroom besides the bailiff and the clerk lady. "I am sorry that I doubted you. Your friend Keemo was innocent and I didn't believe you. Now, I am proud of you for sticking with him even though it was hard on you. You are growing up." Mom had a sad look on her face and then smiled and gave me a tight hug.

We said goodbye to the clerk and the bailiff before walking out into the hallway. Leilani was holding Eric who had his hands up in the air and was cheering. She handed him to my Mom and wrapped her arms around my neck and kissed my cheek and said: "Mahalo Nui Loa, Buzz."

My face turned as red as a tomato.

CHAPTER SIXTEEN
Mahalo Nui Loa

After we finally left the courthouse the ride back home was like a victory parade. As soon as we got back, Kala and Kai loaded our surfboards into their Jeep and took us to a spot where you could catch a wave into the beach and then another smaller wave would shoot you back out to sea. I caught a couple of those waves and only had to paddle a short distance back to the take off spot. Jimbo stood on the beach directing traffic. We had a blast!

"Tonight we are going to celebrate!" Dad announced: "We are going out for pizza!"

That was music to our ears. Dad invited Kala and Kai. My friends and I rode in their Jeep while Dad followed us with Mom and Eric in the van.

"Pineapples on pizza, EWWWWW!" Jimbo spouted his opinion when the waitress brought the large pies we had ordered.

"Try it, you might like it Hawaiian style." Kai, who was sitting next to Jimbo reached for a slice.

There was not very much talking after that. We devoured four large pizzas and countless pitchers of root beer. After we got home, I was completely exhausted and went straight up to bed.

The next morning, we awoke to the smell of pancakes. Mom hugged me when I sat down at the table.

"Good morning my dear keiki." She greeted us in a Hawaiian skirt and blouse with a yellow hibiscus flower tucked behind her ear. I felt a lot better knowing that she finally, truly believed me that Keemo was innocent. "After breakfast we are all going to the beach to meet Doctor Hank and his family and some friends. Buzz and Oz, you may go surfing. Jimbo you can help me, as we discussed.

After the beach, we are going straight to the restaurant with Hannah, Hank and Alika to meet your friend Leilani and her family. So, pack a day bag with nice clean shirts and shorts." Mom advised us before going upstairs to get ready herself. She was back to being her old self again.

"MMMM, these are good pancakes. I'll bet you are glad your parents aren't mad at you anymore." Oz shoved a piece soaked with syrup into his mouth.

"You've got to admit you have a talent for getting into big messes." Jimbo mused with his mouth full.

"I'm glad you guys came to the rescue though. I was worried for Keemo. I knew that he was innocent and seeing him go through everything for no reason was frustrating and scary. Thanks for your help."

"Oh, it was nothing. Jimbo really was the one to figure it out." Oz refused to be interrupted by Jimbo. He punched him on his good shoulder and raised his voice before telling me: "Yesterday morning in the kitchen when you were waiting to go to court, you told us about the funny little crow. Jimbo was convinced the crow stole the ring. Me personally, I thought he was crazy. But then, Kala and Kai came and when Jimbo mentioned his idea they believed it!" Oz became animated. Jimbo was cool as a cucumber nodding occasionally, looking around nonchalantly.

"But, how did you know where the house was?" I wondered.

"Leilani's phone number was still on the message pad on the fridge. Her uncle Lolo answered when I called and told him about the chance we could prove Keemo didn't steal the ring. He hadn't left for work yet, so he came over here and we followed him to the house. That's when Kala took over. He was able to find the nest in that huge tree. Leilani's uncle brought a long ladder from his construction truck and then Maleko climbed up and found the ring in the nest."

"I would have climbed up, but my cast prevented it." Jimbo interrupted Oz.

"Yeah so anyways, Maleko climbed up to the top of the tree and boy that bird was making a lot of noise. Sure enough, when he came back down the ladder, Maleko pulled the ring out of his pocket!" Oz finished recounting the events.

"Okay guys, rinse off your plates when you are done and put them in the dishwasher." Dad came downstairs weighted down with two bulging beach bags, filled to capacity. "Then, bring your stuff out to the van, so I can load it in."

Mom was finally ready. Eric and everything else was loaded up and we were on our way to the ocean. We had to stop at the store for Mom to pick up a few things and were tortured waiting another half hour before leaving there. The van finally pulled up to the beach parking lot. I had never been to this one before. It was more family-oriented than those we had surfed before. There were showers and a large bathroom building. The first look at the ocean revealed lines of white water, so that meant surf!

Mom shouted something out, but I was already far enough away from the beach blanket to ignore her without facing consequences, as we ran through the soft sand to the edge of the water.

After all of the stress over my friend Keemo, when my toes finally touched the water everything was better. My world was back on track, again. I felt normal. The warm clear blue water felt so good; my heart sang as I jumped on the deck of my board and started paddling out towards the incoming waves. The first brush of white water was so light. I paddled straight through it without much effort. Flying over the water surface with ease, it was easy keeping up with Oz, who normally would be way far ahead of me getting out to the take off zone. Jimbo was stranded on the beach with his broken arm. There was no wind and the ocean was glassy as my cupped hands propelled me forward. The silence was soothing. The only sound I heard came from my arm strokes splashing the surface of the water.

The waves at this beach were long and mushy with nice waist high faces. Duck diving through a wave, the force pulling at me got stronger farther outside. Oz was only a few yards in front of me. A few more breakers hit us, before reaching the calm deep. Looking down through the crystal blue water, the contours of the sand below were clearly visible. Tufts of sea grass spotted the bottom.

"The waves look fun." Oz was already sitting up on his surfboard, I stopped next to him. The wind was still and the sun warmed us on our shoulders waiting for the next set. "Wow it's hard to believe we're headed home in just a couple of days. I'll be glad to get home and see my family, but I'm really going to miss this place."

It struck me: "What, just a couple of days?" The thought of having to say Aloha to Keemo, Leilani and Alika and The Big Island hadn't even occurred to me.

"Yeah, we're leaving in a few days. Were you planning on staying? I am sure that Leilani and Alika won't mind. Your mom will be another story, but we'll be sure to come back for the wedding!" My friend chided me squinting while he scanned the horizon. "Here we go!" He dropped down on the deck of his board and began to paddle out towards the approaching set.

Following my friend who was too far out to catch the first wave, I was in perfect position, spun my board around and caught it with just a few arm strokes. Hopping up on my feet, I heard Oz hooting. The wave's face unfolded before me, as I shot up and performed an off-the-lip, spinning Leilani's fluorescent green surfboard back down. Leaning forward at the top of the wave gave me a burst of speed as I dropped down again with arms outstretched. Crouched, I was shooting through the next twenty-five yard section before the entire wall crumbled turning into foaming white water. It engulfed me as my board was knocked out from underneath me. After a short tumble under water, I broke the surface and paddled back out.

Leilani was sitting on her bright pink surfboard talking to Oz, when I got back out to the lineup. "Aloha, Buzz. You caught a nice wave." She smiled.

"That wave you caught looked like fun, I hope there's more." Oz added.

His wish was granted when a cleanup set of waves much larger than the last, came through. My attention wasn't focused on the horizon. Instead, looking at the beach I noticed that Alika, Dr. Hank and Hanna had arrived and were standing by my parents' beach chairs. Turning my gaze back out to sea, Leilani was far enough out and Oz was just scratching his way over the top of the breaking wave, before it came crashing down on me. At the last moment I executed a duck dive pushing the board down under the water surface with my arms and right foot hoping the nose would be pushed deep enough to avoid the wave's force. Then, the idea was to shoot up behind the wave to the surface. Instead, when I pushed down, the nose came up too soon and I rolled head over heels, backwards underwater clinging to the deck of my surfboard. The wave gyrated me around. Rolling under water at a forty-five degree angle, I never lost hold of my surfboard. Two more barrel rolls, and the wave finally released me from its grip as the board and I slowly rose to the surface. My lungs burned as I gasped for air. Looking around, bewildered, it took a few seconds to figure out where the shore was. I turned my attention back out to sea in the nick of time as another wall of white water stampeded towards me. While inhaling a deeply, I grabbed my board and slid onto the deck. After just three arm strokes straight towards the oncoming wall of water, I again pushed the nose deep down and a split second later pushed the tail down with my right foot. Once the deck was as far below the water as it would go, I thrust my body down against it and the force of the wave rolled over, jerking me a few feet backwards. Popping up for air, it wasn't tough to handle the rest of the set after having been pushed far into shore by the force of the breakers. I decided to take a break and rest on the beach for a minute and rode a wave in on my belly. Another wave brought me all the way to the shore and I got out of the water, still panting, in order to rest for a moment.

Jimbo and Alika who was holding little Eric's hand, approached me.

"Hah, you just got worked!" Jimbo teased.

"Aloha, Alika." I ignored him.

"Aloha, Buzz," she moved closer as Eric walked slowly towards me examining the sand. His free hand was clamped down on a shell. This new treasure fascinated my little brother. "How's the surf?" Alika brushed a strand of hair from her face with her free hand. Eric pulled her back a foot upon spotting another shell.

"Oh, it's pretty good." For a moment I thought about staying on the beach and hanging out with her, but the lure of the ocean pulled me back out again. "I'll see ya later." I turned back to the water jumped on my surfboard and glided a few feet before paddling back out.

The waves seemed like they were breaking farther out now. After taking a deep breath, I resumed the paddle. My shoulders were already feeling the burn but I managed to paddle out without a pause. Sitting up for a minute in the calm of the deeper water, Leilani and Oz came into view. They were paddling for the same wave in the next advancing set. Just as Oz got up, the wave curled and knocked him head first into the brine. Leilani was in perfect position and gracefully glided down the face turning at the bottom. With her arms outstretched, she flew up the wall of the six-foot wave, and back down again. The water sprayed like a rooster tail from her fluorescent pink surfboard as she cut back to the curl and turned back sharply. Leilani resumed her graceful glide on the rest of the wave before riding up and over the top of it. I resumed paddling. My shoulders felt rested.

As I was approaching my friends, another set of waves came through. They each picked one off, before I got close enough to speak to them. I could have caught the last wave of the set, but the force of the last wipe out made me a little scared and timid. Waiting for the next waves, I sat there alone. It wasn't long until a new set appeared on the horizon. Leilani and Oz hadn't made the long paddle back, yet. The next set came sooner than anticipated. My heart pounding, I swallowed and headed out towards the oncoming waves. The first wave did not have the power to fully form. The next wall of water rose before me. I turned the board around and with a gulp, started scratching on the water surface as hard as I could. The force gripped the board, jumping to my feet with the sudden forward surge; diving like a hawk I dropped down the wave, and with arms outstretched soared across the unfolding face. All three of us had a great session and decided to stop surfing. We shared stories about our waves on the long slow paddle in.

After the beach, we met Keemo, Hiro, along with Leilani and her entire family at our favorite Chinese restaurant. Our group almost filled all the tables and booths in the place! We enjoyed great company, delicious food, with lots of fun and laughter that evening. It was really late before the party ended and we drove home exhausted.

CHAPTER SEVENTEEN
Aloha Means: "Hello And Good-Bye, …"

The last three days before our departure seemed to fly by. We spent one day back at the Volcano National Park. This time, I was able to really tour the park. We saw lava tubes and some really strange landscapes that looked more prehistoric than modern day earth. It was really cool. We passed the grassy area where Alika and Leilani and the other girls had performed their hula dance. The place evoked fond memories of watching their performance and sitting with Dr. Hank reading his newspaper.

Our final morning arrived too soon. I awoke feeling a lump in my throat realizing that we were leaving soon. Looking around the room I made mental notes of my surroundings. Jimbo was still asleep snoring with his mouth wide open. Oz had cleared the sheets off of his bunk. When I got down to the kitchen, he was already eating cereal at the kitchen table, smiling at Eric's high chair antics. Mom was nervously checking her list of things to do. Looking outside the kitchen window, Dad was loading packed suitcases into the van. A load of trash filled the garbage cans standing at the curb. The two halves of Jimbo's surfboard stuck out of one of the cans.

"Pour yourself some cereal and milk. Then, I need you boys to help clean this place up. Oz, could you please finish stripping down the beds and throw the sheets into the washing machine. Buzz, you are on bathroom duty and don't give me that look.

Where's Jimbo? He is on vacuum cleaner duty. You only need one good arm to operate a vacuum."

"He's still sleeping." I poured some cereal into a bowl.

"When you are finished eating, Oz, please wake him up." Mom commanded.

"Yes Ma'am, I will do that with pleasure." Oz let out a sinister chuckle.

"Who do you think you are going to wake?" Jimbo entered the room and yawned. His hair was sticking up in all directions. His cast was covered in handwriting and signatures of different colors.

"Jimbo, I want you to brush that mop of hair after breakfast." Mom looked at our friend shaking her head. "I am not having you see your mother for the first time in six weeks looking like that."

Jimbo shrugged his shoulders, sat down next to me and reached for the cereal box. He poured the remnants into his bowl. "Hey, what a rip off! You guys ate all the cereal and didn't save enough for me."

"Here you can have a banana, if that is not enough." Obviously annoyed with our friend, Mom grabbed the empty box and threw it into a huge black plastic trash bag in the corner of the kitchen. Oz put his spoon down on the table and drank the flavored milk from his bowl. He got up and rinsed his dishes in the sink before putting them into the dishwasher.

"Okay, Oz please go upstairs and strip the sheets off the other beds and bring them down to the laundry room." Mom came back into the kitchen.

"Aye-aye!" Oz saluted.

"Buzz when you are finished, the cleaning supplies are in the bucket under the sink."

"Okay, mom." I replied complacently.

She turned to our friend: "When you are done eating, Jimbo please finish loading the dishwasher and then vacuum the living room and upstairs bedrooms. Mind you, I already did the whole house including the stairs yesterday while you were at the beach. You are just doing a touch up job, so don't miss anything or think you are being over-worked."

Jimbo shot me a sour look as he peeled the banana, shoved a huge piece in his mouth. He chewed a few times and opened his mouth to show its disgusting chewed up contents. "Hey, Buzz look at my see-food!"

We each performed our tasks to Mom's satisfaction and before we knew it, we were sitting in the van waiting for Dad to lock the front door. It was the last time that we would pass the many familiar landmarks on our way to the airport. Stopping at the terminal curb, Dad got out of the van and pulled over four luggage carts. After we had them all loaded up, he went to park the van. Dr. Hank had agreed to return it to the rental agency for us later that day. We waited for him to return and then walked into the terminal building together where we were immediately greeted by familiar faces. A small crowd stood there waiting to see us off. Alika and Leilani came up to me and handed me a small gift-wrapped package.

"This is a going away present from Leilani and me, and Keemo, too." Alika said. "Go ahead and open it up."

I complied. Inside was a necklace made of small white shells.

"They are puka shells. Put it on." Leilani commanded. I fumbled with the fastener. She took the necklace and stepped behind me. I felt the coolness of the smooth shells on my throat. "There you go."

"Now, you won't forget us." Alika said with a quiver in her voice.

I opened the other brightly wrapped gift. Inside the box was a lei made of feathers. Alika stood on her tiptoes and put it over my head.

"I'll write. You can come to visit." I was at a loss for words, feeling a huge lump in my throat. "Of course, I will come back and visit!" I stammered.

"You'd better!" Leilani looked at me smiling.

Keemo was his usual silent self. We walked as a group to the check-in counter. Hanna was holding Eric. Dad and Mom went up and brought our luggage to the clerk and got our seat assignments. Then our group headed to the gate to wait to board the plane. The whole experience seemed like a blur. I didn't say much. We just stood around each other in a painful awkward silence. Alika and Leilani were wearing matching floral outfits with brown kukui nut necklaces and flowers in their hair.

Alika stepped forward and reached up to hug me. I gave her an awkward squeeze. We didn't hurry to end the hug, I already missed her. Next, Leilani stepped forward.

"Aloha Buzz, you know that means hello and goodbye, don't you." Leilani looked down at me with her beautiful dark brown eyes. "And I love you."

Her hug was even stronger, thinking I felt some bones crackle I said: "UUUHHH-loa Leilani, Mahalo Nui Loa. Thanks for letting me borrow your surfboard. I tried not to get dings in it. If you find any, write me and let me know. I'll send you money to help you take care of them."

She smiled. I felt sad looking up at her. It was really hard to realize that this was really 'good-bye.' I was the last person to get on the airplane. Luckily, Oz saved the window seat for me. Mom later told me that he had to argue with Jimbo to secure it.

And so, we left our friends on The Big Island.

The last thing I remember after getting into my seat and fastening the seat belt was looking down at The Big Island of Hawaii. As the plane rose, it seemed to get smaller and smaller. It had been our Universe for the last six weeks. Looking out the window I was able to make out the familiar attractions below. As the airplane circled and rose higher into the stratosphere, I thought about Alika, Leilani, Keemo, and all the others, who were probably on their way home. My face was squeezed against the window trying to catch a glimpse as the jet liner turned away from The Big Island. All that I could recognize from the aircraft's window were the two giant green volcanoes Mauna Loa, and Kilauea the home of Pele. Then, there was only a huge expanse of shiny gray-blue Pacific Ocean, before the clouds and darkness took over and I fell into a dreamless sleep. I awoke before the landing and was already homesick for Hawaii and my friends.

"Flight crew, please prepare for landing." The captain announced before we touched the ground.

After we got home, I didn't see Oz or Jimbo for at least two days. We agreed to meet at the top of the steps at Main Beach a couple of days after our return home. Oz and Jimbo were already there when I rode up on my bicycle.

"It looks like the surf is bunk." I commented after a quick glance down at the gray shoreline.

"Yes, after surfing in Hawaii for the last few weeks, it doesn't look rideable. Funny, in the past we would have paddled out into that micro mush." Oz remarked.

Jimbo looked bored. He sighed and said: "Once you have been surfing in the islands, it's hard to come back." He gave a sad look at his cast, which was covered with signatures, symbols and caricatures in multiple colors of ink.

"Are you ready to go to Nana's? I've got the present in my backpack." We were all eager to see her and give her the gift we had brought back for her.

"Okay Buzz, we haven't been to The Shack in over six weeks. Let's get settled in again." Jimbo turned the high handlebars of his bicycle. We peddled after him to Nana's house.

"Look at you boys, so strong and tanned. And what happened to you Jimbo?" Nana looked at his multi-colored cast before giving each of us a hug. "Can I interest you in some milk and cookies? I just baked a fresh batch, thinking you might be by. Sit down, I want to hear all about your trip. Did you have any adventures?"

Jimbo and Oz shot me a look so I seized the moment to tell Nana about Keemo and the lost ring, before Jimbo could tell his version of the events. Naturally, he didn't waste the opportunity to tell Nana how 'he' had saved the day. Reaching into my pocket, I pulled out the small gift-wrapped box.

"Well, what is this? You boys shouldn't have." Nana put on the glasses, which she had on a chain around her neck and sat down at the table. Poncho waddled into the kitchen from the backyard. The enormous black and tan canine greeted Oz and Jimbo before giving me a slimy lick and plopping his huge bear-like head on my lap. "Oh, it's beautiful. I am going to wear it Wednesday night to my weekly pinochle game at the senior center. Oh, look I can wear it on a necklace or as a pin." Nana fastened the pineapple broach on the front of her apron.

Oz took the lead in telling about Jimbo's run in with the lady at the pineapple cart. He tried to change the subject, but it was gratifying to hear Nana scold him for his rudeness. It was nice to see him squirm for a change. Nana didn't dwell on it very long though, and got up to serve us her delicious chocolate chip cookies with a glass of ice-cold milk.

"Your friend Stephanie and two of her girlfriends helped around the yard while you were gone. She left on vacation with her grandmother and Uncle Rudolf. You remember him, don't you boys?" Nana let out a deep yodel of a laugh. "I'll never forget the look on his face when you barged in on that dinner party." She reminded us about our prior adventure at Turtle Cave. We laughed and munched on the cookies, while she spoke. The girls used The Shack while you were gone, I let them store their beach things there, too." Jimbo stopped chewing and looked at me with desperation with his mouth full. I was not going to object. We finished the cookies, thanked Nana and went out to The Shack.

"You chicken!" Jimbo whacked me with his cast.

"You'd better watch it." I rubbed my arm angrily, while Oz opened the door to The Shack.

"Why didn't you speak up? Oh no, look, they have invaded our space!" Jimbo stomped around the shack pointing out the girls' beach umbrella and folding chairs. "And look at this!" He grabbed a green bikini top off of the surfboard rack that Oz had built out of bowling ball pins.

Oz frowned: "That's not yours, and The Shack belongs to Nana, anyway. We can't tell her who can come here and who can't."

They continued bickering for a little while until we all decided to go home. Stephanie was out of town, so I figured I would give her the gifts I had gotten her in Hawaii at school. That turned out to be a mistake.

A few weeks later, back at school, I caught up with Stephanie on the second day in the hallway before class.

"Wow, pretty wrapping." Stephanie's eyes lit up when I handed her the little boxes. She opened the one with the necklace first. "Oh this is real pretty, thank you Buzz." She put the box and paper into her pocket unfastened the locket and put the necklace on. "What do you think?"

Just then, I felt a slap on my shoulder. "Hey, Buzz Aloha." Fortunately, Jimbo already had his cast removed so it didn't hurt much. Oz, who was next to him, greeted me with a nod. "Looks like Buzz gave you the necklace his two girlfriends in Hawaii gave him, as a going away present; nice re-gifting, Buzz!" Jimbo snickered sarcastically.

Stephanie shot me a sour look. Some other kids were joining the surrounding group.

"UH, ER, no, this is the one they gave me." I pulled the collar of my hooded sweatshirt down to show her the puka shell necklace I was wearing. "Jimbo doesn't know what he's talking about." My face was turning red.

"I see." Stephanie smiled coyly. "Well don't forget you promised me surfing lessons, too."

I nodded: "Sure, maybe after school this week."

"Now, tell me more about these two girlfriends in Hawaii." she probed. A few chuckles came from the kids around us.

Just then: "BRRRRRRRIIIIIINNNNNNGGGGGGG."

It was the sound of ringing announcing the beginning of first period. I guess you might say that I was saved by the bell!

GLOSSARY

Autism – a bio-neurological disorder that is often first observable in early childhood with symptoms including a lack of response to other humans and by limited ability or disinclination to communicate and socialize.

Boa constrictor – a large tropical American snake that attacks and sometimes kills its prey by squeezing it.

Circumstantial evidence – evidence providing only a basis for a belief regarding the fact of a dispute.

Detention – the temporary time that a student is confined as a form of punishment.

Direct evidence – evidence (usually a statement or testimony by a witness) directly related to the fact in dispute.

Insolence – insulting behavior or attitude.

Knucklehead – *slang* – Someone who is hardheaded, stubborn

Marine biologist – someone who studies organisms that live in the sea.

'Ohana - Part of Hawaiian culture, 'ohana means family (in an extended sense of the term, including blood-related, adoptive or intentional).

Porter – a person who carries luggage and related objects.

Rottweiler – a muscular breed of dog with black fur and tanned markings.

SCUBA – an apparatus carried by a diver, which includes a tank holding a mixture of oxygen and other gases, used for breathing underwater. (Acronym for: Self-Contained Underwater Breathing Apparatus)

Shenanigans – mischievous play, especially by children.

Stewardess – a female flight attendant.

Take-off spot – the area where surfers catch waves.

Ten-gallon hat – a large cowboy-style hat.

Tsunami – a very large water wave formed in the ocean and can destroy buildings and people, usually due to an earthquake or volcanic eruption.

Turbulence – state of agitation or disturbance in the air, which is disruptive to an aircraft.

Wing flaps – devices mounted on the trailing edges of the wings of aircrafts to improve the aircrafts ability to lift characteristics of a wing and are of a fixed-wing aircraft to reduce the speed at which the aircraft can be safely flown and to increase the angle of descent for landing.

10592039R00141

Made in the USA
San Bernardino, CA
21 April 2014